# INFATUATION

March Foster lit a cigarette. He looked at
Nicola in her rose pink velvet dress sitting at the
top of the table beside her newly acquired
fiancé. He turned to Verona.

'Do you see this working out?'

Verona nodded in the direction of the engaged
couple.

'What . . . those two? Certainly not. I warned
her indirectly . . . and when Denny told me I
warned him. She's a sweet thing, and though
Denny is charming this marriage could never be
a success. He'll get sick of her and break her
heart.'

March's gaze returned to Nicola's face, rapt
and dreamy in the candlelight. She looked
bewitched. Denis Avon had bewitched her. Nic
was a sensible girl. She *couldn't* be as silly as
this . . .

**Also by the same author,
and available in Coronet Books:**

# Infatuation

## Denise Robins

**CORONET BOOKS**
**Hodder and Stoughton**

Copyright Denise Robins

First published in Great Britain by
Hutchinson & Co. Ltd

*Coronet Edition 1963*
*Third impression 1977*

---

Printed and bound in Great Britain for
Hodder and Stoughton Paperbacks
a division of Hodder and Stoughton Ltd,
Mill Road, Dunton Green, Sevenoaks, Kent
(Editorial Office 47 Bedford Square, London WC1 3DP)
by Richard Clay (The Chaucer Press), Ltd,
Bungay, Suffolk

ISBN 0 340 12783 X

ON most mornings, Nicola was the first person to get to the shop.

The shop! *Her* shop!

On this mild April morning after the brisk walk from home through the quiet streets of Welbridge, Nicola's cheeks were pink and her eyes were glowing. The pink glow and the colour were not only because of the ten minutes' walk from her home, which was in the residential part of Welbridge. It was due to the thrill—still so new—of seeing that little newly painted shop with the freshly painted name:

*NICOLETTE.*

Her business name. . . . This was her own little business. . . . The Beauty Parlour which she had dreamed about for the last three years, and which was now an established fact.

As she unlocked the door and stooped to pick up the morning's mail her heart beat with the warm strong satisfaction of a person who sees an ambition fulfilled and knows that she has worked and saved for it.

Of course she had been lucky. And the family had been so wonderful. Mummy and Daddy paying for her training at a well-known beauty salon in London. Brother Ron, who had been in the R.A.F. during the war, helping with his generous cheques. They had all encouraged her when she had shown signs, even as a youngster, of being clever and soothing with her hands, and interested in 'beauty'. They were all darlings, including her young sister Frances (more commonly known as Flip), who used to suffer in silence while Nicola experimented upon her with creams and lotions and make-up until she was qualified to give Mummy a really good 'facial' in professional style.

And last but not least, dear kind Aunt Winnie's legacy which had come just at the right moment. A week after Nicola finished her training. That small but important sum of money, together with Nicola's savings, had enabled Nicola to take the lease of this little shop and gamble on it being a success.

*NICOLETTE* had opened two months ago on February first. Since then business had been brisk. Nicola could not expect to make a profit yet. There were many overhead expenses in any business, no matter how small, and there had been all the equipment to buy . . . furnishing and decoration, and a margin for the salary of Ann, the young assistant whom Nicola was training; and wages for people like Mrs. Deakes, who cleaned the shop every evening after they closed down.

But it *was* a success. Everybody said so. The Welbridge ladies were beginning to come to Nicolette for treatment and seemed satisfied with the result. All the pinching and scraping before she had started, the risks and the worries and the hard work, now seemed worth while.

March had really been a most exciting month. Starting with the arrival of Denis . . . Denis Avon, actor, who played lead in the Welbridge Repertory Company.

Nicola's mind and thoughts had recently swerved rather significantly from work to play because of Denis. But no, play was the wrong word. It was too serious to be called that. The thought of Denis was deep and thrilling and *real* . . . not only the Denis who appeared on the stage . . . a most handsome and attractive young man with a golden voice which would wring a tear out of the most hardened playgoer, but the Denis whom one met away from the stage and his work. The friendly, irresistible, gay yet sympathetic companion who had in an unbelievably short time disturbed Nicola's peace of mind and threatened to change the whole world for her.

To be a success at your job is one thing. To be a success in your love-affairs is another and much more emotionally disturbing.

Before Denis Avon came to Welbridge to storm the citadel of the feminine hearts in the town (and hers in particular!) Nicola had prided herself on being a level-headed business girl. It was her business capacity which had enabled her to 'get going' in this beauty parlour all on her own. But she was beginning to wonder what had happened to that Nicola. The cool calm practical Miss Boyd threatened to become a romantic schoolgirl—lovesick for the hero of her dreams. Why, she could remember teasing seventeen-year-old Ann who helped in the shop, because she had hung about the stage door waiting for Denis to come out and sign her autograph album. And laughing at young Flip who cut Denis's photograph out of a programme, framed it and hung it over her bed. Smiling too, in rather a superior way, when dear sentimental Mummy sniffed into her handkerchief while Denis played that last poignant scene of the erring husband reconciled to the young wife he had wronged and deserted.

But now Nicola could not afford to laugh at anybody. She herself was crazy about Denis. It seemed that she had been born with a silver spoon in her mouth. Like the beauty salon, her love-affair was prospering. The great, the much-sought-after, the heart-shaking Denis appeared to be just as much in love with her.

Nicola pulled up the blinds, filled the little shop with spring sunshine and sat down at her desk in the tiny office which adjoined the room in which she gave her beauty treatments. She gazed around her with an ecstatic expression.

It all looked lovely . . . the pale peach-coloured distemper and paint; the soft fleecy blankets to match, folded on the couch whereon her clients relaxed while she massaged, patted and smoothed away the wrinkles, then added the glamorous make-up which helped the old to recapture the impression of youth and made the young even more beautiful.

Aunt Winnie's legacy had only just bought the lease of the shop and paid for the expense of doing it up. But Nicola had had to save and plan and forgo quite a lot of personal luxuries in order, for instance, to buy those gleaming satin curtains, the cream Wilton carpet, and the beautiful gilt-framed mirrors which reflected rows of exciting-looking jars and bottles on glass shelves. As for her clothes . . . oh, what a time she had had, trying to make old things look more fashionable, working late at night . . . anything rather than spend money which she needed for all her beauty preparations, and the fabulous cost of getting all those lids and labels printed with the name—*NICOLETTE*. But it had been worth

7

it. Women in Welbridge were beginning to say, "Have you tried Nicolette's massage cream" . . . or "skin lotion" . . . or "muscle oil". And of course when the Rep. Theatre opened and Verona Dale, the leading lady, discovered Nicky's salon and came in for a 'facial' and approved of it, Nicola's success was assured. All the girls at the theatre came to her at least once a week, besides which Miss Dale had ordered heaps of creams and lotions on which there was a goodly profit.

Verona was a darling; one of the warm-hearted generous kind of her profession, *and* Verona had introduced Nicola to Denis.

This morning as Nicola sorted her letters and prepared for the morning's work, her mind would keep reverting to the memory of that first wonderful meeting.

Miss Dale had given a small party in her flat, which was in that new big block facing the river. It had been to celebrate the opening night of a new play that had just been well received.

Nicola had at first felt shy and out of things in that theatrical crowd; people whose talk seemed a little exaggerated and artificial; they all appeared to be sophisticated, widely travelled and experienced. Whereas Nicola, beyond the fact that she had had her training in London, had spent all her life in this sleepy little Berkshire town which was of no importance before the war. It was now rapidly growing, because a large aircraft factory had been built on the outskirts.

Population and trade had increased quite a bit since the days when Nicola's family first settled there. Mr. Boyd was then a junior clerk in the Civil Service. He had worked in the Town Hall; joined the Army Pay Corps during the war, returned to the Town Hall in 1944, and since retired with his pension.

Nicola had led the life one might expect the daughter of a man in such a position to lead. Hard working, quiet, uneventful, with few excitements except the annual family holiday (usually spent in Wales where Aunt Winnie had lived) or in Scarborough with Granny, Mrs. Boyd's mother, who had died a year ago.

Nicola had never been abroad.

But all Miss Dale's friends—members of the Rep. Company —talked eloquently of the South of France, of tours in the Swiss mountains, of visits to Rome and Paris. Exciting and rather dazzling for Nicola. And the most exciting and dazzling thing of all was the personality of Denis Avon.

Nicola had a swift vision of him as she had seen him that day, threading his way through the crowd in Miss Dale's sitting-room, cocktail glass in one hand; greeting this friend and that in the boyish gay manner which was one of his chief charms. She had seen him often on the stage before but never at such close quarters. Without the actor's make-up, she had decided, he looked even more attractive. His profile was classic and had been much photographed. A fine head with waving chestnut hair, chiselled features, dark blue eyes with very black lashes. He had a beautifully shaped mouth (a little spoiled, perhaps . . . even weak . . . but charming) and a cleft chin and graceful figure. He was to Nicola as handsome as a young Greek god, and as he drew near her she had the exquisite thrill of receiving two quick interested glances from him. Then he came up to her and said: "Hell . . . why aren't you drinking?"

When she had answered, shyly, that she never 'drank', he laughed and said: "How very unusual!" . . . then brought her an orange squash, asked her name and afterwards stayed talking to her for quite a long time.

She could hardly remember anything he had said at the time. Mostly about the new play and his part in it. He was obviously self-centred but one could forgive Denis for being an egoist, Nicola thought. He was so delightfully, honestly pleased with himself and his reception in Welbridge. She had wanted to go on listening to him. But Miss Dale had taken him away to introduce him to somebody else. Only when the party ended, Verona had teased Nicola about him:

"You were quite a success with our Denis. That's because you are so fresh—really radiant compared with us," she had said in her generous fashion. "We actresses suffer from late nights and too much grease-paint and limelight. But you look about seventeen—definitely not twenty-four. In fact, Denis

9

thought you *were* in your teens. But watch your step, Nicky, my sweet. Don't believe a word he ever says. He's a terror."

Nicola had tried to profit by that advice, but when she got home she found that she wanted to believe all the nice things Denis had said to her. She had even felt anxious lest he should have thought her *too* young and awkward, compared with his glamorous theatrical friends. She had feverishly experimented on herself with a new beauty treatment, and wondered if she could indulge in a really expensive new dress this spring. For she was bound to meet Denis Avon again. In fact he himself was giving a party that next week and had asked her to it.

She had gone to the party. Once again Denis attached himself to her side, and after that quite an intense friendship had sprung up between them. Her parents invited him to their home. He had supper with them . . . made himself most charming to her mother, and talked so intelligently about politics to her father that he had afterwards admitted "that actor chap knew a thing or two"; then conceded to Nicola that, although he did not approve of the stage as a career for a young fellow, Denis Avon seemed a normal healthy-minded chap outside his profession. He forgave him for not having seen war service, because he had been getting over a bad attack of rheumatic fever which had ruled him out for any of the Services. But he had travelled through the Middle East and Germany with E.N.S.A. and nearly been blown up once or twice, entertaining troops in serious zones of war.

As a rule, Nicola was delighted to look at the engagement pad on her desk and note that she was booked up for beauty treatments from ten o'clock onwards. But she was a little irked today to find bookings for the whole afternoon.

Denis's new craze was rowing on the beautiful river, which ran through Welbridge. Yesterday he had begged her to get away early and go out with him. Exercise, fresh air and sunlight were what he needed, he said, before the show opened. And tomorrow, Saturday, there was a matinée and he would be working all day. So would she.

Nicola gave a brief impatient sigh as she slipped into the pale pink overall which she wore when giving treatments. She would never be able to meet Denis at half past four if she was to do that last 'facial' properly. And she loved her work. It was most important that it should be done well. But Denis Avon had become important, too.

Last night for the first time he had kissed her.

Bill Venning, the theatre manager, had given a supper party after the show and Nicola—now firm friends with the whole Rep. Company—had attended. Denis saw her home. It was a cold but perfect spring night, with a clear moon shining on the river. They had walked along the towpath to Regent Square where Nicola lived. And Denis had suddenly stopped and swung her into his arms and said in that thrilling, golden voice of his:

"Nicky, I am crazy about you. I don't know what it is, but I find you more attractive than any girl I have met in my life."

Utterly in love with him, she had felt herself melting into his embrace. It was more than she had dared hope for: that the great Denis Avon should love *her*! She had hung back a moment in his arms and whispered: "Why should you find *me* attractive, Denis?"

His answer was ready; his voice vibrant with sincerity:

"Because you are genuine . . . so absolutely honest and to be relied upon. I can't imagine you ever lying or deceiving a fellow. And you've got courage. I admire the way you've built up that business and how you run it all on your own. I admire the practical streak in you as well as your adorable touch of glamour. I adore your cool slenderness, the sensitive way you blush when I say nice things to you. The way those fascinating pupils of your big grey eyes grow large and dark when you are excited. Your funny little laugh, your trick of wrinkling your small nose when you are amused. And your hair . . . that fair smooth head of yours with its shining coil in the nape of your neck. There is something very chaste, almost Madonna-like, about you which sets you apart from other women in my eyes. I don't wonder you have been a success as a beauty expert. *You are a beauty.* Beauty its very self!"

Could she ever possibly forget a single one of those lovely poetic things which he had whispered against her mouth . . . or the burning kiss which had followed, and revealed to her, suddenly, the whole essence of loving and being passionately loved? She went home deeply and irretrievably in love with Denis Avon. He left her with the words:

"It's quite obvious that you and I were meant for each other, little Nicola. I didn't think I would get married for years. But I want to marry you . . . soon . . . as soon as you'll have me."

He wanted to take her out this afternoon and talk it all over. She had not slept, because she had lain awake hour after hour, remembering his kisses and everything that he had said.

It was all so wonderful, she could not speak of it—did not breathe a word about it to the family. But here, in her little shop this morning, some of the rapture faded and gave place to more prosaic, sensible reflection.

This Beauty Salon was her own shop . . . the business which had been her dearest ambition and to which she had meant to devote the next few years of her life. Denis had said that marriage had not entered his head until he had met her. Well, it was the same with her. Perhaps she had thought about marriage at times. But only casually. With that strong streak of ambition and her love of work, she had never seriously contemplated getting tied up to any man and forsaking her job for a domestic life.

The more she thought about it all now, the more uneasy she became. But surely, if she *did* decide to marry Denis, he would not want an immediate marriage? They could be engaged and she would be able to carry on with her work, while he carried on with his. She was only twenty-four; he was twenty-six. There was plenty of time for them both.

When Ann Williams came into the shop, Nicola bade her good morning, tried to drive the thought of Denis from her mind and concentrate on her job.

She said:

"We want some ice for Miss Dale's pack this morning, Ann. Run along to the MacFisheries and make sure they are sending our block early."

Ann, a nice-looking girl, still rather in the plump stage and trying anxiously to 'slim', went off to carry out orders.

Alone again, Nicola opened a cupboard and began to take

out towels, bottles and bowls and prepare for the first treatment which was to be for Miss Deborah Greene—one of the girls in the Rep. Company. But try as she would, Nicola could not stop thinking about Denis and last night. That wonderful moment in his arms . . . that breath-taking, undreamed-of proposal of marriage. She could hardly wait to see him again.

Somebody opened the door of the shop. Nicola parted the curtains of the cubicle in which she had been standing, and saw a broad-shouldered young man wearing grey flannels and a tweed jacket. He had a pipe in one hand and was holding an enormous Boxer puppy on a lead with the other. The Boxer was panting and straining at his leash and lunged playfully towards Nicola.

"Hi, Kimbo," exclaimed the young man, "down you get! Behave yourself. You're in a Beauty Parlour now, and if you are not good Miss Boyd will cut off your whiskers and remove all your wrinkles."

Nicola burst out laughing and immediately went down on her knees and embraced the Boxer.

"Oh, what a darling!"

"My latest love," said the young man with a grin and added: "I say, Kimbo, you're in luck. Our beauty expert is allowing you to kiss her. She has never been so nice to me."

Nicola, still laughing, stood up and smoothed her crumpled overall.

"Ah, you've not got nearly such a winning way as Kimbo."

He bowed from the waist and stuck his pipe between his teeth.

"That does it. I will say good morning, Miss Boyd."

She smiled up at him.

"Idiot! How are you, March? I haven't seen you for ages."

"No, I have been away on business. Not finding it easy to get used to this business racket. It doesn't suit me. I'm taking a long week-end off and that is why Kimbo and I dropped in, to ask if you would like to come on the river and have a sort of picnic with us on Sunday. I'm getting up a party."

"Oh, thanks awfully, but I—I've already got a date," she said.

She hadn't. But nothing would have induced her to get booked up before seeing Denis again. He would be sure to want her to spend Sunday with *him*.

March Foster (he had been christened thus by a fanciful mother because he had been born in the month of March) forced the Boxer down into a recumbent position, then looked at the girl with mild disappointment. Somehow he had banked on Nicola joining the Sunday picnic. He liked to have her around. They had both been brought up in Welbridge but March had been in the Army for a few years and away on active service. It was not until his demobilization that he had led any kind of settled existence and begun to see his old friends down here regularly again.

He came out of the Commandos with the rank of Major and several ribbons on his tunic, including the Military Cross. His father was a man of some means and owner of a chain of prosperous stores, the biggest of which was here in Welbridge.

It was Mr. Foster's ambition that his one and only son should settle down to the business so that he could retire and hand over the general management to March. But, so far, March Foster had found it immensely irksome trying to settle down to civilian life. Even a job as a 'high-up' in the most successful chain of stores spelt monotony for a young man who was highly trained and skilled in Commando tactics and used to the company of a crowd of tough young officers who, like himself, adored the thrills and dangers of life. After the war first ended, he had managed to stay on with the Army in Palestine. But in the end he had to retire. The old man had become impatient and demanded that his son should come home. So, reluctantly, March returned to Welbridge. But he had not settled down yet, and there was generally a 'row' on with 'Pop', who was a solid conventional business-minded old man. He had little patience with March's spirit of adventure and unbusiness-like ways.

Nicola looked upon March with a somewhat benevolent gaze. She liked him. Everybody in Welbridge did. They had had some good parties together and many of the girls in the locality found him attractive. He was tall and strong and had a brown hard face with rather blunt features, rough dark curly hair and a pair of merry hazel eyes. Nicola thought March a first-rate person and, in her opinion, good to look at.

But he never seemed to her to be serious. Perhaps she had never had a chance to get to know him really well since they 'grew up'. His courage she certainly admired. He hadn't earned his medals for nothing. And she often heard his mother say that March had an artistic side. Wrote short stories as a hobby. Clever little sketches about people he knew. Not that Nicola could ever connect the war-scarred young Commando with art any more than one could imagine him as a business man, and none of his stories had so far been published.

But she liked him. They always got on well. And he made her laugh. Before Denis Avon came to Welbridge . . . she had gone on one particular party with March which was quite memorable. They had danced together and talked seriously for the first time. The evening had ended on quite a sentimental note. He had become suddenly gentle and sweet and she had gone home thinking more than twice about March the ex-Commando. But he had never followed up that evening. He had gone away again, and Nicola, immersed in her own job, had forgotten that episode.

Here he was again. Her feelings towards him were of the friendliest but casual. In the middle of their conversation, Ann came back with the ice, followed by Nicola's first client, so she had to bundle March and Kimbo unceremoniously out of the shop.

As he left her, March said :

"The old man is sending me on a tour of inspection of our shops on Monday but I will be back the following week-end. What about keeping Sunday free for me? I have just had delivery of my new Riley Sixteen. It's a peach. Pop got it for the business. I would like to take you out. We might run down to Hungerford. I know a jolly good pub there for lunch. . . ."

Once again Nicola stammered a refusal. March looked slightly surprised but waved her a cheerful good-bye and departed.

As he walked down the High Street, however, it struck him suddenly that he was not making the grade with Nicola Boyd.

She had turned him down flat this morning, twice. Why? What had he done? He used to think they got on rather well. And that last time they went on a party together he had found her decidedly attractive—a woman to be regarded seriously instead of the little girl he used to play with and 'rag'.

Of course he hadn't tried to make the grade very hard. He had never really pursued any girl with persistence. He got too much fun out of life as a bachelor; especially while he was in the Services.

His mother was always urging him to get married and settle down. One day he meant to do so. He knew he had a love of home and would want a wife, and he adored small kids. He could see himself as a family man—but not for years —say when he was well over thirty. A beautiful girl for the moment was hardly as exciting to March as a new car! But he found himself thinking quite a lot about Nicola once he left the Beauty Salon that morning. He was really darned disappointed, he thought, that she wouldn't join the picnic on Sunday, or the Sunday afterwards. She was really one of the most attractive girls in Welbridge, and strange to say, despite the fact that she ran a beauty shop and was a success, she was not in the least bit conceited or exacting like some of the glamour girls he had taken out in his life. There was something very fresh and sweet about Nicola. He considered her grave grey eyes and the almost silver fairness of her hair; her sound common sense and good judgment. Yes, she was *sensible* as well as a good-looker. A rare combination. Why had she turned him down? Had she a boy-friend . . . some affair in progress? He must make enquiries.

March found himself suddenly strangely interested in Nicola Boyd.

## II

DENIS had moored the boat in one of the quiet backwaters. Quite a crowd had been drawn out of doors this lovely April afternoon and lured on to the sparkling water.

But it was growing a trifle late now the river. Despite an impatient Denis who kept coming to the salon to see if Nicola was ready, she refused to hurry her last client. But here she was at last, alone with *him*. The shadows lengthened and the last golden rays of the sun filtered through the fresh green lace of the trees. It was an exquisite tranquil hour and Nicola was not conscious of the cold. She listened to yet another declaration of love from Denis.

This time the word 'marriage' came into it, in no uncertain manner.

"I must see your people and talk to Papa in the good old-fashioned way and tell him that I want to marry you by special licence at once!"

Nicola was dazed. For a moment she could only stare up at him. She was in his arms, both of them leaning back against the red cushions in the boat which rocked gently with the current. Her whole body was warm, trembling a little in his embrace. He had kissed her until she was breathless and now he was taking her breath away again by all these amazing things which he was saying to her. He turned her head a little, with his marvellous good looks and the apparent sincerity of his love-making. But Nicola's cautious streak bade her beware. Flushed and shaken, she put one cool slim hand against his urgent lips.

"Wait, Denis . . . darling, really! We can't possibly be married at once. We haven't known each other nearly long enough. It's *crazy*!"

Denis pulled her back into his arms.

"I adore you in that grey flannel suit," he said irrelevantly, "and the little yellow jumper is sweet. Don't tell me you knitted it yourself. Do you knit? You do everything. I can hardly believe you are so capable and can still look so glamorous."

She laughed and shook her head, still trying to reason with him.

"Denis, you are impossible. We are supposed to be having a serious talk about marriage."

"Very serious," he nodded, "and I mean what I say. I am madly in love with you and you have got to marry me next week."

She gasped.

"Next week!"

"Yes."

"But it's out of the question!"

"Oh, no, it isn't, darling. You see, I am now going to tell you my big secret. I am finishing with the Welbridge Rep. perhaps in two weeks' time. I have been offered a wonderful part in a London production. It will have six weeks' provincial tour first. You know my ambition to get on to the London stage. I'll tell you about my part later. It isn't a lead, of course, but it's a good one. Suits me. What concerns me now is *us*. I refuse to go away and leave you here in Welbridge. You have got to come with me—on my tour—as my wife, and later on, if I am a success in London, I can promise that you will have a wonderful time. I'll make money. I'll be able to buy you gorgeous clothes. We'll have a superb flat . . . and . . ."

"Oh, Denis, my darling, wait!" Nicola interrupted, thrilled and yet dismayed. "You're forgetting the shop."

"You mean your Beauty Parlour?"

"Yes, of course. After all, I have only just opened it. I am only just beginning to make a success of it. I can't walk out on that."

Denis yawned and then picked up one of her hands and kissed the pretty polished nails.

"My little beauty expert," said he in a teasing voice. "Ah no, my sweet, you'll have to chuck the business. Sell it. Give it away. Or find someone to run it for you. I want you to marry me. Isn't that more important to you than being *NICOLETTE*?"

For a moment she did not speak. She sat quiet in the curve of his arm, her heart throbbing, cheeks on fire. He went on reasoning with her . . . airily dismissing *NICOLETTE* as though it were of small consequence in her life and none in his. He enlarged on the subject of his own career. Already he was seeing the name DENIS AVON in neon lights outside a West End theatre. And he built up a fabulous picture of the marvellous life she would lead with him in London after what he called her 'provincial drudgery' down here.

The more she listened, the more uneasy Nicola became. One

side of her—the human emotional side—was stirred and captivated. She longed to put her lips against that beautiful vain mouth of his and whisper: *"Very well, I love you. Take me to London as your wife. Nothing else matters."*

But there was still that other side of her, reasoning, rebelling. He could not altogether change the Nicola who was independent and level-headed, and who did not want to be dragged willy-nilly from the business she had started and which, in its small way, was prospering.

Try as he would, Denis could not get a definite answer from her that afternoon. She refused to be swept right off her feet. She must think things over, she told him. It was her whole life's work and ambition which he was trying to demolish in a single moment. When, disappointed, thwarted, he accused her of not loving him, she almost surrendered, there and then. She loved him so much that she hardly knew how to refuse to give him the promise he asked for. She still could not believe that the great Denis Avon could possibly be so much in love that he should wish to marry her, carry her off like this. She begged him to be patient, to wait, to give her time to think.

With that he was forced to be content. And his failure to beguile her into immediate concession seemed only to fire his enthusiasm. He told her that he needed her; and that his wonderful chance of making good in London would mean nothing to him unless she was by his side. He needed that calm strong nature of hers . . . that rare combination of beauty and efficiency which would make her a perfect wife which set her apart from other women in his eyes.

Later she left him at the theatre, then went home hardly able to think straight. She passed her salon on the way and looked at the name *NICOLETTE*: that name which stood for independence and security, for her personal achievement and triumph. How could she throw it all up for Denis? And yet without him life would have little meaning now. Her heart beat to suffocation at the mere memory of his eager arms and lips. Denis was overwhelming as a lover.

*But was he just a stage-lover?* Were his ardours merely superficial? Would he change in time? Oh, if only she knew all the answers! If only somebody would tell her what to do!

That night she informed her family of Denis's proposal. Her young sister, Flip, was the only one to shower her immediately with congratulations.

"Oh, you are lucky, Nic! Just fancy . . . *Denis Avon* . . . and he'll be my brother-in-law . . . how too, *too* thrilling!"

But neither Mr. or Mrs. Boyd were ready to encourage their elder daughter to marry the young actor. Mr. Boyd's opinion was that, nice though the young chap was, he *was* an *actor*; perhaps fickle and unstable. He would never make her a good husband. He would lead an unsettled extravagant life and always be hard up. Mr. Boyd enlarged on the financial side of the matter. Mrs. Boyd was less voluble. She was by nature a quiet woman of few words. But she looked with troubled eyes at her eldest daughter. In her opinion, Nicola was just a wonderful girl and absolutely dependable. Somehow she did not want to see her swept off her feet by the handsome young actor; and it would in her opinion be a tragedy for Nic to throw up the little business for which she had worked and planned ever since she started training.

"You haven't known Mr. Avon long, dear," she said. "I think you ought to have an engagement first, anyhow—not rush into marriage."

That was all that Mrs. Boyd said, but it was enough to increase Nicola's own doubts and apprehensions.

She found it hard to sleep that night, and when she did she dreamt that she sent Denis away, then she wanted him back and could not find him and was desperately unhappy. She woke to find the tears streaming down her cheeks—she was seized with an intense longing to see Denis at once, throw herself in his arms and tell him she would leave everything, everybody, for his sake. She could not bear to send him away alone.

She was in no state to do her work that morning. Denis was taking her out to lunch . . . going to insist upon a definite reply from her. But she still didn't know what to say. She looked pale and heavy-eyed, and felt sick with worry. And her first client this morning was the great Miss Verona Dale herself.

Once the treatment commenced and Nicola sat smoothing cream with her cool clever fingers into the face and throat of the lovely leading lady, Miss Dale noticed suddenly that something was wrong with the girl. She was usually bright and talkative. This morning she seemed dejected, even gloomy.

"What's happened to you, my dear?" asked Verona. "Are you depressed?"

"It's nothing—just a headache," stammered Nicola.

Verona Dale looked up through her long lashes at this girl who was such a favourite with all of them in the Rep. Company. Nicola was much younger than Verona herself and very much less experienced. Verona thought she understood exactly what was wrong with Nicola. Bluntly she said so.

"I think it is your heart rather than your head that's giving you trouble, isn't it, Nicky darling?"

Nicola blushed crimson.

"I . . . Oh, no, of course not."

But within the space of a few minutes Verona Dale had cunningly extracted half the truth. Yes, Nicola admitted that she *was* in love. But she was not prepared to name the man. So Verona resorted to less direct methods of discussing Nicola's troubles.

"Whoever you choose, whoever the lucky man is, for heaven's sake don't let it be an actor, darling," she said glibly.

She did not see Nicola's burning flush but felt the slim fingers quiver and stop work a moment.

"Why not, Miss Dale?"

Then of course Verona knew. . . . With deliberate casualness she added:

"Take someone like our leading man, for instance. I wouldn't be married to Denis Avon for all the tea in China. He's terrifically attractive. And there's something awfully nice about him. We *all* like Denis. But no woman should take him seriously."

Nicola stopped the massage and turned to wipe her hands with a face-tissue. Her pulses were racing, her lips compressed. She spoke rather stiffly.

"I don't doubt if Denis Avon ever fell really in love . . . he . . . he'd change. He'd settle down."

"H'm," said Verona. "Well, I'd hate to see a nice girl fall in love with him. She'd only get hurt. He's too unstable. I know his type. I've met them on the stage all my life. Think of the awful life he'd lead his wife. No roots or security. Nothing lasts with a chap like Denny. I can well imagine that to start off his wife would have raptures, but, my goodness, what miseries she'd end with!"

Nicola closed up like a clam. Nothing would induce her to go on discussing Denis with Miss Dale. But after the friendly, charming actress had gone Nicola sat down weakly and put a hand to her throbbing head.

Everybody was against her marrying Denis. There seemed to be a general conspiracy to make her feel she would be crazy to throw up the world for him. Well, perhaps they were all right and yet . . . love was not meant to be a dull prosaic thing, set along smooth lines. Where there were raptures, there must also be heartaches. If she married Denis she would have to expect difficulties. But wouldn't they be worth while, with and for *him*?

Ann Williams went out to lunch. Nicola was left alone. Almost in despair she looked around the pink, perfumed salon. She loved it. She wanted to go on with her job. Yet without Denis Avon now, life would have no real significance.

Let the whole world be against her. But somehow she was encouraged rather than put off by opposition. Her fighting blood was up. And she loved Denis—whatever Miss Dale said about his lack of stability. She loved him. And he loved her. If it was true, that he was unstable, real love would change him, bind him to her side.

The door opened. Denis came in the salon to fetch her for lunch. She slid out of her overall and stood facing him, looking rather small and defenceless and with a mute appeal in her grey earnest eyes. He on his part looked eager and handsome enough to captivate any woman's heart. His eyes were glowing with love and longing for her.

He came towards her, a huge bunch of violets in his hand. "For you, my sweetest. They reminded me of you . . . I'd like to make a wreath of them for that golden head of yours. Then you would be a nymph—the incarnation of spring."

Foolish flattery. Yet she found herself unable to resist the sweetness of his words and the magic of his touch. And suddenly she was crushed in his arms, violets and all, and he was covering her face with kisses.

"I love you so much, Nicola," he whispered huskily. "Tell me that you are going to marry me, my darling."

After that there could be no more doubts. No further room for hesitation. Between those long kisses, she heard herself whispering 'yes' and 'yes' again. She seemed now to be swept along on an irresistible tide. Denis did all the steering, and she had little or no volition of her own.

Later that day Denis approached her parents and managed to convince even that practical unsentimental couple that an immediate marriage with Nicola was essential to Nicola's happiness as well as his. That very evening Nicola found herself officially engaged to Denis. Mummy was ready to send a notice there and then to the Welbridge daily paper, and a beautiful ruby and diamond ring gleamed on Nicola's finger: a ring on which Denis had spent obviously more than he could afford.

That was what one loved about him . . . his bursts of generosity . . . his boyish charm . . . his apparently sincere wish to look after Nicola for the rest of her life and make her happy.

He talked of a wedding next week. . . . She must, he declared, find an immediate buyer for NICOLETTE . . . then a flat in town.

What money had he? What security? Nothing as far as Nicola could judge. What background? What did he offer his wife? She did not know. She discovered little or nothing about his private life except that he had no parents, and when he wasn't in a job he lived with an old aunt in Putney. He would take Nicola to see Aunt Emma as soon as possible.

But for the moment he did not propose to be bothered with family duties. He wanted to celebrate his engagement. Everything with Denis must always be now. He lived for the present, rarely considered the future.

After the show that night, he held a celebration supper party on the stage.

Feeling as if she was in a kind of feverish dream, Nicola sat at Denis's side and tried to enjoy the hastily organized party as much as Denis was enjoying it.

23

He was in tremendous spirits. He had had a particularly good reception from his audience, and he had won his Nicola. He was content. He had never looked more handsome or been more delightful to everybody. And he made Nicola feel that she was the only woman in the room who really counted. They exchanged long deep glances. He stood up to propose a toast to her.

"To my future wife, who is, I am sure you will all agree, beautiful enough to be in herself an advertisement for Beauty."

There were cheers and applause. Everybody had something nice to say. And yet Nicola sat rather silent. A little of the mad excitement of becoming publicly engaged to Denis evaporated as she listened and watched.

The whole Company had been warmly generous in their acceptance of her as Denis's future wife. But was she dreaming, or did she sense that the general enthusiasm was a trifle guarded . . . that one or two curious looks were thrown at her by the girls in the cast.

And as for Miss Dale, her blue eyes had looked even reproachful—pitying—when she had kissed and congratulated her.

Down at the end of the long supper table Verona Dale sat beside March Foster. March was here—had been asked to the supper by the leading lady herself. He had taken her out once or twice since the Rep. theatre had opened in Welbridge. Verona had a weak spot for the young ex-Commando, and as he was an old friend of Nicola's, felt that he had a right to be in the engagement party.

Once or twice Nicola caught a long strange look from March. His personal congratulation when he first saw her this evening had been abrupt, even cool, but tinged as usual with flippancy.

"Kimbo will be enormously jealous," was his only remark. "I think he thought when you kissed him this morning he was to be the big thing in your life."

She had laughed back.

"Oh, you can tell Kimbo he still holds a large portion of my heart."

Then March had turned rather abruptly away.

She wondered what he was saying to Verona. She wished this supper party would end. She was beginning to feel nervy and not as happy as she had expected to be. Denis held one of her hands, full of warmth and radiance, as excited as a child who had got his own way. He adored her, he said, in that rose pink velvet dinner-dress. He snipped two pink roses from a vase and pinned them in her silver-fair hair.

"You really are exquisite and I can't wait until next week," he said with an ardour that made her tremble.

*Next week!* Was it possible that she was going to turn her back on Welbridge and her job, and marry Denis, *next week?*

She had a suffocating feeling which she did not altogether understand. She only knew that she wanted to get away from the laughing joking crowd, here on the stage . . . away from the drinking and frothy chatter, and be alone with Denis.

March Foster lit a cigarette. As he put down the burnt match he looked through half-closed eyes at the girl in the rose pink velvet dress sitting at the top of the table beside her newly acquired fiancé. He had watched the young actor pin the roses in that fair shining hair with consummate skill. Somehow it had annoyed him intensely. The man himself annoyed March. He was too smooth and, in March's opinion, too darned insincere. How the devil did he manage to get hold of Nicola? March had never anticipated such a thing.

He turned to Verona.

"Do you see this working out?"

Verona nodded in the direction of the engaged couple.

"What . . . those two? Certainly not. I warned her indirectly . . . and when Denny told me I warned him. She's a sweet thing, and though Denny is charming this marriage could never be a success. He'll get sick of her and break her heart. But there is nothing to be done about it. The kid's crazy about him. It's a shame, but it's too late now."

March's gaze returned to Nicola's face, rapt and dreamy in the candlelight. She looked bewitched. Yes, that was the word. Denis Avon had bewitched her. It wasn't a healthy sort of affair. Nic was a sensible girl. She *couldn't* be as silly as this. . . .

"Nobody can do anything about it," Verona Dale said again.

"H'm," said March profoundly, "*I wonder* . . ."

And quite suddenly, still watching Nicola, his pulses quickened and the light of battle began to kindle in his eyes.

## III

THE supper party on the stage was over. The last bottle of wine had been drunk and the last cigarette smoked. Denis rose to his feet and made a little speech with an expression of mock gloom.

"Owing to present controls, ladies and gentlemen, we must now either attempt to continue this gaiety by quenching our thirst with lemonade and dreaming of the days when Virginia cigarettes fell freely into our laps at a shilling for twenty, or . . . we must drift homewards and seek consolation upon our Vi-spring mattresses. . . ." He coughed and added: "The Vi-spring Company has paid me handsomely to include this in my speech."

Laughter greeted the sally. Everybody rose. Nicola slipped a hand into her fiancé's and stood beside him, her over-excited mind still only half able to grasp her happiness.

Then March Foster said:

"The night is still young and all the ladies are so beautiful, I think it would be a shame to break up the party. After all, you don't have many, you hardworking souls. But I have a house—or rather my parents have a house—with a large room which has a parquet floor and a radiogram. Why not all of you come back and dance?"

Judy Morris—the small pretty red-haired girl who played juvenile leads in the company—clapped her hands.

"What a marvellous idea!"

Bill Venning, the big, red-faced, cheerful-looking manager, said:

"Very nice of you, old boy, but how about disturbing the household?"

"Oh, my parents don't mind that sort of thing. My mother is away and Papa sleeps soundly. And I may add that you need not drink lemonade nor only dream of cigarettes at home. There is plenty of both by courtesy of my revered father and, of course, the Black Market."

Another ripple of laughter. Nicola joined in it but she saw March's gaze fixed upon her. He was giving her a long, rather curious look which she did not understand. She felt a little sleepy. She wanted to go home, or be alone with Denis. But Denis, holding her hand tightly, edged through the crowd towards March.

"I think it's a first-rate idea, old boy," he said. "I'm definitely in the mood for a night out. What do you say, folks? Shall we take advantage of the offer and follow the gallant Commando whither he leads us?"

Shouts of "Yes!" The party mood was still 'on'. Verona Dale, as she put her silver foxes round her shoulders, stifled a yawn and said:

"Well, for a short time perhaps, but it's matinée day tomorrow and I don't want to look like a hag when I wake up."

"You couldn't, darling," said Denis and lifted one of her hands as he passed her and kissed it.

March Foster watched, and thought, not for the first time that night:

"Too smooth . . . too much the matinée idol and ladies' man ever to make a faithful husband. No, Verona is right . . . someone has got to weigh in and save Nicola. . . ."

Was it only that he wanted to 'save' her, or did the thought of her marrying Denis Avon arouse another instinct in him . . . a challenge which he could not resist . . . the invitation to a fight? *A fight for Nicola.* He knew as he looked now at Nicola that he was in love with her. He always had been but he hadn't known it. He had been too busy—first of all fighting the war and then settling down to civilian life. But he loved her, and he was utterly dismayed by the thought that she meant to marry Denis.

The little company of actors piled into various cars and drove to the Fosters' home, which was on the outskirts of Welbridge. Heron's Hall was one of the showplaces of Welbridge, partially old, partially modernized, but retaining its Georgian character. A glorious garden stretched down to the river's edge, where there was a boathouse. March, as a boy, used to be keen on rowing. He had won a sculling contest for his college. The Fosters also had a motor-boat which they had not been able to use lately because of shortage of petrol.

There was a time when Heron's Hall was full of servants and run on luxurious lines. Even now they had more domestic help than most people. But they did little entertaining these days. March was always away and Mrs. Foster, a delicate woman, was more often than not in the hands of doctors, in expensive nursing homes.

Nicola had not been inside this house for a very long time, although as a child she had been asked to all the parties that the Fosters gave for their young son. Despite being a self-made man and, nowadays, a rich one, George Foster (Welbridge knew him as Old Georgie) had none of the unattractive qualities of the *nouveau riche*. He was a generous host to all the old friends who had known him when his father before him had started the first shop in this neighbourhood, and neither loud nor ostentatious.

Nicola could remember some quite wonderful parties in Heron's Hall. As they drove up to it—Nicola and Denis had squeezed into March's Riley with him—March flung her a mischievous look and said:

"I can remember you climbing up that apple tree over there in the orchard to pick the reddest apple at the top of the tree. It was when you were about ten and I was a good bit older."

Nicola laughed and nestled closer to Denis.

"Goodness! I remember that, too. I can even remember I was wearing blue overalls and I tore them and cried and you laughed at me."

Denis laughed.

"Are you the sort of girl that climbs trees?"

"Oh, you don't know nearly as much about her as I do," put in March airily. "Our demure little beauty specialist used to be the tomboy of the crowd."

"I *wasn't*!" Nicola denied ungrammatically, "but you dared me to go up the tree after that apple, so I did, that's all."

"Commando tactics, eh?" said Denis in a slightly bored voice. He was not interested in the fact that March Foster had known Nicola as a child. But March continued with his reminiscences, then drove the Riley up to the front door, got out and opened the door for Nicola. The other cars were behind—just turning into the drive. March always drove faster than anybody else.

"It's far too long really, Nic, since you were at Heron's Hall, but I've been away so much, haven't I? And since Mother's operation last winter we've had hardly anybody here."

"Are you sure it won't disturb Mr. Foster if we make a noise in the house?" asked Nicola.

"Quite sure. The drawing-room is on the river side. Father's room is nowhere near. Come along in."

The party filed into the drawing-room, where March hastily switched on some lights. He told the others to roll back the rugs and put on the radio while he went in search of drinks.

Denis looked a trifle curiously around. It had three french windows looking out on to the river. It was certainly a lovely spacious room full of lovely things, with a big French crystal chandelier shedding brilliant light; rich old rugs, pale green satin looped curtains, and fine antique furniture. It had a gracious air.

"Nice place," Denis observed to Nicola; "plenty of cash here, eh?"

She nodded.

"Yes, but they're awfully sweet people . . . no vulgarity. March's mother is an angel. His father is a bit rough, a typical hard-headed business man, but Mrs. Foster is rather artistic and she did all the *décor* and arranging of the house. Goodness!" she added with a sigh, "I've been here such heaps of times in my life."

"So you know March Foster really well?"

"We were both brought up in Welbridge but in recent years . . . since I've grown up . . . I've seen very little of him."

"He doesn't appeal to me much. I don't really like the way he looks at you," Denis said in a low voice.

Nicola stared and then broke into a laugh.

"Darling, don't be silly! The way March looks at *me*? Why, he hardly looks at me at all."

"Oh, well, I have my own opinion," said Denis.

Nicola opened her lips to argue and then shut them again. She had yet to learn that when Denis formed an opinion it was generally the outcome not so much of intelligent consideration as of his mood at the moment. She had also to learn that there was a strong streak of envy in him and that he didn't like anybody to have anything that he hadn't got. It rather annoyed him to come here and see March Foster's beautiful home while he, Denis, struggled in cheap, theatrical 'digs'. But he wasn't going to struggle much longer. He spoke his thoughts aloud:

"I'll soon be in a position to give you a much more marvellous home than this, darling," he said, and bent down and dropped a kiss on her hair.

She smiled up at him but she was a little puzzled. How absurd of Denis to say that March 'looked at her' . . . and yet had she not intercepted a 'look' from him which had puzzled her, just before leaving the theatre? But it was all nonsense. Everybody knew that March had no time for girls.

Then March came back with some interesting-looking bottles and several packets of cigarettes.

The little crowd surrounded him, laughing and ragging. Bottles were opened. Someone found a dance-band on the radio. Bill Venning put an arm around Judy Morris and began to dance.

The celebration party continued with zest under the Foster roof.

Denis quenched his thirst and then led Nicola on to the floor. Like most actors he danced perfectly. Nicola was light and graceful, but as she had had so little chance of dancing in her busy life she found it hard to follow Denis's intricate steps. After fumbling once or twice she stopped, flushed and apologetic.

"You're far too professional for me, Denis."

"I'll soon teach you," he said. "I adore dancing. We shall dance a lot together in the life we'll lead."

Nicola drew a sigh.

She still felt bewildered and a little uncertain as to what

kind of life she *would* lead in the future with this handsome and glamorous man.

Now he had left her and was dancing with the leading lady. This time it really was a professional exhibition. Everybody clapped and cried 'Encore'! Somebody said:

"Come on! Give us a Ginger Rogers–Fred Astaire! . . ."

March came up behind Nicola.

"Come and look at this, Nic," he said.

She turned. He had opened one of the french windows which led on to a paved terrace. A full moon was shining. The garden looked exquisite in that ethereal light and the river was like a broad band of silver flowing past at the end of the lawn. Nicola shivered a little as the cold night air struck her cheeks but she said:

"Oh, how lovely!"

He thought that she looked lovely too, her fair hair bleached by the moonlight and her eyes as big and radiant as the stars themselves. A radiant girl in a rose petal gown with lips made for kisses—tender—serious—yet passionate. And he had let her go! . . . In his casual way he had 'missed the boat' . . . forgotten that such youth and beauty do not stay alone and unchosen for long. Denis Avon the stranger, the interloper, had snatched the prize from under his very nose. What a blind fool he had been all these months!

*"It's too late,"* Verona Dale had said, for she, too, had seen the folly of Nicola's choice.

But March could never accept defeat at any man's hands.

Now Nicola turned to him, her eyes still full of that unearthly radiance which made his pulses quicken at the very sight.

"It's a lovely night from every point of view, March, and sweet of you to let us all come here and carry on with the celebration."

He leaned against the lintel of the glass door, cigarette between his lips, hands in his pockets, brooding gaze fixed on her.

"I don't know that I care much for it."

"For what?"

"Your engagement to Denis Avon," he said abruptly.

31

She looked startled and felt it.

"Good gracious, why not, March?" she asked with an embarrassed laugh.

"I just can't see you married to him, that's all."

"Oh, March, don't you like him? Everybody does!" she exclaimed.

He suddenly adored her for her simplicity. That unspoiled freshness which marked her out from every other girl he had met. He said in a low voice:

"Denis Avon is handsome and charming, Nic. But he's an actor."

She bit her lip. Her heart beat a trifle resentfully. She resented any criticisms of Denis. But March—with whom she had played as a child—whom she knew so well—she mustn't mind what *he* said. It didn't matter anyhow. She protested mildly:

"How Victorian of you, dear! There's nothing wrong in being an actor. It's as good a profession as any other."

March shook his head, his eyes narrowing.

"No, my dear. An actor remains . . . an *actor*. Doesn't *that* scare you?" He nodded in the direction of the room. Nicola turned and saw her fiancé still executing some exciting steps with Verona. They had both simulated an abandoned pose, dancing cheek to cheek, moving in perfect unison.

Nicola turned back to March. He saw that now the radiance had left her eyes. Perhaps she *was* scared, but she wasn't going to say so. She tossed back her head.

"Oh, that sort of thing! I couldn't care less. It means nothing to Denis. It's just what he calls 'theatre'. Why should I mind?"

"You've always been a quiet little thing. I can't imagine you as the wife of a successful actor."

Nicola felt annoyed. She had a vague idea that March was perfectly right but she didn't want him to say these things. She was madly in love with Denis and she was going to learn to dance with him just as well as the glamorous Miss Dale. She was going to be the perfect wife for a successful actor.

"I shall make a home for him and look after him," she declared.

He saw that she was on the defensive now. He continued the offensive.

"Oh, but you won't be allowed to give way to your domesticated side. It will be parties and parties and parties; rehearsals and first nights and so on—no free time to think. No *NICOLETTE*!—no independence. No more personal life for *you*. You'll just have to live for *him*."

The colour rushed to her face and her breath came unevenly.

"March, you're being horrid. It isn't a very good way of entertaining me on the night of my engagement."

Now he took the cigarette from his mouth and flung it out on to the lawn.

"I'm sorry, Nic. I'm not very tactful and I never act; you know that. I'm always just my blunt self. I've known you a long time and . . . perhaps I've overstepped the mark but I felt privileged to speak as I felt."

"But why do you *feel* all this? Anybody would think from what you say that the wife of a successful actor has to become a sort of *slave* to him."

"And if that were so—would you like it?"

Nicola glanced at Denis, so slender and handsome, fair gleaming head close to Verona's which, in contrast, was as black and smooth as a raven's wing. She wasn't jealous of Verona. Or of any of the women who acted with Denis. But could she ever be jealous of other women . . . of the *world* . . . of the success which would claim so much of his time and energy? She said:

"I don't think if you really love anybody that you would mind being a slave to them."

That answer disarmed March for the moment. It also alarmed him. For it showed that little Nic was pretty serious about her love-affair. Somehow he felt sick at the thought of her becoming Denis Avon's slave.

"It would never suit you!" he exclaimed. "You're much too independent by nature. You always were. And what about your own business? You were so keen on it. Is he going to make you leave Welbridge and close down the salon?"

33

He saw her wince. He had hit a vulnerable spot. Her lashes drooped and she struggled for an answer. Then she said:

"I don't want to chuck the business just when it's beginning to do well, I must admit. But Denis's profession is much more important than mine."

"No," said March curtly, "it isn't. Every man's profession is of equal importance to him—if he likes it and has spent everything that he has in building it up. I've been so full of admiration of the way you've struggled and fought for yours, Nic. Don't give up too easily. You'll regret it if you do."

She was about to argue, then suddenly laughed, her usual amiability returning.

"Oh, don't you worry about me, March. I can manage my own life. I just can't understand why you're so concerned."

He bit his lip.

"Are you telling me to mind my own business?"

She laughed again but the expression in his bright hazel eyes startled her a little . . . it was so full of a determination inexplicable to her.

"I know you're just speaking as an old friend," she said, "but I repeat . . . don't worry about me. I'm going to be terribly happy with Denis."

March silently raised his brows. For the moment there seemed nothing else to be said. But he was conscious of a crazy longing to take her out there into the moonlight away from the crowd, to kiss that defiant young mouth until the complacency, the confidence, left her eyes. He wanted to say:

"But I love you. Dammit, *I* love you, and could give you the sort of life you want—*I would take care of you*. You're not as strong as you think you are. Nor as weak! You're not the 'squaw' type. And that blond glamour boy playing to the gallery, here at this very moment, will only make you unhappy."

Yes, he wanted to say that, to force her to become conscious of another man and another love . . . *his, March Foster's*.

But for the moment he refrained. He echoed her laugh lightly, put an arm through hers, and said:

"O.K. I hand it to you. You will make a perfect wife for

Denis Avon. And now, Miss Boyd, may I have the pleasure of a foxtrot? The *danse seul* is over."

As he put an arm round her and they moved on to the floor, Nicola glanced quickly over her shoulder at Denis. She was no longer annoyed with March but she felt depressed. He *had* depressed her, even though she refused to agree with a word he said. But she wished he hadn't said it. And she wished she could be alone with Denis . . . feel his lips on hers in one of those deep thrilling kisses which made her feel so utterly his. He was not even looking at her. He had gone towards the radio with Judy.

"Let's find a samba. Judy's the samba expert. We'll show you!"

Nicola couldn't samba and March was no dancer. They were walking round together to the lilt of the foxtrot . . . just an easy swinging walk in time to the music (she could do that without stumbling). March wasn't being difficult or analytical now. He was grinning in the old mocking way.

"I'll bring Kimbo in in a moment. He and I'll give an exhibition together. Ever seen Kimbo dance on his hind paws?"

The party continued. Dancing, drinking, laughing.

March was being the perfect host. He danced with everybody in turn, in his masterful and solid fashion. But it was Denis who held the attention, as usual. His exhibition of the samba with young Judy was a triumph which everybody applauded. Nicola looked on admiringly and applauded with the rest. But she was conscious now of desperate fatigue and of wanting him to herself.

It was she who finally broke up that party.

"Denis, I must go home. You can all sleep, but I've got an early job tomorrow morning. Do you know it's past two and I've got to be up again at seven?"

He put an arm around her carelessly.

"Oh, just don't turn up at your job. Stay in bed, angel. Give yourself a holiday. You're the boss."

She laughed at him.

"I can't cancel all my appointments, darling."

He shrugged his shoulders.

"The sooner you shut down that place the better."

35

She felt a trifle discouraged and rather resentful. *NICO-LETTE* meant so much to her. But Denis seemed to wipe it off the map airily as though it was of no importance whatsoever.

But he took her home, as she asked.

When she had said good night to March and thanked him for the extra party, he gripped her hand very tightly for an instant and looked at her with a faint expression of apology.

"Have you forgiven me for speaking my mind?"

"Oh, of course," she said.

He grinned and put his tongue in his cheek.

"It's the green-eyed monster, you know. I'm rather annoyed about this . . ." and he lifted her hand and tapped the ring on her engagement finger.

"Idiot!" she laughed.

But as she drove away with Denis in Bill Venning's car she remembered those words. He was annoyed . . . because she was engaged to Denis Avon. *March* was annoyed. But why should he be? He wasn't in love with her, himself. He never had been.

Yet *Denis* had said that he did not like the way March looked at her . . .

Nicola would not have been human if she had not considered all these things with a slight thrill of interest. It put March in quite a new light.

Perhaps he had put up that argument against her chances of happiness with Denis because he *was* jealous?

Oh, but she would be happy with Denis. She must be . . . she couldn't bear it to be otherwise.

When he took her in his arms for a moment outside her house she clung to him and closed her eyes in response to his passionate good-night kiss.

"Oh, Denis, Denis, I do love you!" she whispered.

"I love you too, darling," he whispered back.

"Will you always?"

"Always," he said, "you're absolutely perfect."

"Except that I can't dance," she said with a little laugh.

"I am going to teach you. I'm going to teach you every-thing," he said loftily; then he added: "And tomorrow we must fix a date for our wedding."

She drew back from his arms and gave him a worried look.

"Denis darling, I don't see how we can possibly get married in such a rush. I simply can't shut down *NICOLETTE* in two minutes."

"No, but you can in two weeks," he said, and would brook no further argument. He kissed her again, then was gone, confident of getting his own way.

She let herself into the little house where she had lived a peaceful and rather dull existence for so long. She felt quite exhausted. Her brain refused to work. She kicked off her shoes. Her feet ached with so much dancing. Not Verona's or Judy's sort of dancing, but the sort she did with March and the other boys in Welbridge.

How could she ever hope to come up to Verona's or Judy's standard? And how *could* she close the Beauty Parlour down and marry Denis and go away from Welbridge in a fortnight's time?

She was too tired to think or worry any further. She would have to see Denis and talk about it tomorrow.

But somehow as she went up to her bedroom, stumbling with weariness, lips still burning from Denis's last kiss, she felt that tonight's party—from her point of view at least—had not been an unqualified success.

IV

MRS. BOYD commented on the fact that Nicola looked pale and heavy-eyed the next morning when she came down to breakfast.

Overnight there had been one of those rapid changes of weather which help to make the English climate so difficult. The silver brightness upon which Nicola had gazed with March at Heron's Hall six hours ago had vanished with the dawn. Now it was raining steadily.

In the grey gloom of the early morning she faced her mother in the kitchen unable to conceal her yawns as she helped to make the toast.

"You were very late last night, darling," observed her mother.

"I was rather, I'm afraid. We all went on to Heron's Hall," said Nicola, "and had a party there."

Mrs. Boyd, busy making a dried-egg omelette, glanced quickly from the frying-pan to her daughter.

"The Fosters' place! Why did it end up there?"

"March took us. He's quite friendly with the Rep. Company. He knows Miss Dale and he was at our celebration supper on the stage."

Mrs. Boyd nodded and continued with her cooking. She had little to say on the subject of the engagement party. She did not approve of it. But it was her policy—and her husband's—not to interfere in the lives of her children once they were of age. In her opinion it was her duty to protect and guide Flip, her youngest, who was still at school. But her son was a grown man and Nicola quite old enough to take care of herself. Indeed, Mary Boyd had the highest opinion of her eldest daughter and a great admiration for the way she had launched into business after her beauty training. But she was bitterly disappointed in Nicola's choice of a man.

She had been discussing it with Nicola's father last night, after the girl had gone out. Flip, of course, was full of enthusiasm about the handsome engaging young actor. But the parents were of the opinion that he would never make Nicola the sort of husband she deserved. They were quite surprised that she had allowed herself to be carried away by his good looks and the glamour that must always surround a promising young actor.

"I always thought that Nic was level-headed and practical," Mary Boyd had sighed.

But John Boyd had thrown her a quizzical look and said:

"Very few women are level-headed in love, my dear. And Nic's no exception. I'm not altogether surprised. And one can't find anything really wrong about the fellow. He has nice manners and I should think he has been well brought up."

"Who knows?" had been the mother's reply. "We know so little about him. He's a stranger to Nic, really."

"Well, cheer up. He may be the Sir Laurence Olivier of the future," Nicola's father had consoled her.

He was a cheerful optimistic man. But Mary Boyd was a pessimist and in her silent way suffered hideous untold agonies about all her 'brood'. It had been torture to her during the whole time that Ronald was in the R.A.F. She had been sure he would be killed during the last year of the war when he was on active service as a pilot. She suffered daily because she was sure that Flip would have an accident on her bike going to and from school. And now she was quite certain that Nicola was going to ruin her life.

But it was her way to say nothing much—to endure in silence.

Nicola had some understanding of her fond and harassed mother and she was quite aware of the silent opposition to Denis. It had the effect of strengthening her determination to marry him, to show Mummy and everybody else (including March!) how wrong they were.

Rather defiantly, during breakfast, she gave the family an enthusiastic description of the party.

It was young Flip, with no tact and little wisdom, who said:

"I say! I bet March Foster is fed up because you're going to marry Denis. My friend, Pam Butler, says her brother Chris knows March and he thinks that March has been getting keen on *you* lately!"

A short silence followed these words which were accompanied by a giggle from Flip. Mr. and Mrs. Boyd exchanged glances. The latter looked a trifle melancholy. But John Boyd concealed a smile behind his morning paper.

Nicola flushed crimson, then she turned a little angrily on the tall lanky figure in the green gym tunic and school blazer.

"Don't repeat silly things, Flip."

Flip giggled again.

"I say, Nic, if darling Denis hadn't popped the question, would you have married March?"

A deeper red burned Nicola's face.

"Oh, go on with your breakfast or you'll be late for school!" she snapped.

Flip sniffed.

"You *are* in a huff! Sorry I spoke. I was only ragging. But Pam *did* say that was what Chris said. Pam said . . ."

"Finish your breakfast, dear," Mrs. Boyd broke in hurriedly, seeing the light of battle dawn in her elder daughter's eyes.

"I didn't mean anything," said Flip with another sniff, "although I quite like March Foster. Everybody says he was wonderful when he was a Commando, and I simply *worship* Kimbo. I wish I could have a Boxer. Mummy, when can I have a dog?"

"When you're able to look after it properly yourself, dear, instead of leaving me to house-train it," said Mrs. Boyd mildly, with recollections of the awful state of the home when Flip had last introduced a pet animal into it.

Nicola was thankful that the conversation had turned from herself.

"I've got an early 'facial'. I must be off," she said and rose from the table.

As she passed Flip, she pulled one of the long brown plaits. She was sorry she had snapped at her. Flip was a darling and although at the moment disfigured by a gold band over her teeth and already taller than Nicola—much too tall—she showed signs of developing into a handsome girl. Denis himself, after meeting the family, had said how good-looking young Frances was, and remarked that she had the same 'soft grey eyes' as Nicola, and the same sweet engaging smile.

Just before she left the room, Mrs. Boyd, with all her worries and anxieties gnawing at her, could not resist asking one question that lay heavy on her mind.

"Have you made . . . have you made any definite plans for the future . . . I mean about your marriage, darling?" she asked.

Nicola paused and turned to her mother. That troubled beseeching look in her mother's weak soft eyes irritated her slightly because it called continually for pity. Nicola was a strong character and had her father's philosophical outlook. She was sorry for Mummy because she agonized herself— often unnecessarily—about them all. Yet she was such a good mother, and never interfered; Nicola loved her and was grateful to her. She said:

"Nothing is definite, Mum dear. I've got to talk things over with Denis. But in view of the fact that he may get a job in London instead of with the Rep. he may want an early wedding."

Mrs. Boyd caught her breath.

"How early, darling?"

Nicola realized that she somehow did not want to answer that question. It weighed so heavily on her own conscience.

"Oh, in about . . . a few weeks . . . perhaps . . . June . . ." she stammered.

Mrs. Boyd looked stricken. Behind his paper John Boyd raised an eyebrow. Flip, as usual, spoke her mind.

"Whoopee! Then I'll have darling Denis for a brother-in-law jolly soon. And I'll be a bridesmaid. Nic, I *will* be your bridesmaid, won't I?"

"Yes," said Nicola.

But she was eyeing her mother through her lashes, and was once again filled with a mixture of pity and irritation. Mrs. Boyd looked so anguished. Nicola added: "Nothing's definite. Don't anybody, *please*, start flapping."

Then Mr. Boyd spoke.

"I shouldn't rush into anything if you can help it, my dear. There's your business to think of. What about that?"

"I want to see about selling it," muttered Nicola.

Mr. Boyd wiped his grey moustache on his table napkin, cleared his throat and eyed his elder daughter over the rim of his spectacles.

"Humph! Pity! You put a lot into that shop and it's just starting to do well."

"I must go or I'll miss my appointment," said Nicola rather violently, and escaped from the house before the family could make any more disturbing remarks.

They *were* disturbing. This sudden engagement to Denis Avon had completely upset the calm and even tenor of her existence and had inevitably upset the family too. She would hate to leave them all. Poor anxious Mummy; dear kind Pop; darling Flip—and Ron when he was at home.

She felt especially troubled about Ron. She knew she must sit down and write to him today without fail. He was on an engineering course in Bristol. She wished he were here so that she could talk to him. He was so sensible and understanding. Yet she dreaded writing to him, because it was largely the money which he had sent in the past which had paid for her training. She owed it to him for making a success of *NICO-LETTE*. She had meant to do so and repay every penny he had contributed.

Times were bad and although she had, on the face of it, a success in the salon, a growing clientele . . . she might not be able to sell the goodwill easily. That meant she might never be able to repay Ron. And she knew he would not approve of Denis. Ronald Boyd was a bit like March Foster . . . a masterful and thoroughly masculine type. He had no use for actors, except on the stage.

All through that morning Nicola was depressed. Increasingly so because one or two of her clients made further appointments—a course of beauty treatment—dates which would carry her far into June. How *could* she do as Denis asked and just close down *NICOLETTE* as though it were of no consequence, and dash off to London with him?

Ann, her assistant, brought her in a note as the shop closed for lunch.

"You do look pale this morning, Miss Boyd . . . are you all right?" she asked anxiously as she looked at her young employer.

Nicola slipped out of her pink overall and forced a smile.

"Oh yes, I'm fine . . . it's just the weather . . . it's so damp and muggy this morning. There was a mist over the river when I came along."

With fast-beating heart, she opened the note. It was from Denis. But it did nothing to raise her spirits. On the contrary it flung her into something approaching panic.

*Darling,*

*Will call for you at your home after the matinée. Have definite news about London. They say that May marriages are unlucky. But we'll show them the reverse.*

*I adore you.*

*Denis.*

The line 'They say that May marriages are unlucky' danced in front of her tired eyes. So Denis *meant* her to marry him this month. He took it for granted that she would do so. He had definite news about London and he was going to force a definite answer from her—after the matinée today.

With eyes full of dismay she looked slowly round the gay pink fragrant Beauty Parlour which until now had been the pride and joy of her young life.


## V

As soon as Nicola saw Denis that afternoon she guessed that the news he was going to give her was not quite so good as his excited note had suggested. His handsome face looked a trifle sulky. (She had yet to learn about the sulky trait in Denis's nature and the almost breath-taking swiftness with which he passed from one mood to another.)

He called for her as promised, but not either to stay for tea or take her out as had been suggested.

"Pop on your things and come back to the theatre with me, will you, sweet," was his somewhat terse greeting. "Everything's gone wrong. It *would*—just when I most want to talk to you."

"Won't you come in?" she asked.

"Can't possibly. Got a taxi outside. Verona packed up directly after the matinée. Temperature high—'flu they think. She collapsed after the show. She can't possibly go on tonight. That means a rehearsal now, at once, and we've only just found an understudy."

"Oh, Denis!"

Quickly Nicola picked up a sports jacket and scarf and followed him into the taxi, without further questioning. Driving through Welbridge to the theatre that cloudy close afternoon —a storm had been threatening all day—she slid a hand into his and listened while he grumbled. She was full of sympathy for him. It must be a bore to have one's leading lady out of the show at a moment's notice. (Not a word of sympathy for poor Verona, of course. It was all from the egoist's point of

43

view.) It would spoil *his* performance, he said. That difficult bit in the third act which Verona played so well . . . the farewell between husband and wife—Verona was an excellent foil for him because she was restrained. He was supposed to be the nervy, excitable one. Irene Hale, the new-found understudy, would probably be useless. She had looks and a figure, but no brains. Never could restrain her emotions. That particular scene, which she had played once before, had ended in them both shouting at each other. The company had been trying to find a better understudy but Bill Venning did not do much about it, and it was Denis's belief that he was rather keen on Irene.

In silence, Nicola listened to all the back-stage gossip and grousing. It was all so new to her. For the moment she found it rather amusing and she could quite see that it must annoy poor Denis dreadfully to have his best scenes spoiled by playing opposite an inferior actress.

It was only when they reached the theatre, and Denis jumped out and gave her a hand, that he seemed to remember their personal affairs. Then with a quick ardent look, he whispered:

"I'm not always on the stage. You can come and sit in the wings while we rehearse. We can talk between scenes. You got my note, didn't you?"

"Yes, thank you, darling."

He tucked his arm through hers. They walked up to the stage door through the narrow lane at the side of the theatre.

"Love me, darling?" he murmured.

A little pulse beat in her throat as it always did when Denis looked down at her like that (she could remember when she had first seen him look that way at Verona Dale during their big love scene, and thought that it must be wonderful to have a man throw so much passionate tenderness into a single glance. Here it was . . . not play-acting but reality and all for *her*.)

"I adore you, Denis," she whispered back breathlessly.

He had forgotten his ill-humour. He had a charming smile for the old man at the stage door entrance who respectfully greeted Mr. Avon; a few gracious words for one or two of the cast whom they passed, not forgetting to include Nicola.

"You know my fiancée . . . Miss Boyd . . ."

It was a thrill for Nicola . . . a very new and youthful thrill to come here like this and attend a rehearsal as *his* fiancée. Now, in the draughty wings, it really seemed to her that she was part of the Rep. Company . . . much more part of it than she had been on the night of her engagement party. She had felt that night as though she were in the clouds.

This was exciting . . . but much more down to earth. It was bitterly cold after the warmth of the May sunshine outside; dimly lit and dusty. She thought how garish the set (supposed to be the drawing-room of a London house) looked at close quarters. No lighting effect, no glamour. No—just the crude scenery and well-worn furniture, the old stage 'props' which had seen a great deal of use and travel . . . the Rep. Company could not afford to put on an elegant show in these after-the-war days.

The Company was here in full, all grumbling. A hired hand was passing round cups of tea. Some of them nodded and smiled at Nicola but with indifference. Their attention was on the rehearsal. At eight o'clock the show must go on with Irene in Miss Dale's place; just one of those things . . . but aggravating; and all meant extra work and strain tonight.

Nicola settled herself on a packing-case. She watched Bill Venning, coatless, shirt-sleeves rolled up, red face perspiring, shouting directions from the front of the stalls.

"Come on, Irene . . . you're on, you're *on*, my dear! Ready, Denis? *Albert!* Get that something table out of the way. What the hell is it doing there? You'll have someone tripping over it. Further to the right . . . *come on!* Get going . . ."

Nicola watched. Denis was on the stage now, lighting a cigarette. How cool and debonair, how disdainfully handsome he looked! Completely at his ease. Her enraptured gaze rested on him. Nobody could teach Denis. He was just a wonderful natural actor. Now Irene Hale was moving towards him . . . saying *'Give me a cigarette'* . . . her first line. She had quite a nice voice and she was younger and prettier than Verona Dale. Red hair, big eyes . . . graceful hands. But she was pitifully nervous. Nicola pitied her. She hoped everybody would be patient with the poor little thing. It couldn't be easy or pleasant even though it *was* her chance . . . the chance all newcomers to Rep. prayed for . . . but it must be terrifying . . . at least until one got back one's self-confidence, thought Nicola.

With breathless interest she watched the rehearsal proceed. Most of the scenes were with Denis (the rest of the cast were on at intervals). All word-perfect except Irene, who broke down several times. Twice Venning shouted to her "*Speak up*" or "*Repeat that*" . . . twice it seemed to the sympathetic Nicola that Irene looked on the verge of bursting into tears. But Denis was quite patient . . . at his best on the stage. Acting for the benefit even of the rest of the company and the single man in the stalls. Conscious of his ability. Immensely vain. Patronizing Irene now and again. "*Come on, dear . . . you're doing quite well . . . let's go through that one again . . .*"

Through the veil of infatuation which clouded Nicola's usually shrewd vision she saw only Denis's better points . . . Denis's magnificence. . . . If he was conceited, why not? He had a right to be.

She would have been flabbergasted could she have seen Miss Dale's understudy when that rehearsal ended. In floods of tears in the arms of her friend who played the minor part of a domestic.

"I'd be perfectly all right if it wasn't for Denis Avon. I can't *stand* him . . . the way he sneers . . . you can see it behind his smile . . . and when I *am* good, he hates me stealing his thunder even for a second. I think he's a *pig*!"

The friend, one of Denis's admirers, thought it best to agree and consoled the weeping Irene by assuring her that she would be 'a terrific success tonight'.

At last the emergency rehearsal was over. Lights were switched off. The stage was shrouded in darkness and silence once more. The cast vanished to get a hasty 'breather' and a bite of food before the next performance.

"It certainly isn't all fun and games," remarked Nicola as Denis emerged from his dressing-room outside which she awaited him; "you have to work terribly hard!"

"It's always hard work playing opposite somebody who can't act," he said.

"I didn't think she was too bad, although naturally not up to Miss Dale's standard."

Denis yawned.

"I think she's appalling. But you get these girls in a Rep. Company. They usually come from some dramatic school where they have been told they are better than Edith Evans. It makes me tired. I shall be thankful when I get to London."

Nicola gazed at him.

"When do you expect to go to London, Denis?" she asked in a low voice.

He did not answer. He was about to switch off the light in his dressing-room. He hesitated and said:

"I shan't have time to come home with you now . . . I've got to nip back to my digs for a quick bath and a sandwich. Come in here just a moment, darling, and let's talk."

Slowly she followed him into the little room. The leading man's dressing-room! Exciting—an open cupboard revealing a row of suits; silk dressing-gown behind the door; mirror and long dressing-table covered with pots and bottles . . . greasepaint . . . rouge . . . suntan . . . hair oil . . . and of course a dozen or more photographs of Denis in various costumes and positions pinned to the walls. And two of his most prized possessions, framed, signed photographs of 'stars' . . . names to conjure with in the London theatres. Nicola had often heard him speak of them—listened with respectful admiration while the christian names dropped with such light familiarity from his lips.

"I was talking to Ivor Novello the other day . . ." or . . . "had supper with Larry and Vivien Leigh . . ."

She could not possibly know that he had only met these people at public theatrical parties. He made it sound as though each name revived memories of an intimate rendezvous to which he, alone, had been invited.

Now Nicola was in his arms. Alone for a moment, he held her close, kissing her soft red lips, her flushed cheeks and the eyelids which closed under the touch of his eager lips.

47

"Nic, my little darling . . . it's heaven to have you to myself for a moment . . . the whole afternoon has been devilish. Nic . . . I do love you!"

She put her arms around his neck, drawing him close with all her young impetuous passion.

"I love you, too. I don't know why you love me so much . . . but it *is* wonderful. *You're* wonderful. Oh, Denis, *darling* . . ."

He caressed her, his eyes dreamy and content. He needed a little love and admiration. He was in the mood for it. Then after a moment, with one of his swift transitions of mood, he stopped making love to her and sat on the arm of a chair, lit a cigarette and became more businesslike.

"Now, darling, we've got to get down to this question of ourselves. Let's forget the theatre for a moment. When are you going to marry me?"

Her heart leaped. She had been waiting for this. It filled her with a thousand doubts and fears and yet the most delicious anticipation. It was still so new and so exciting to know that Denis was anxious for an *immediate* marriage. In an unsteady voice she said :

"Don't you believe in . . . in engagements, Denis?"

"We are engaged, aren't we?"

"But I . . . I mean . . ."

"Long ones, no," he broke in and flung back his handsome head in that arrogant way he had. "I think they are dull and dreary—an invention of Queen Victoria. This is the modern age of speed, my sweet."

She gave a helpless laugh.

"Speed, yes, but not in marriage. It is so frightfully important, Denis. One needs to be sure . . ."

"Sure of what? Of love or financial security?"

"B-both . . ." she stammered.

He laid his cigarette on an ash-tray on his dressing-table, cast one of those quick looks at himself in the mirror (a habit of Denis's) then put out a hand and drew her towards him. Now his eyes grew irresistibly tender. He raised each one of her hands in turn to his lips.

"You are a darling, Nic . . . there's something so essentially sane and *good* about you. I more than love you. I respect you from the bottom of my heart."

Nicola grew quite white with emotion.

"Oh, Denis!" she said under her breath.

"Yes," he nodded, "I think it is your integrity, as well as your physical loveliness, which makes me want to fall at your feet and stay there."

She found it impossible to speak, she was so unutterably moved. Behind the extravagance of his words there seemed to be sincerity. It won her as nothing else could have done.

And Denis Avon genuinely believed that this girl was necessary to life's happiness . . . that he must carry her off quickly before any other man could get her. He was sick of artifice. He needed her absolute honesty . . . and perhaps because he knew his own weaknesses, he needed her strength. Of all the girls he had lightly loved in his stage career he had never found one to command his respect in the way that Nicola did. That feeling, coupled with the fascination of her smooth fair head, those melting grey eyes, that perfect skin . . . entranced him. He was madly in love. Of that there was no doubt. He wanted Nicola for his very own. And when Denis Avon wanted a thing, he must have it—at once.

She was back in his arms now. His voice was wooing her . . . confusing her with plans and demands. They seemed to fall from Denis's lips in a veritable cascade of rich promise.

There was no object in their waiting, he said. She must sell *NICOLETTE* and give her life and herself to him. If they married at once and he was still in Welbridge, she too would be here to settle up her affairs. But at least they would be *together*. Life was so empty for him now once the curtain rang down and the show was over.

He wanted her to make a home for him.

*"You'd be so nice to come home to . . ."* He sang the words of the old popular song in that pleasant baritone of his (singing was another of Denis's accomplishments), and as she listened in the circle of his arms, and his blue eyes smiled down into hers in that boyish bantering way (the expression he adopted for most of his lighter publicity photographs because women liked it), she felt her whole being melt towards

49

him. She thought no more about her Beauty Parlour and all that she had built up. She only knew that she loved Denis Avon and must follow him to the ends of the earth.

She heard herself saying in weak surrender:

"I'll marry you whenever you want . . . just tell me when . . . if it's really what *you* want, I want it too, Denis darling."

He kissed her—triumphant—and having got his own way, his worries seemed to fall from him like a cloak. In his volatile fashion he soared into the highest spirits.

"You are an angel and I adore you. And I do want you more than anything in the world. I'd marry you tomorrow if I didn't know that your ma and pa would strike. How about a fortnight's time? Is that too soon?"

He took her breath away. She protested, breathless:

"*A fortnight!* Oh, Denis, it *is* rather soon. I've got no new clothes. I've never *thought* of such a thing. I've absolutely nothing ready."

He tossed his handsome head.

"Who cares? One can't buy a trousseau these days with present prices and no cash—and a big wedding is a hideous waste of money. I'd like just to walk with you into a Registrar's Office and walk out again and say: 'This divine creature is Nicola Avon, my wife. . . .'"

She caught her breath—*Nicola Avon*—that sounded too marvellous to be true! But she managed to keep her head. She shook it at him decidedly.

"No, darling. You're quite mad, but you're not going to make me as crazy as that. Three weeks is the *very earliest* I can be ready. Anything earlier would upset my mother and father terribly. They are conventional people, you know, not used to the theatre and lightning marriages. And they have done a lot for me. I owe them something. Besides, it would break Mummy's heart if she couldn't give me a proper wedding, no matter how difficult things are these days. And from my personal point of view, I'd hate to be married anywhere else but in a church, Denis."

He looked at her more solemnly. Now it was his turn to capitulate. Anyhow, the actor in him found her suggestion appealing. He was not a particularly religious type, but it would be quite wonderful . . . he thought. Little Nicola, a white bride with a veil over that glorious pale gold head of hers . . . himself in a morning coat (thank goodness he had had one made for the last theatrical garden-party at Buckingham Palace). He visualized the swelling organ . . . the flowers . . . the admiring congregation . . . the photographers at the church door. It would be good publicity. He'd get it in the London papers . . . that pal of his on the *Mirror* . . . *"Denis Avon and his beautiful bride."*

He bent and kissed Nicola's anxious young face.

"Okay, my beautiful. It shall be as you want. Three weeks' time and a church wedding. And now I'd better get along home. You break the news to the family and I'll come over and do my stuff with Papa in the morning; ask for his daughter's hand, and all that. . . ."

Like one in a dream, Nicola followed Denis outside. It was dark now, still close, even hot, after the cool theatre. Black clouds hung over Welbridge. There was a sinister threat of thunder in the air.

"Damn," muttered Denis, "you can't get one decent day in this country without it ending in a storm! Will you forgive me for not seeing you home, Precious?"

"Of course, you must have a rest."

"I'll see you in the morning."

"Don't forget I'm in the shop all morning, darling."

Now his brows contracted.

"Oh, that darned Beauty Parlour! I'll be glad when it's disposed of. Can't you skip *one day*?"

"Darling, I'm booked right up. . . ."

"Oh, all right . . . then I'll fetch you before one o'clock."

Her face cleared.

"Thanks, darling, and I'll get Mummy to give us both lunch and we'll all discuss the wedding."

They were standing on the pavement outside the theatre. At that moment a few large ominous drops of rain hit Nicola on the nose.

"Ugh! You are right. We *are* going to have a storm. I'd better run."

He muttered under his breath. A thunderstorm and drenching rain meant no queue for the pit or gallery, and half-empty stalls. He hated playing to a half-filled house. Still, it had its points tonight, with the impossible Irene in Verona's shoes.

Then suddenly Nicola said:

"Denis, do you realize we have never discussed anything about where we're going to live, for instance? Mummy and Daddy will hurl questions at me. And when *do you* take the London job?"

He frowned and pulled up the collar of his coat. He greatly disliked the thought of his suit getting wet. Hurriedly he answered her:

"I meant to tell you, darling, only the rehearsal and Verona going sick took it right out of my mind. I heard from my agent this morning. Things are delayed in London. The show they were going to cast me for doesn't look like going on until the autumn. They can't find a theatre. I expect I'll hang on to the Rep. here for a month, anyhow."

Her big eyes glowed at him.

"Oh, Denis, then couldn't I keep on with my salon, even if we do get married? It's making a profit now. It seems a shame to chuck it. And it means we'd both have a job for a bit. . . ."

"My darling," said Denis with an exaggerated bow, "forgive me, but I really *cannot* discuss our future in the middle of a deluge. We might come to some agreement about your salon as long as it doesn't take you away from me too much. But we must talk it all over tomorrow. Okay? Quite happy, sweet?"

"Oh, quite!" she breathed.

They kissed—then she was running home through the darkened streets. Now the rain came down in earnest. The first flash of lightning threw the steeple of St. Giles' Church into sharp relief, followed by a low growl of thunder.

In a daze, Nicola let herself into her home.

*Quite happy*—yes, she supposed so. Deliriously in love with Denis . . . certainly. But did that mean perfect happiness? This love seemed in fact to bring quite a lot of worries and problems in its wake. She just couldn't recognize herself as the hard-headed business girl who had been trained as a beauty specialist. Denis had swept her right off her feet.

That business about London . . . how unexpected, and a bit

bewildering, too. In the first instance, he had suggested an immediate marriage so that he could take her to London with him. Now it seemed that he was not to play in a London show as soon as he had anticipated. (Something else to learn about Denis . . . that so many of his swans turned out to be geese . . . and so much of his big talk came to nothing. But she couldn't know that yet. She just thought there was an unexpected delay.)

Of course it suited her not to be rushed off to London, she reflected, in an effort to concentrate. Especially if she could persuade Denis to let her keep on with *NICOLETTE* for a bit. Then there was another vital point to be settled. *Where would they live?* In theatrical digs here in Welbridge? Or in her own home? There was plenty of room. But it did not seem the best start for married life.

There was *so much* to be thought over and talked about.

If she had been able to sit down coldly and dispassionately and dissect it all, she might have started to see a dozen snags and hear a dozen warning voices. But she was in the grip of a powerful force . . . more powerful than anything in the world . . . her first big love-affair . . . which it was . . . and with a man as experienced, handsome and glamorous as Denis Avon, Nicola did not stand a chance.


VI

IT was young Flip who first gave March Foster the news.

She had had the most thrilling lunch with her hero (so soon now to be her brother-in-law) with him in the family circle, Nicola had staggered everybody by announcing that she and Denis were to be married on the first Saturday in June—barely three weeks from now.

It had been really exciting—lunch specially cooked by Mummy; Daddy had chosen a bottle of white wine, and there were flowers everywhere. Denis seemed to have bought up half the florist's shop, arrived with the bouquet and presented it to his future mother-in-law with one of his most charming speeches.

Flip was now on her way back from school where she had been twice reprimanded for whispering and giggling in class. But she didn't care. Her mind was full of the bridesmaid's dress which she was going to have made; and of the ceremony in which she, Flip, would play an important part. How *could* she listen to Miss Eccles' geometry lesson? It was essential she should tell her best friend about the lunch, with Denis as the honoured guest.

Cycling towards her home, she saw March Foster's car coming down the street. She waved to him, wobbled perilously and stopped. March pulled up and got out. He liked Nicola's young sister. Even now with the disfiguring band over her teeth and the ugly school uniform, there was much in her to remind him of Nicola.

"Hello," he greeted her, pulled a pipe from his pocket, stuck it between his teeth and grinned, "where are you off to on that dangerous-looking machine of yours?"

She grinned back at him and pushed her straw hat on the back of her head.

"Home, thank goodness. I say, March, *have you heard*?"

"I hear all sorts of things. What is it this time?"

"Nic's marrying Denis Avon three weeks from tomorrow," announced Flip, crimson with excitement at being able to impart such news, "and I'm going to be bridesmaid. Isn't it *super*? I shall have my first long dress and perhaps be allowed to go to the theatrical party that the Rep'll give for the bride and bridegroom after they come back from their honeymoon. They'll only have a week-end, because Denis says the show must go on . . ."

She chattered along breathlessly. March Foster stood like a graven image, listening, his square hard face a trifle white, his eyes narrowed. Slowly he took the pipe from his mouth and examined it. Then he said:

"Why the ugly rush?"

Flip tossed a brown plait over her shoulder.

"I expect because they're so mad about each other, don't you, March? Denis says he won't wait. Isn't it thrilling?"

The merry giggle that followed found no echo in March's heart. He felt as though he had been dealt a mortal blow.

Now Flip was pouring out the story of the lunch. Through her young schoolgirl mind he saw a complete picture of it.

It had been a bombshell exploding in the midst of the family when Denis told Daddy that he wanted this speedy marriage, Flip declared. But in spite of any suggestions that they should wait until they got to know each other a bit more, Denis had insisted, backed up by Nic, of course. They didn't want to waste time in a long engagement, they said. They knew their minds. They were sure of each other. Nic had been terrifically excited all through lunch and Denis, too, and he had said a lot of *lovely* things . . . how much he wanted to become one of the family, etc., etc. Daddy had been a trifle glum, and Mummy had kept quiet, too, and looked upset. But in the end everything was agreed upon. The wedding here at St. Giles' . . . a week-end honeymoon in London . . . then back to work for Denis at the Rep.

"He expects to go on in a London play quite soon," Flip announced. "Isn't it super for Nic to be marrying such a *gorgeous* actor?"

March drew in his breath. Two ominous little lines appeared on either side of his mouth. He could not find words to answer that artless question. He only knew that he felt strangely angry . . . angry with Nicola for allowing herself to be swept away like this on a tide of infatuation (he was sure it could be nothing but that), it could only sweep her out to perilous seas. The theatrical life was not her *métier*. She would wither up and die in it. Even the thought of that week-end honeymoon in London hit March like a blow. Nic, who adored the country and quiet lonely places . . . Nic now choosing to begin life in a whirl of excitement *in London*. Then back to what?

Flip supplied further information.

Mummy, anxious not to part with Nic, had suggested that while Denis was with the Welbridge Rep. the young couple should live at home, but Denis had thought this a bad idea, and in that Daddy had backed him up. Young married people must be independent, he said. Besides, actors kept late hours . . . difficult hours for meals and so on. Denis did not particularly want Nic to live in 'digs', so he suggested, grandly, that they should start their married life in the Welbridge Park

Hotel. It was a large ornate house of Georgian style which had recently been converted; at one time belonging to a peer of the realm, and very comfortable and well run. It had an acre of garden and, like the Foster house, had its own uninterrupted view of the river which ran through the grounds. Of course it was very expensive there, but Denis said he earned a good salary and Nic had decided to carry on with her own job for the moment, so between them they could afford it.

This news further troubled March Foster. Why *should* a girl have to go on working when she was married? Of course many did so and shared expenses nowadays. But March disliked the thought. And could married life be a success with the pair both working at different hours? Nic and Denis would see little of each other.

Why the devil couldn't the fellow have been content with an engagement for a few months and let Nicola find her feet . . . get her bearings? March asked himself savagely.

"You'll come to the wedding, won't you, March?" said Flip's eager young voice. "Won't it be *exciting*?"

"Very," said March abruptly, then excused himself, climbed back into his car and drove on to the garage. He had been on his way to get petrol.

Flip went home. Nicola had just got back from the Beauty Parlour. She looked tired. It had been a long and exciting day and there was more thunder about. The storm last night had not yet cleared the air. She was in the bathroom rinsing through a pair of nylons when Flip burst in on her and said:

"I say, Nic, I met March Foster and told him about you and Denis and he looked *furious*! I *know* he's keen on you, and he's livid because you're getting married so soon."

Nicola coloured then laughed.

"Don't be silly, Flippet."

But after Flip had departed, whistling *Here Comes the Bride*, Nicola thought about March and once more had an uncomfortable memory of his flippant remark . . . '*I'm rather annoyed about this*' . . . and he had tapped her engagement ring.

*It just couldn't be true that March had ever thought about her seriously?* . . .

56

But she had little time or inclination to worry about him. There were so many other things to think about. The die was cast. She was actually going to get married to darling Denis in three weeks' time.

She and Mummy had made a list of '*Must do's*'. There were the invitations to be printed; they must get hold of the Misses Burton tomorrow—two sisters who ran a high-class dressmaking establishment in Welbridge. The elder one had been a cutter in a big London tailor's and was considered excellent. The younger one made beautiful lingerie. They had known the Boyd family all their lives. They would most certainly do what they could to make some of Nicola's trousseau quickly. The rest could be bought. Daddy had already made a generous offer of a cheque. On Monday, Nicola *must* close down the shop and go up to Town with Mummy and buy the material for her wedding dress. She *must* look her most beautiful for Denis, who liked one to be glamorous and wonderful.

Already Nicola had decided on a classic gown with low neck and long tight sleeves in rich creamy satin . . . and Aunt Frances (after whom Flip had been called and who had 'the money' in the family) was sure to offer the loan of her veil. She had always said she would. A real Limerick. It was all wildly exciting. The parents had been dears . . . quietly falling in with her wishes because they believed in allowing her to run her own life at her age. Yet she knew they were troubled . . . not too happy about this lightning affair. And there were moments when Nicola stopped to think and was herself a little scared and apprehensive.

But as soon as she thought about Denis as a husband, reason fled . . . she was crazily in love and enraptured by the thought that he, of all the men in the world, was anxious to share his life with her.

Think of living at the Welbridge Park . . . as Mrs. Avon! Intoxicating reflection! And at the same time it was a colossal relief to think that she could carry on with *NICOLETTE* for a while. She was so anxious to pay back Ronald. Brother Ron would, of course, get a couple of days' holiday and come home for the wedding. She was going to put a telephone call through to Bristol tonight.

When she *did* start to concentrate on details, now and again, she was a little bewildered about the financial side of her forthcoming marriage. Daddy had asked Denis about his income, apologizing in that nice way Daddy had. . . . *I'd just like to know that my Nic is going to be all right, although I'm not one to money-grab, and I think it's good for young people to have to fight a bit. Nicola's mother and I had to do it . . .* and so on.

But Denis had never come down to definite figures. In his airy way he had just said, "Oh, they pay the leads pretty well in a Rep. Company these days . . . we'll be all right."

But none of them really knew how much he had, and they were still a bit in the dark about his background, although for the first time at the family lunch today he volunteered the fact that his mother had died when he was born, and that he had been brought up by his grandmother (now dead) and had only this aunt—Miss Emma Robinson—who lived in Putney. Laughing at Nicola with his handsome eyes he had added:

"So you see Nicola won't be bothered with a lot of in-laws and I can give her all my time, and it's going to be wonderful for me to become one of this *heavenly* family. . . ."

He had ended by blowing a kiss to young Flip, who sighed with rapture.

Nicola thought it rather touching that he should be so much alone and long for a family life. It seemed all the more essential that she should marry him at once and give him some domestic comforts. She would make a 'home' out of their room at the Welbridge Park.

But still she felt uneasy when she remembered the look she had seen her parents exchange during one of Denis's extravagant speeches. Somehow she *knew* he did not go down well with them, and that he was not the son-in-law they wanted.

It was as well that she could not have heard her father's remarks once he was alone with her mother.

Mr. Boyd had said:

"Well, I hope it will turn out well for our Nic. She's such a good, honest girl. But somehow that fellow is too smooth for my liking. I just can't get on with him."

Mary Boyd had answered:

"I do feel it's all much too hasty and yet—he's very nice. It was sweet the way he brought me those flowers, and he's sweet to Flip. . . ."

"A bit too sweet," growled Mr. Boyd, "but you women like saccharin."

"Oh, dear," said Mrs. Boyd, "don't you feel he is trustworthy? You know, he *is* an actor, so if he's a bit artificial it does not necessarily mean that he's insincere."

Mr. Boyd had vouchsafed no further opinion. All women were the same in his opinion . . . carried away by charm. But he feared for his elder and much-loved daughter. Nevertheless it was *her* life. She must make or mar it.

But Nicola knew none of this and could only guess what her parents were thinking.

That same evening the Boyds went out to play bridge—the one pastime which they enjoyed regularly with friends of theirs down the road. Flip had been called for by her best friend, Pam, and Mrs. Butler, her mother. They were going to see a Walt Disney which was showing in the town.

They had wanted Nic to go with them but she had refused. She had far too much to think about and do. And tonight she *must* look at some business accounts *and* get that 'phone call through to Ronnie.

There was a delay on the line, and while waiting for the call to come through Nicola received an unexpected visitor— March Foster. As soon as she saw him her pulses gave a funny little tremor . . . she remembered what Flip had told her.

Certainly he looked a bit solemn. He had brought Kimbo with him.

"I was going to take him for a walk, and I wondered if you'd like to come with me. That is, if a chap may suggest such a thing to another fellow's future wife."

Nicola laughed at him. But there seemed some slight bitterness in his voice rather than the usual humour. She excused herself from the walk and told him about the telephone call.

"Stay and talk to me a bit, March, do," she said.

"May Kimbo come in?"

"Of course."

They returned to the sitting-room. The Boxer, obeying an

order, turned a couple of circles and then seated himself on the hearthrug and began to lick his huge paws. Nicola sat down again and March took the chair beside her. His gaze rested on her with mixed feelings. It seemed incredible to him to think that this friend of his youth . . . little Nicola . . . should be on the verge of marrying that fellow who was at this moment playing his part in the 'Rep'. He could not accept it. And he could not quell the turbulence in his own heart and mind at the prospect. Since Flip had told him the news, he had felt as devilishly uneasy and perturbed as he used to feel when he was in the Commandos . . . in those small dark hours before the dawn when they were just about to make an attack which would mean grave danger . . . perhaps death. Indeed, he felt 'like death' this evening, he told himself. And a dozen times or more he had railed at himself for leaving things so late . . . for not realizing, long ago, that Nicola Boyd was the one girl in the world whom he wanted to marry.

He stared at her . . . the fair charming head bent over her cash-book . . . the slim tall figure in the flowered cotton frock and short-sleeved woolly cardigan, and those graceful fingers which she kept so beautifully manicured and which were at the same time such . . . clever, capable hands.

Passionate possessive thoughts raced suddenly through March Foster's brain, and set his heart racing madly. She couldn't marry that actor fellow, he thought desperately. He was going to tell her so. He was going to tell her here and now how much he loved her. That she was his and always had been. He would beg her to reconsider things . . . to marry *him* instead of Denis Avon.

VII

NOBODY had ever accused March Foster of cowardice where physical things were concerned and he was no coward now in a situation which other men might have found slightly formidable. He plunged straight into battle, albeit he felt himself breaking out into a sweat as he did so.

"Look here, Nic," he said, "I may have no right to say anything to you . . . on the other hand, I've been brought up to believe that all's fair in love and war. If you were married it would be different. But you're not. And an engagement is supposed to be a period of trial—isn't it? You and this actor chap are on trial with each other until you're married. No doubt *you* may pass the test with him. But is he going to pass it with you? Haven't you been a bit precipitous about this whole affair?"

So surprised was Nicola that she was reduced to speechlessness for a moment. Fountain-pen suspended in her hand, she looked with wide-open eyes at March; her face and throat suffused with hot pink colour. March stared at her and chewed his lower lip. He added in a blunt voice:

"I'm in love with you myself. That's the honest truth and I suppose the fact gives me some right to speak up."

Nicola laid down her pen. Her heart was plunging. But it was with anger as well as amazement. She was about to tell him that he had no right to 'speak up' in such a way and that she resented his half-scornful allusion to Denis. 'Actor chap' indeed! How dared he? And how absolutely fantastic to hear March Foster saying that he was in love with *her*! Then she recovered her sense of humour and decided to treat this thing as a joke.

"Really, March, I've never heard of such a thing! In love with me . . . *you*! Are you being funny?" She gave a nervous laugh.

He scowled.

"You have a warped idea of what's funny. Why shouldn't I be in love with you?"

Her lashes fluttered. Her cheeks were still flaming. So March was serious! The hints that young Flip had been throwing out were not from imagination after all. She stammered:

"Really . . . it can't be true. We've known each other for years and years . . . you've been a sort of brother to me."

March Foster in love was much the same as in all his dealings with life . . . determined and indefatigable. At this moment he might be suffering from doubt—first as to his own wisdom in laying his cards on the table like this—secondly in his chances of victory. He knew suddenly that he adored this girl, but her flippant attitude infuriated him. He thrust his hands in his pockets.

"Brother, my foot!" he snapped. "We've been friends, but we haven't really seen each other for ages, and up to now I've never thought of you as anything but a sweet girl whom I was fond of, neither have I taken any girl seriously. But these things alter, suddenly. *I've* altered . . . about you. I've decided that I want to get married and to *you*, and no other woman in the world."

Nicola gasped. These were certainly Commando tactics. They were without romance or thrills. But there was something very impressive and breathtaking about such an honest-to-God proposal of marriage, she thought. She couldn't go on laughing at him. Not with *that* look in his bright hazel eyes. She felt floored. She also felt a natural feminine pleasure in being thus elevated in March's fancy from 'just a sweet girl he was fond of' to the one woman in the world whom he wanted to marry. Now he was speaking again—on a softer note— leaning a little towards her.

"Have I knocked you for six, Nic? I'm sure I've put my case very badly. I'm not a chap who finds it easy to show his feelings or make flowery speeches, as no doubt your Denis can do. But I do love you. And I do want you to give me—as well as Denis Avon—a chance."

Once more there was that slight quality of scorn in his allusion to Denis which roused Nicola's ire. She stopped feeling flattered, sat bolt upright and exclaimed :

"It's *quite* absurd, March. Anybody would think you were suggesting that I could be engaged to you both at the same time and then choose."

March gave a brusque laugh.

"Not a bad idea."

"Don't be ridiculous. You really are a bit crackers."

He managed a grin.

"Fell on my head when I was young, I believe. You ought to be sorry for me. And instead you're cross."

"Oh, March, don't be difficult. If I'm cross, it's because you are trying to suggest that *I* am not serious about Denis and that you can come into my scheme of things in *that* way."

March's heart was sinking. He felt that he had gained nothing and was in danger of losing what he used to have in the way of friendship with this girl. But he covered his chagrin and disappointment by laughing.

"*That way!* Dear, dear! Sounds very sinister and awfully like a bit out of a play ... *forgive me ... I don't love you that way* ..." He broke off and shrugged his shoulders. "Oh, well, I suppose I've 'had it'. But I somehow couldn't help asking you to give me a break."

She could not go on being angry with him. There was something nice and natural about March. She had always liked him a lot. And he was one of her brother's greatest friends. Ron had a tremendous admiration for March. Uneasily she thought of Ron and what she was going to tell him on the telephone tonight when her call came through. He was another person who might be a bit contemptuous about 'actor chaps'. Oh, *why* must being on the stage mark poor Denis down as an inferior being, in the opinion of all these super-masculine, athletic young men? She felt resentment on Denis's behalf. At the same time she was touched by what March had just said and sorry because she must hurt him.

She gave him a sweet and appealing smile.

"March dear ... it's terribly nice of you ... I am honoured ... honestly I am. But I never dreamed you would ever feel like this about me."

"Nor did I," he muttered, "that's the hell of it. I seem to be two weeks too late on the job."

She tried to laugh.

"Well, if I'm the 'job', I'm best forgotten, March. You see I ... I'm frightfully in love with Denis and I *want* to marry him, terribly."

March winced. There was something so final about that simple ingenuous statement.

"Are you quite sure?" he asked. "I mean it's all very sudden and one wants to be certain of such a thing. Look how long I've taken to make up *my* mind. And now I'm darned well positive about it."

She looked and felt embarrassed—and there was an expression of compassion in her beautiful eyes which made March even more certain that he had lost ... even before he had begun . . . with Nicola. If a girl started to be sorry for a chap . . . it was hopeless.

Gloomily he said :

"I wonder whether you'll like the theatre life—even if your husband becomes a star. I should think it will be worse if he does. You'll never have any home life at all. Look at these famous stage marriages . . . nine out of ten of them crack up."

Nicola looked and felt indignant.

"Even if that's so—it is probably because both husband and wife are on the stage. But *I* am not and I can make a home for Denis wherever we go."

March hunched his shoulders.

"You certainly seem all set to be the perfect wife. But every time you've talked to me lately you've appeared to be wrapped up in your Beauty Parlour. That's another thing. It's the end of that for you."

"It would be, whoever I married," she parried. She was not going to admit to March that the business was the one sore point in her relationship with Denis. She added, "Anyhow, for the time being, I am keeping on my shop—at least until Denis leaves the Welbridge Rep."

"So you really are going to marry him, Nic?"

"Yes, March."

March drew in his breath. Defeat never came easily to him. He writhed under it. He looked at Nicola suddenly with great bitterness. She was a sweet thing . . . one hundred per cent good and kind, and lovely with it. He hoped to God that fellow would make her happy.

"Well, here's where I make a graceful exit," he said.

She stood up. She felt curiously depressed.

"Oh, March, I don't want this to make a difference to us . . . I mean we've always been friends. Do let us stay so."

He was on the point of telling her that he never wanted to see her again. That he couldn't bear to, now that he was so completely in love with her. On the other hand, he thought, that would seem a trifle churlish. It would not be easy to see Nicola go right out of his life—or walk out on her family. He liked them all so much.

"It will be a bit awkward," he said with a shrug of the

shoulders. "I don't suppose your husband and I will ever get on. We don't speak the same language."

Her face grew pink with distress.

"Oh, March, I want you to be friends with Denis. Do try. You don't know him yet. I'm sure you'd get to like him. He's great fun. Even Daddy, who doesn't care for the stage, admits that Denis is terribly nice. I do want you to stay friends with both of us, March."

"Do you?"

He stopped caressing the Boxer's head and suddenly put out a hand and caught one of Nicola's and held it a moment against his cheek.

"Oh, hell!" he said under his breath. "Why didn't I wake up to the fact that I loved you long before that fellow came to Welbridge? You may not think it, Nic, but this has hit me rather badly."

She felt an absurd inclination to cry. She was suddenly overcome by March's sincere display of feeling towards her. She said:

"March, I am so sorry."

He laughed, dropped her hand and rose to his feet.

"I suppose I ought to say 'let the best man win'."

"Let's stay friends," she begged again.

He gave his charming schoolboy grin and ran a hand through his thick rough hair.

"If that's the way you want it, okay."

"I do," said Nicola earnestly. "When one marries one doesn't want to lose one's friends."

He wanted, madly, to pick her up in his arms and kiss her until she begged for mercy. But he resisted the impulse. Poor little Nicola! He had distressed her enough already. But suddenly he said:

"Will you promise me something . . . if you *do* change your mind . . . will you give me a chance?"

She shook her head.

"Oh, March, I shall never change . . ."

"No," he thought gloomily, "but Avon might. It's that actor chap I don't trust. I have a feeling that he isn't fit to clean her shoes. Verona Dale as good as said he wouldn't stick to any

65

woman. It won't be Nic who will change her mind. It will be him. He'll get his head turned and then she'll suffer. . . ."

But he said none of those things. When he spoke again it was in a casual voice :

"Well, I'll always be around if you want me at any time."

Now her eyes filled with tears. She brushed them quickly away with the back of her hand.

"Thanks awfully, March. You really are nice. And you will try and like Denis, won't you?"

"Yes," said March in a rather violent voice and then whistled to his dog. "Come on, Kimbo, I think we've out-stayed our welcome."

"Oh, wait!" exclaimed Nicola; "there goes the telephone. That will probably be my call to Bristol. Wait and let me tell you what Ron says."

"Okay," said March briefly.

While Nicola went into the hall to answer that call he brooded over the thought of Nicola and her forthcoming marriage; all his fears for her future and the tragedy of his own loss. A while ago he might have stood a chance with Nic. What a fool he had been . . . what a blind fool! Too thick-witted, he told himself savagely, to recognize through all these years of friendship and affection for the Boyd family that his heart belonged to Nicola. What a lot of good times they had had together in the past! Ronald, too, was one of the nicest chaps he knew. A first-class airman . . . easy-going . . . amusing . . . they used to meet on leave occasionally and 'beat it up' together, and Ronald adored Nic. She was his favourite sister and he was one of her greatest admirers. Now that March came to think of it, he could remember an occasion when they had met in France after D-Day. . . . Ron was then in a squadron on operational duty which included March's company. They had spent an evening together before the attack . . . drinking beer in a little wayside *estaminet*. Ronald had read a letter from home and shown March a snapshot of Nicola, taken on her nineteenth birthday. She was then in V.A.D. uniform, working in the Welbridge Cottage Hospital. Ron had said :

"Dickens of a fine kid, young Nic. I reckon she'd make a

66

damned good wife for you, old boy. How about taking her on when the war's over and having me as a brother-in-law?"

March at the time had guffawed and shaken his head.

"I'll do anything for you except get married, old boy," he had answered. "I'm a born bachelor!"

Fool, *fool*! To discover too late how much he loved her—and now that chap Avon had weighed in and won.

Nicola was away for ten minutes. When she came back March thought that she looked flushed and slightly perturbed, but she said in an airy voice:

"It *was* Ron. He sends you all the best."

March felt that he had better not ask what Ron felt about his sister's plunge into matrimony.

He said:

"Thanks. How is the old so-and-so?"

"Fine," said Nicola; "he says he looks forward to seeing you at the wedding."

"Don't rub it in," said March.

Impulsively Nicola held out her hand.

"I didn't mean to. But please come to my wedding, and let's all be happy. I want everybody to be happy."

"Nice child," he murmured, grinning to hide the emotional storm that her touch, her sweetness, aroused in him. Then with a rough gesture he pulled her hand against his lips and dropped it again. He gave a mock bow.

"I'm becoming quite the cavalier! I shall be on the stage myself soon," he said. "Oh, well—good night, my dear. See you some time."

She wanted to ask him to stay and talk to her, but thought it best that he should go. She followed him to the front door and closed it after him. When she returned to the sitting-room, she sat down in front of her ledger again but found it impossible to concentrate. Her mind was too full of conflicting thoughts.

March's outburst had come as a shock and left a deep impression. At the same time she was positive that she was utterly in love with Denis and that she could never for a moment think of March as anything but a friend. Might she have fallen in love with March had Denis never come into her life? As a friend he was marvellous. And he was strangely attractive. For the first time he had made her conscious of her sex and of his masculinity. And she knew that she could never again think of him in an entirely platonic way. What he had said tonight had, in fact, spoilt their friendship. At the same time she did not want him to go right out of her life. She genuinely wanted him to make friends with Denis. Yet she had to confess that she felt decidedly uneasy about it. The two men would never really see eye to eye. That applied to brother Ronald, too.

Tonight, she told herself, the stars seemed to be against her. First the upheaval with March . . . then Ronald's disappointing reception of her great news. She would not have admitted it to March, but Ron had been just as dubious about this forthcoming marriage as March himself. In a brotherlike fashion he had put it a trifle more bluntly.

"Good lord, you must be cuckoo, my poor Nic!" he had said over the telephone wire, "you haven't known the chap a couple of minutes. And what do you want to marry an actor for? He doesn't sound your cup of tea. I don't want to be a wet blanket, but I can't say I'm impressed by the news."

When she had argued and protested and explained how wonderful Denis was and how much she loved him, Ronald had added:

"Well, he may be a wizard chap for all I know, but I think you're rather rushing into it and you ought to have a longer engagement. Don't Mother and Dad think so?"

She had told him exactly what their parents felt and added rather resentfully that she felt Ronald was taking a gloomy view. Whereupon he said:

"Well, it's not like you to rush into anything and I do take rather a dim view of the fellow not giving you a bit more time. And anyhow, what about *NICOLETTE*?"

That had been much more difficult for Nicola to discuss over the telephone—or justify. Ron didn't speak from his own point of view—he wouldn't. He was much too generous. But she knew that he must be feeling a bit concerned, as he had helped her so considerably to start *NICOLETTE*. She had made haste to assure him that when she had sold the business she would pay him back. And he had said:

"Don't let that worry you. What I'm really concerned about is *are* you marrying the right chap?"

Her fervent declaration of love for Denis had been cut short by the operator telling her that she had had 'six minutes'. She had another three—he asked after March, and then told Nicola that he would write, and rang off.

Remembering it all, Nicola felt profoundly depressed. Ron had not even wished her luck. He seemed more against her marriage than anyone, so far. And he was the one being in the world whose approbation she most wanted. She had always adored Ronald.

She lit a cigarette and smoked it, feeling nervy and troubled. Of course she knew her own mind, and had no doubts about how much she wanted to marry Denis. But this sort of thing *was* upsetting. At the same time it was a challenge. But she would show them all, she told herself. Ron, March and the family—she would prove to them that her choice was the right one; that Denis was worthy of her love, and that she would be the happiest woman in the world once she was married to him.

VIII

THE date of Nicola's wedding to Denis Avon had been fixed for the tenth of June. During the three weeks following the engagement there had been little time for Nicola to think of anything much except the terrific excitement and thrill of it all. Rushed between preparations for the wedding and her job at *NICOLETTE* she often had no leisure in which to think at all.

She saw Denis every day and every day she seemed to fall more in love with him. It was a delirious time for any girl and Denis just then was at his best—an eager, impetuous lover—all that her heart could desire. If there had been a remote feeling of doubt within her as to the wisdom of her choice—a doubt planted by brother Ron's disapproval—and March's—it was soon eliminated by Denis. The handsome

69

popular young actor, apart from his work, seemed to have eyes and ears only for Nicola. People like Ron and March did not know or understand Denis, she kept telling herself, but she would soon prove to them what a marvellous man he was and what a wonderful life she would lead as his wife. There were sure to be difficulties. But what marriage was easy these days? Anyhow—to love and be loved by Denis would make everything worth while.

June was not a good month so far as weather was concerned. It was colder and wetter than May had been. But even that fact could not cast a blight upon Nicola. Her mother, watching in her silent devoted way, remarked one day to her husband that 'Nic had blossomed like a flower' during her brief tempestuous engagement. She had never been so gay, so radiant to look at, or so self-confident.

"Somehow I hope and believe she is doing the right thing and that we need not worry too much," Mary Boyd observed.

John Boyd said nothing. He had his own personal views on the matter. And he could not but believe that this hasty marriage was a mistake.

But Nicola was no child. She must decide for herself. The marriage was arranged and John Boyd was prepared to play his part.

Even Ronald Boyd, who had been so dead against the marriage when he first heard about it that night on the telephone, later admitted that 'perhaps he was mistaken' once he met Denis. He could see how happy and sure of herself his sister seemed to be.

Ron came home for a week-end at the beginning of June especially to make the acquaintance of his future brother-in-law. Before Nicola introduced Denis to him, she had told Denis how much she had always loved her brother . . . what a lot Ron had done for her . . . and impressed upon him her desire that the two boys should 'get on'.

When they met, Denis, if anything, showed up the best. He shook hands warmly with Nicola's brother, proved himself eager to be friendly and evinced a tactful interest in Ronald's job (although engineering bored him and he knew nothing about it). Perhaps he sensed that Ronald was not particularly pleased about this rush marriage, so Denis, who so hankered to be liked and admired by the whole world, worked enthusiastically to win Nicola's brother over to his side.

Ronald started off by being a trifle gruff and unresponsive. He eyed the handsome young actor with suspicion and—incapable of dissembling (for he was a candid, rather blunt young man without a trace of hypocrisy in his nature)—declared that he thought they were 'rushing things'. But Denis did not take offence. Smilingly he pleaded guilty, but maintained that they could not wait because they were so much in love, and that as he might so soon be leaving Welbridge, he wanted to take Nicola with him as his wife.

"I quite understand that I'm robbing her family. Nobody would want to part with Nicola," he said with his most delightful smile, "but you'll have to try and excuse me, old boy, and I can assure you our home will be open to you at any time."

Ronald felt a little mollified by this and before the weekend was over was half inclined to think that Denis was a 'good chap'. 'A bit smooth', but that was probably his stage training. And he couldn't be called 'wet' even by Ronald—used to thoroughly masculine R.A.F. types—personal friends like March Foster. Denis took him to the Welbridge Arms, filled him with beer, and, always at his best in a crowd, entertained the whole bar with racy stories and was a great success. The next morning, when Nicola spoke to her brother about Denis, she was delighted to find him a bit more satisfied with the idea of her marrying the 'actor chap'.

So Nicola glowed, and was proud of Denis and content. The invitations had gone out and the presents poured in. Flip came home with bad marks from school because she was in such a state of excitement that she could not concentrate. All she could think of was her bridesmaid's dress.

Nicola—usually rather a retiring and simple person—found herself quite the centre of attention in the little sleepy town of Welbridge. Work increased in the salon and she had all she could do to get through it. She went home tired out every evening but was pleased with her own progress. And of course the job was made even more agreeable because the main subject of conversation between herself and her clients was THE WEDDING! All the girls who came for a 'facial' were enthusiastic about it and fervent in their praise of Denis. The little Rep. Company was playing to packed houses most nights. Miss Dale had recovered from her 'flu and returned to the cast and Denis, in happy mood, was giving his best performances.

There remained only one person in Welbridge who shared none of the enthusiasm and was frankly gloomy about the whole affair. That was March Foster. He saw Ronald Boyd and had a drink with him, but they discussed the approaching marriage only in a fleeting fashion. March was pleased to see his old friend although it gave him a pang. He had never before really noticed the similarity between Ron and Nicola. Brother and sister had the same slender build and fair hair and several of the same mannerisms. There was, however, nothing girlish in Ron's appearance. He had a much harder mouth than Nicola's and a squarer chin, and one side of his face was badly scarred—legacy of a crash in his Service days. He asked March bluntly what he thought of 'young Nic's choice'. March guardedly replied that he hadn't really formed an opinion because he had scarcely seen Denis.

"What do you think?" he asked Ronald in his turn.

"Seems an amusing chap and he's certainly crackers about Nic, but I rather wish she would give things a bit more time," was Ronald's reply.

March looked bitterly and blankly in front of him and said:

"I couldn't agree more . . ."

And that was as far as the discussion went.

March had seen Nicola only once since the evening when he poured out his heart to her—an evening which he had since regretted because he was proud and was also a person who did not change his mind easily. He found it hard to accept the fact that Nicola was going to belong to another man. But when he met her—which was in the High Street—he greeted her with his usual flippancy, as though they had never had that intimate 'scene'. She had looked fatigued, in his opinion, but seemed in high spirits and full of praise for the wedding present which his parents had sent her. Certainly, she said, it was going to be the 'star' gift, for it was a Crown Derby tea-set and one of Mrs. Foster's treasures.

"I feel sure she oughtn't to have parted with it," Nicola said to March.

He looked at her without a trace on his hard brown face of the pain in his heart.

"Why not? My mamma is very fond of you, my dear Nic. . . ."

That was all he had said. Then he had walked on. By some ironic chance he met Denis Avon coming out of a matinée that same afternoon. March nodded to him and would have gone on, but Denis insisted upon stopping and talking. Denis cared nothing for March Foster—in fact he sensed hostility in that quarter. But he was always on the side of money and he had never forgotten the magnificence of the Foster home. The Fosters were people to 'keep in with' in Denis's opinion. So he clapped March on the back and said :

"Nice to see you, old boy. When are you coming to see the show?"

"I'm not much of a theatre-goer," was March's reply, and he could hardly explain the resentment that the patronizing smack on the shoulder roused in him.

Then Denis mentioned the wedding present and thanked him profusely for it.

"It was from my parents—not me," said March shortly. "I, myself, haven't yet decided what to give Nicola."

"Oh, well, see you at the wedding," said Denis airily and moved away.

March walked on, conscious of absolute hatred for Denis Avon and then reproached himself for being a jealous fool.

And when he thought about the wedding present he felt even more wretched. He would have liked to have given Nicola the earth—not a mere present to celebrate her marriage to another man. He would like to choose something rare and beautiful for her. Something *personal*.

And in the end he decided that he would give her a dog. A dog like Kimbo. She had always loved Kimbo and expressed a particular liking for Boxers. So he found an expensive but beautiful puppy of three months old—the same strain as his own Boxer—and took it down to the Boyd home two days before the wedding.

It was his bad luck that Denis should be there at that precise moment. March had an absurdly sentimental wish to present the puppy to Nicola when she was alone. But it was a fine day and the whole family was out in the garden at the time of his arrival. Flip was the first to see the puppy and rushed to it with a squeal of delight.

"Oh, what an *angel*! . . . what a *poppet*! . . . Nic, look!"

Nicola, who had been sitting in a deck-chair beside Denis, making a list with him of people whom they must thank for presents, got up and greeted March. He put the Boxer into her arms, and grinned, in a strangely embarrassed fashion.

"He ought to be wrapped in tissue paper and tied up with white ribbon, I suppose. I didn't know what to give you but I thought you might like him. Wishing you every happiness and all that."

Nicola flushed and gave a little cry of pleasure. The puppy immediately cuddled down into her arms and thrust its ugly charming little face against her hand, which he began to lick fervently.

"Oh, March, what a beauty! Is it really for me?"

He nodded. His regretful gaze drank in the sight of her charming gesture as she put one cheek against the Boxer's small head. Her pleasure moved him deeply. But he gave one of his careless laughs.

"Glad you like him. He's a nephew of Uncle Kimbo's. I've got his pedigree for you. He's quite a lad. Uncle's markings, too, as you see."

"Oh, he is like a tiny Kimbo—he's adorable!" exclaimed Nicola.

The family crowded round. Mrs. Boyd expressed her admiration. Nicola added :

"Has he got a name?"

"A kennel name, yes, but most unsuitable. I forget it now. You must rename him," said March.

Nicola turned to her fiancé.

"Denis, do look! . . . March's wedding present . . . the most beautiful Boxer."

74

Denis rose with languid grace from his deck-chair and took a look at the puppy. He was not a dog-lover. He thought the puppy a ridiculous present and he couldn't stand March Foster anyhow. However, he put on his usual 'act'.

"Jolly little fellow," he drawled, "thanks, old boy." Then could not resist a barb : "But I'm not quite sure what we shall do with him . . . living in hotels and rooms and so on."

Nicola, already infatuated with the baby Boxer, cuddled it tightly.

"Oh, I shall take him with me everywhere, Denis darling! He can walk with me to the shop, and I'll make love to Mrs. Gunter who runs the hotel, and ask her to let me have him. I am sure she will. I've seen guests there with dogs."

"And I can see all our nice new shoes being chewed up," said Denis with rather an acid laugh.

But nobody took any notice of him. Nicola had set her new treasure down on the grass and everybody was laughing at the nervous way in which big Kimbo backed a pace from his tiny obstreperous nephew.

March felt his heart warm slightly at the delight which Nicola showed in his choice of a present, and he took a faintly malicious and human pleasure in Denis's obvious distaste for it.

Mr. and Mrs. Boyd asked March to stay to tea but he murmured an excuse that he already had an appointment. In reality he could not bear to stay and be a looker-on, for now Denis, in possessive fashion, had put an arm around Nicola and was giving her that warm sidelong glance which women found so attractive and which made March feel that he wanted to be sick.

So engrossed was Nicola in her new live wedding present that she hardly noticed the departure of the giver. When she looked up and found him gone, she exclaimed :

"Oh, what a shame!"

"What's a shame?" murmured Denis.

"March ought to have stayed to tea."

He whispered against her ear :

"I'm jealous. You're not to want anybody here but me."

She looked up into his handsome sparkling eyes.

"Silly! You know I don't really. But Denis . . . *isn't* my puppy adorable? What shall we call him?"

He frowned faintly at the little Boxer who was now growling and tugging at a piece of string which Flip had thrown him.

"You don't really want to drag it around with us everywhere we go, do you, darling?"

Nicola looked up at him quickly.

"Oh, but yes! I adore dogs. Don't you?"

"I think they're all right in their place—in a kennel," he drawled.

She stared at him. A faint colour stole into her face. It was the first time she had ever felt conscious of any difference of opinion between this adored lover and herself. She was vaguely disappointed and not a little astonished. She had never really met anybody before who didn't like dogs. She had been brought up with animals. It was only her job which lately had kept her from replacing a much-loved cocker spaniel which the Boyds had had for nine years and which they had had to have destroyed. (She could remember how the whole family had mourned poor Tessa.) She had longed to have another dog, and March could have given her nothing she liked more than Kimbo's charming and ridiculous little nephew.

"Oh, dear!" she said with a faint indrawn breath.

Denis gave a lazy laugh and gently pulled the lobe of one of her ears.

"Don't look so hurt. You won't have any time to waste on puppies. You'll be much too busy making love to me. It was a damned stupid present, anyhow. I suggest you send it back —or sell it and buy something more suitable."

Now Nicola's cheeks were decidedly red. She found the latter suggestion hateful. And much as she adored Denis, she had very decided views of her own, and was not willing to be too submissive, even to him. She said :

"Really, Denis, I can't dream of selling the puppy or giving him back. What would March think?"

"Is it so important to you what March Foster thinks?"

Nicola's heart gave an uneasy little jerk.

"It isn't a question of just *March*. Don't be absurd. I'd be the same no matter who gave it to me. Besides, I don't want to part with the puppy."

"I see," said Denis, drawing away from her, "and if I do—what then?"

Silence followed this ultimatum. Nicola was thoroughly startled now; conscious that a shadow had fallen between her and her former complete happiness. It was such a little thing . . . such an unimportant matter . . . yet to hear Denis talk like that . . . look at her so coldly . . . threatened to destroy the absolute belief she had hitherto cherished that she and Denis could never, *never* seriously disagree.

## IX

It was impossible to continue the discussion here and now with the rest of the family watching and listening. So Nicola, with that cold feeling of disappointment in her heart, and heightened colour in her cheeks, bent down to pick up the puppy and pressed it against her, kissing the top of its square silky head.

She was in the mood to be defiant and show the world that she had a mind of her own. Nicola never had been the 'door-mat type'. She said in a loud clear voice :

"You are Kimbo's nephew, my little sweetie, so I think we'll christen you Kim."

"That's a super idea !" exclaimed Flip with enthusiasm.

Denis narrowed his gaze. Inwardly he was furious. He did not like being defied. And he was also amazed that Nicola should put his wishes second to her own. He had fully expected her to give way at once. Behind the façade of his usual charm and amiability he had a quick and sometimes ungovernable temper. It was a temper he generally controlled when necessary for his personal advancement. He did so now, much though he wanted to snatch the dog out of Nicola's arms and demand that she should give it back to March Foster at once. He grew a little white and his lips tightened. Then he managed to laugh.

"Dear, dear ! These dog-lovers !"

77

Flip goggled at him.

"But don't *you* adore dogs, Denis? I think they're *sweet*. I've been trying to get Mummy to let us have a new one and she says I can for next birthday if I promise to house-train it. I think I shall have a lady Boxer like Kimbo and Kim, then we'll marry them and have dozens and dozens of little Boxers."

Mary Boyd laughed at her youngest daughter.

"Oh, Flip!"

Denis then did what was expected of him.

"Very excellent scheme, poppet," he said.

Nicola, her heart beating quickly, turned to him. She was about to ask him a question but changed her mind. After a moment or two Mr. and Mrs. Boyd went indoors and Flip, who prided herself on being of a romantic disposition, threw a soulful glance at her sister and the handsome young actor, and made herself scarce.

Nicola drew near to her fiancé.

"Did you really mean that you want me to get rid of my new puppy?" she asked in a low voice.

Denis hesitated. He let his narrowed gaze rest on her. She was looking particularly lovely with that bright colour in her cheeks and the rather mutinous curve of red lips. And she really had the most delicious hands, he thought, as he watched her long slender fingers, with their rosy polished nails, stroking the puppy's head. He couldn't be cross with her for long. Not today, anyhow, when so soon she was going to be his wife. And secretly he admired her spirit—and for the moment he was inclined to be amused by the way she had stood up to him.

"Do you want the dog so much?" he asked.

"Yes, I think I do. And I should hate it if I really thought that *you* felt the right place for a dog was a *kennel*," she said with frank distaste.

He raised his brows. Well, well . . . he did not want to incur Nicola's displeasure. Let her keep the dog. If it annoyed him later on he would get rid of it. But it wasn't worth quarrelling about now, and he said so. Putting an arm around Nicola, he added:

"Darling . . . I can't bear to see you look so upset. The Boxer is a nice little fellow . . . but is he so important to you that you want to fight with me?"

Nicola gave a nervous laugh. She was relieved to see the warmth and love in his eyes again but she was not quite ready for surrender. She said:

"Denis, darling, it isn't really the importance of the *dog* . . . but your attitude. You seemed . . . so unsympathetic . . . demanding that I should give the little dog back to March and that sort of thing. It didn't seem *like you*."

Denis put his tongue in his cheek. He drew her nearer to his side.

"Oh, my *angel* . . . I didn't mean to be unsympathetic. I was only expressing my views, in the same way that you have expressed yours."

She knit her brows. He was beginning to make her feel that she was just as difficult as he was, and yet . . . she could see that, if he could, he would certainly have wiped March's present right off the map.

"Oh, Denis," she said, "I hoped you would like animals, because I do so much. Apart from that, I don't want anything to come between us even in a small way. I want us to agree about everything."

Now Denis's temporary ill-humour evaporated. He was allowing himself to be thoroughly amused. He laughed heartily and dropped a kiss on her cheek and then one on the tip of her nose.

"Sweet thing! What an infant you are at times behind the 'big business' woman. Quite enchanting. But you know perfectly well that no two people can agree over everything, no matter how much they love each other. I am sure we shall find lots to argue about. And I shall just seize you in my arms like this . . ." he pulled her right against him, regardless of the puppy, and kissed her more possessively . . . "until you beg for mercy and give in to my whims."

The touch of his lips on her mouth, as always, roused all her passion and sent every other thought but him flying from her head. When she drew back from him, breathless, she put the squirming puppy down on the lawn and smoothed her crumpled dress, her face bright pink, her eyes soft and full of that shy surrender which always pleased Denis. He adored the mixture of passion and shyness in this girl; the exquisite freshness which set her apart from all other women in his life (and there had been many). The others had been 'too easy' . . . or too cold and mercenary. But Nicola was the perfect mixture and would, he felt, make the perfect wife. And Denis Avon wanted everything in his life to be perfect. He decided now to subjugate his wishes to hers completely.

"Angel, you shall have your puppy and fill our house with Boxers if it makes you happy," he said tenderly.

"You really won't mind me keeping little Kim?"

"Of course not, silly. I didn't think it meant so much to you when I suggested getting rid of him. Very decent of Foster taking the trouble to find the sort of breed you like."

Nicola's spirits rose. The air had cleared. The anxious moment passed. When Denis left for the theatre she was quite happy again. Only when she was in her bedroom that night and the baby Boxer lay curled beside her bed in the dog-basket which had once belonged to the beloved Tessa, and had been routed out of the attic by Flip, did slight anxiety creep back into Nicola's mind.

She lay awake for a long time recalling all that Denis had said when March first gave the puppy to her. His surrender had been unconditional. Yet she could not quite forget that first scowl he had given and his remark about the 'right place for a dog being a kennel'. Was there a Denis she did not know? Would she find him difficult, and inclined to want his own way all the time? Then she reasoned with herself that she was equally apt to want hers and that Denis had as much right to his ideas as she had to her own. No man could be perfect. She had no right to make a little god of Denis. He was only human . . . her darling Denis . . . bound to have faults. She had criticized other marriages in which one side or the other demanded everything. It mustn't be like that with theirs. It must be a case of fifty-fifty, and if Denis really didn't like dogs, she ought perhaps to refuse to keep little Kim. Then, as she heard the small animal's breathing, she sighed, and felt unutterably relieved to think that Denis had given way on this matter. She adored him for it. And she was an idiot to have let this small matter trouble her at all.

She remembered his farewell kiss and thought :

"Only one more day and I shall be *his*, for ever!"

The blissful vision of life and love with Denis obscured any further desire to reason or worry. She fell asleep with a tranquil mind, confident that she loved Denis more than ever.

Only one other small cloud temporarily shadowed the horizon for Nicola before her wedding. That was when she walked with little Kim (who was now her slave) up to Heron's Hall. It was after she had left the salon, having put a notice up outside to the effect that *NICOLETTE* would be closed for a week. She had decided to give herself the week's respite and honeymoon, even though Denis must continue to play his part at the theatre. She had not seen March since he gave her Kim and felt that she owed him a few more words of thanks. He had slipped away so suddenly that afternoon.

She also wanted to call on his mother, who had only yesterday returned from a nursing home.

March was not at home but his mother was there, and Nicola found her on the terrace lying under a rug in a long basket-chair.

Catherine Foster was a small frail woman whose hair had gone snow-white before her time. Nobody knew how she had managed to produce her 'tough' young son. She was a delicate creature who passed from one illness and operation to another.

Nicola looked at her with pity. Every time she saw March's mother she thought how quickly she was ageing, for she was barely fifty—and how unhappy she always seemed to be in spite of money and position. March had inherited his good health and spirits from his Yorkshire-born father—a big boisterous man. But Catherine Foster had an unhappy disposition which had not been improved through the years by her long bill of ill-health. This marriage, as Nicola and everybody in Welbridge knew, had been ill-assorted from the start. George Foster had met his bride during a holiday in Cornwall. Catherine was Cornish born and bred, and thirty years ago had been a lovely girl of the Spanish type so often found down there; dark-eyed and raven-haired. But she also had that reserved, rather difficult temperament and moodiness of the Cornish. And she had never really loved George Foster. But as a younger man he had swept her off her feet with his terrific energy and determination. Eventually he had carried her off to Huddersfield, where March had been born. It was in Huddersfield that George Foster had first started his chain of stores, later carrying them down to the South, where he had finally settled while March was still a little boy.

From the beginning, Catherine Foster had been homesick, hated the North and spent most of her time pining for the West Country. She had had two other children who had both died, then no more. She had grown almost to dislike her hearty, successful husband, who was patient and warmly generous to her—and ever grateful for his fine son. But she rarely said 'thank you' to him for anything. She had stayed with him only because she was a religious woman who believed in the sanctity of the marriage tie. She had become, in her own mind, a martyr—and not a cheerful one. Many illnesses had left her with a warped, embittered outlook. March was the only being on earth for whom she now cared. She loved him with all the passion of her distorted nature, which was fundamentally warm, but had frozen over with frustration and disappointment in the man she had married. She was fastidious, dreamy and fond of books. She found her husband crude and materialistic. She had suffered agonies all through the war when March was with the Commandos. Now she was thankful to have him home safe and sound and was encouraging him to write. She gloried in his literary qualities, which she believed he had inherited from *her* side. Her father had kept a bookshop in Newquay.

Her main ambition was that March should marry the right type of girl and give her grandchildren in whom she could live again. She was in his confidence (he was always particularly gentle and kind to her) and she knew that of all the girls in Welbridge he had favoured Nicola Boyd. It was a choice that Catherine Foster approved. Nicola was a beautiful girl— not only sweet, but sensible. At first, when she had heard that Nicola was going to marry Denis Avon, she had been furious on her son's behalf. She would never forgive Nicola, she had said with indignation. March had tried to talk her out of that state of mind. Nicola had a right to choose her own husband, he said, and it was his wish that his mother should always be friends with Nic and her family. So Mrs. Foster caved in and had sent Nicola that treasured Crown Derby tea-set for a wedding present. But she looked at Nicola with slight resentment this afternoon. The girl was really lovely . . . no doubt happiness gave her that special radiance. . . . Tomorrow she was going to be married. But why wasn't it to poor March? Catherine Foster asked herself. She made an effort to smile at Nicola.

"Very nice of you to come and see me, Nicola."

"It's terribly nice to have you back home, Mrs. Foster," said Nicola. "Have you seen the darling puppy March gave me?"

Mrs. Foster eyed the little Boxer and nodded.

"No, but he told me he was getting it for you."

"I came to thank March for him, as well as to see you, and to tell him that we've christened the puppy Kim as he is Kimbo's nephew."

Mrs. Foster sighed.

"Well, I'm afraid March is out. I think he's taken Kimbo into the country for a really long walk. He said he mightn't get back to supper."

"Oh, I'm sorry," said Nicola, and added: "How absolutely gorgeous Heron's Hall looks this evening."

Mrs. Foster sighed again. Sunset was always the loveliest time at Heron's Hall. The beautiful garden full of beautiful trees and the green lawns stretching down to the water's edge were bathed in golden light at the close of the June day. The roses were just coming out. The rockery was a blaze of aubretia, mauve and pink, and there were still rows of tall scarlet tulips fringing the flagged pathways. Lovely garden and lovely house. On the table beside Mrs. Foster stood a pile of the newest novels and magazines. There was an excellent maid-companion waiting to take her indoors and help her to bed up in her luxurious room overlooking the river. She had everything that money could buy her. But she felt ill and wretched.

She did not really want to upset Nicola on her wedding eve, yet could not resist thrusting a few barbs at her.

"What's the use of all this, just for Mr. Foster and myself, and March so often away? It would be different if he had a wife and some children here to cheer the place up. But now he can't get you, I doubt he'll ever marry."

Nicola flushed scarlet.

"Oh, Mrs. Foster, I'm sure that isn't true."

Catherine Foster's dark eyes, sunken in her thin face on which the parchment-like skin was drawn tightly across the bones, regarded the girl bitterly.

"I wouldn't be surprised. He was crazy for you."

Nicola stared at the ground, her heart jerking uncomfortably. She had never felt more embarrassed.

"I . . . I'm very upset to hear you say that . . ." she began to stammer.

Mrs. Foster interrupted :

"I shouldn't think many girls would be upset to know that my fine handsome March with his winning ways and his gaiety was crazy about them."

"No, but I meant . . . I mean . . . I wouldn't want to think he was going to stay unmarried because of me," said Nicola. "And believe me, I'm *terribly* honoured to know that March ever wanted to marry me."

"It's broken his heart. He's not been the same since you became engaged. So much quieter. Always going out for walks alone, like this afternoon. He never says anything, but *I know*, because I'm his mother. He really doesn't want to go to your wedding tomorrow. It's just his nice nature that's making him do it."

Nicola raised eyes full of distress to the older woman.

"I'm most awfully sorry, Mrs. Foster. I like March so very, very much. But I'm afraid I can't help it. One doesn't do these things deliberately. I . . . fell in love with Denis Avon— that's all."

Mrs. Foster said nothing for a moment. A little wind blew coolly across the terrace. She shivered and pulled a silk scarf which she was wearing more closely about her throat.

"It's about time I went in," she said in a sombre voice.

Nicola did not know what to say. Every word spoken by March's mother had cut her to the quick. And a few minutes ago she had felt so utterly happy. There was the thought of the marvellous tomorrow . . . of the small but delightful trousseau which her mother had helped her collect . . . the thrilling wedding dress which the Misses Burton had made so beautifully . . . the little coronet of seed pearls, and Aunt Frances's veil . . . all waiting in her room for the great event.

Why must she feel disturbed because this notoriously discontented woman resented her refusal to marry her son? And yet . . . there was so much kindness and genuine warmth of feeling in Nicola . . . she could not bear to hurt anybody. Especially March, who had been such a good friend most of her life.

At length she brought herself to speak.

"Please don't be angry with me because I love Denis," she said. "I honestly can't help it. And I'm sure March will find someone very much better than me . . ." she broke off, clearing her throat in an embarrassed way.

Catherine Foster relented. There was something so simple and frank about Nicola. She reached out a hand in which Nicola immediately placed one of hers. The older woman thought: "What warm strong young fingers . . . how full of life and hope she is . . . and I feel as cold as death. I am useless. I can do nothing for my own son any more. He will have to break his heart for this girl and I can't prevent it. . . ."

But she felt remorse because March would have been furious with her for speaking to Nicola as she had just done. She said:

"That's all right, childie. I shouldn't have discussed my boy with you. And nobody can blame you for choosing the man you want. Only be sure he is the man you want."

Nicola's cheeks crimsoned. She pressed Mrs. Foster's cold hand for a moment, then dropped it and gave a nervous laugh.

"I'm quite sure . . . really I am, Mrs. Foster. I wish you knew Denis. He's quite wonderful."

"He could not be as wonderful as my son," Mrs. Foster blurted out the words before she could restrain them.

Then Nicola laughed again, but gently. She said:

"*Dear* Mrs. Foster, naturally March must seem the most marvellous person in the world to you. I expect I shall feel like that about my son if I ever have one, and be jolly angry with any girl who refuses him. But I still assure you that my Denis is exceptional. I am so very lucky."

There the discussion ended. Mrs. Foster called to Jenny, her maid, to help her indoors, then said good-bye to Nicola.

"I'll tell March you came. I'm sorry I shan't be well enough to come to your wedding. But I dare say I'll see the local report and the photos and I wish you all happiness, my dear."

Nicola walked home, pulling a rather reluctant but playful puppy after her. It was growing dark. She felt curiously downcast after that conversation with poor Mrs. Foster. What a blight the woman must cast over the whole household! she thought. No wonder March was always out . . . trying to get away from that lonely big house—from his materialistic old father who bullied him, and that poor sick mother, sick in mind and body, drenching him with her hungry, futile devotion. And everybody said that March was so sweet to her. March would certainly make a good husband for some girl some day. But, Nicola argued with herself, each to his own taste . . . and she had chosen Denis with his golden voice and charm; all the glamour of his theatrical success; his irresistible attraction for her. She must put March out of her mind . . . not allow herself to be upset by what Mrs. Foster had said.

But she could not entirely banish the memory, and each time it returned . . . and she heard the echo of those words : '*Be sure he is the man you want* . . . ' she had an indefinable and inexplicable feeling of unease.


## X


*Extract from the diary kept by Miss Frances (Flip) Boyd, written on the evening of the tenth of June in her home at Welbridge.*

"MY SISTER'S WEDDING DAY! I shall never NEVER forget Nic's wedding because it was absolutely scrumptious and as super as the weddings you see on the films and Nic looked just as super as any film star and of course Denis was terrific. It all had a marvellous beginning although the end was just what Miss Eccles puts at the bottom of most of my home-work—'disappointing'. But I'd better begin right from the beginning.

Mummy let me take Nic's cup of tea in to her at eight o'clock and we laughed and talked. We were all livid because it was raining which I said would spoil everything. Daddy said it would clear up before twelve so we hoped for the best as the wedding was to be at twelve. Nic didn't seem at all upset. I would have grumbled like anything but she has the sweetest disposition (much better than mine) and she just said she was so happy she wouldn't care if it snowed.

I sat on the end of her bed and she pulled my hair and said I was to stop looking 'soulful' and laughed at me. But I couldn't help it because I thought it was all so romantic. Denis gave me a sweet little locket yesterday. It's going to be in the local papers as 'the bridegroom's gift to the brides-maid'. It's a little heart, gold, with a ruby in it, on a chain. Mummy says it's Victorian. Denis says it's the only bit of heart that he can give me because all the rest belongs to Nic, which I thought was frightfully romantic. He's given Nic some gorgeous clips which he got in London. At least Nic and I thought them gorgeous but I heard Daddy tell Mummy that 'he didn't reckon much to them' and said they weren't real. But my private belief is that Daddy doesn't like Denis because he's always dropping those sort of remarks and I've often heard Mummy say 'Shush'. She says Daddy's too out-spoken. And Nic says Denis is only an actor in a Rep. Company and not a star yet and hasn't any money and had already spent too much on her engagement ring so couldn't afford real diamonds for her clips. But I don't care whether my gold heart is valuable or not. I like it because it's so romantic.

The house was terribly exciting last night. Full of people and all the lovely presents. Aunt Frances is staying with us. Daddy says she's 'got lots of money tucked away', and that we must all be nice to her. I don't mind trying because she's not bad but she's Daddy's oldest sister and has been a widow for twenty years and looks terribly old and isn't nearly as well dressed as our char, Mrs. Tunny. But she lent Nic her gorgeous veil and gave her a huge cheque and said I was growing into a very nice girl. I think I'm her favourite because I've been called after her. And she simply FELL for Denis. He was terribly sweet to her and she told Nic she thought he was very handsome and charming but I heard Daddy say 'that young man knows which side his bread is buttered'. I don't think he thinks Denis is sincere.

The Rep. Company clubbed together and gave Denis a super portable wireless for a present and some of the girls in the Rep. and Ann Williams from *NICOLETTE* did all the flowers in St. Giles'. It looked gorgeous. Mr. Smyth, the organist, told me he hadn't seen so many lovely flowers since the wedding of Lord Farrandale's daughter last summer and she was very special because *he* owns nearly all the land around here!

Ron came home yesterday and it's super having him in the house. But he grumbled at having to wear a stiff collar and 'tog up' and although he says Denis is okay he is awfully sick about him marrying Nic because he wanted her to marry March. But I don't think March would have made such a gorgeous bridegroom as Denis, although I like him awfully, and I still think darling little Kim much the nicest wedding present Nic got from anyone.

I've never known our house to be so full of excitement as it was last night and this morning and I do hope my wedding day will be the same. At least the same as it was at the beginning, because I still haven't come to the AWFUL END.

I was allowed to stay and help Nic do the rest of her packing and now and then she seemed rather sad because she was saying good-bye to her old home, she said. And Mummy was a bit odd and kept sniffing into her handkerchief. But Mrs. Tunny says all mothers cry on their daughters' wedding day, which I think very stupid as they ought to be pleased.

Daddy was quite right about the weather and it did clear up about eleven. The sun came out and it was quite hot and Nic was thrilled. Mummy said she looked terribly tired and had been doing too much and tried to make her stay in bed but Nic said she couldn't. I expect she felt nervous. I know I would if I was a bride. I asked her what it felt like to know that she wasn't going to be Miss Boyd after this morning but would be Mrs. Avon and have to live with Denis, and if it scared her. She said 'not at all' because she loved him so much and she thought it would be heavenly. She didn't see Denis yesterday as it isn't supposed to be the right thing but he sent her a letter during breakfast. I was with her when she opened it. I saw her blush like anything but she wouldn't tell me what was in it, mean thing. I bet it was a passionate love-letter. Denis makes terribly passionate love on the stage so I bet he does when he's alone with Nic. Daddy says that love isn't the only thing that counts and that friendship is just as important in marriage. Nic says Denis is a wonderful friend and I bet he is. So I don't know what they're all bothering about, except that March Foster looks grim and so does Ron. Ron wanted Nic to marry March. But Nic can't help what she feels and I'd have chosen Denis too.

It was a terrific moment when we came to dress the bride. Nic looked absolutely wonderful when we'd finished—frightfully slim, and all shining, with starry eyes and her hair gleaming like gold under her veil. Mummy said looking at Nic made her want to cry and even Daddy paid an unusual compliment and spoke to her in quite a husky sort of voice. He said: 'You look beautiful, my dear, and very happy and I hope you always will be.' Ron left for the church first because he was going to be an usher. I heard him mutter something about he didn't know what he was going to do about putting the bride's friends and relations on one side and the bridegroom's on the other, because our side would be full up as we know everybody. But Denis only has his Rep. friends and his actor friend from London who is his best man. By the way, his name is Maurice Gould. I've never seen him in a play but he is super to look at, with big dark eyes and long lashes. Ron said his hair needed cutting and I'd better offer him a kerbi grip, but he doesn't understand actors! Anyhow I felt thrilled because Maurice was to be my opposite number, *me* being the bridesmaid. When I asked Nic why

Denis had so few friends and relations, she said he was an orphan and his Aunt Emma was much too old to come down to Welbridge and that some people didn't have many relations like us. We seem to have dozens and dozens.

I don't want to be conceited but I must mention that I looked awfully nice. My dress was net over blue silk with a low neck and lacy fichu like Princess Margaret wore when Elizabeth got married! Denis sent me a Victorian posy to carry, as well as the super bouquet of white roses and carnations with a lot of feathery fern for Nic. Mummy let me take the gold band off my teeth so that I wouldn't look so awful, and I had my hair waved, and Ann Williams gave both Nic and me a 'facial' last night, so my skin didn't look as awful as usual, and Nic powdered my nose. I wore a wreath of real flowers to match my posy.

Well, after Ron left, the cars came for Aunt Frances and Mum and me, and later Daddy came on with the bride. Old Pop looked terrific in his striped trousers and morning coat, and darling Mum was scrumptious too, in a blue and white flowered silk dress and jacket which she bought in London and Miss Burton altered for her. She wore a big straw hat with roses on it. Only Auntie looked frightful, but she always does. She has all that money and won't spend it. She had an old brown dress with frightful lace which she said she'd had for twenty years and worn for all her nieces' and nephews' weddings. Mum made her buy a new hat when she got here but she chose the cheapest she could find and it was grim— with pink ribbon the same colour as her nose. But she was in a jolly good temper and I don't suppose anyone looked at her anyhow. Not with Nic going up the aisle in all her glory.

Heaps and heaps of our Welbridge friends filled the church and lots more were outside, waiting with confetti. I knew Nic would be livid about that, but they meant well, Mum said. And Denis had lots of photographers there, even one from a London paper he told us afterwards.

Oh, the wedding was *terrific*. Mummy started to cry and I almost cried too because it was so lovely. St. Giles was all dim and holy, and the flowers were so terrific and Mr. Smyth played the organ his *best*. I felt jolly nervous going up the aisle behind Nic holding my posy. It was shaking—like me. I nearly died. But Maurice Gould whispered, 'You're doing splendidly . . .' and that helped. Denis was gorgeous, standing there before the altar with the sunlight shining through one of the stained-glass windows on his chestnut hair, making him look like Sir Galahad. At least I thought so. And when he and Nic smiled at each other, it was *terrific*. Everybody said they made a gorgeous pair.

Coming down the aisle after the wedding, I suddenly saw old March in a back pew. He was following Nic's figure with his eyes and he looked jolly rotten. I did feel sorry for him. But he grinned at me as I passed him and when we met outside, while the photographers were all taking the newly-weds, March squeezed my arm and whispered how beautiful I looked, and that I'd be the next Welbridge girl to 'get off'. Isn't he *awful*!

I got my photo taken with the family group. And I was jolly proud, standing next to my famous new brother-in-law. I heard people call out to him, 'Good luck, Mr. Avon! . . .' He's jolly popular as an actor.

Then we all drove home. Nic was actually *Mrs. Denis Avon*. We had a terrific spread at home. Champagne and everything. Only intimate friends were invited to the reception because a quiet wedding had been agreed upon. But it was all jolly nice and Denis made a speech and said how lucky he felt to have won the most beautiful girl in Welbridge and Nic blushed and everyone clapped and said 'hear hear'. I ate too much wedding cake and felt jolly sick but I did enjoy it. And Maurice was terrific to me and said he'd come and propose to *me* one day when I grew up. But when I told Daddy, he stopped smiling and said one actor son-in-law in the family was quite enough, but that I needn't repeat that to Nic, and of course I wouldn't.

March was at the reception. I saw him raise his glass to Nic and heard him say: 'Best of luck, Nic.' And she looked rather funny as she thanked him. Then he went over to talk to Mummy and didn't speak to Nic again. It was so warm and sunny that everybody wandered into the garden and wanted to take snapshots of the bride and bridegroom. Denis seemed to like that. Of course he's used to posing. I tied a white ribbon on baby Kim. And Nic held him and said she wanted to be photographed with him. She was looking all pink and happy talking to everybody and showing them her wedding ring. Then Miss Dale, the leading lady of the Rep., said she wanted to snap the couple with her special camera, and just as she did so, Kim who was chewing at his ribbon and growling like puppies do, twisted himself round Denis's leg and Denis nearly fell over just as Miss Dale snapped them. He looked awfully cross and went quite red and said something—I couldn't hear what it was—to Nic. But it made her go red, too, and look upset for a moment. But that wasn't what made the *Awful End* to the wedding. It was while the bride and bridegroom were changing into their ordinary clothes. They were going up to London for the night to the Savoy Hotel. Nic had a lovely going-away suit which was her one really expensive model. Aunt Frances paid for it. It is a heavenly dusty pink tie-silk with a blue design and she had a little pink hat to match, with a veil, and a pale blue gaberdine coat. She had just come downstairs, looking super, and was putting on her gloves when we heard a fearful *yelp*. Everybody stopped talking and listened because the yelping was simply *awful* and came from upstairs. Nic said; '*It must be my Kim*. Where's *Kim*?'

Then March came forward and said he'd been climbing up the stairs trailing his white ribbon after him. At that moment Denis came down. He looked awfully handsome in a new grey suit and he was gay and smiling. Nic rushed at him and said: 'Where's Kim? What happened?'

Denis said he hadn't the least idea, so Nic rushed upstairs and then came down with Kim in her arms. She was stroking him and he'd stopped yelping but Nic's eyes were full of tears and she looked frightfully upset and she said she'd found him under the bed in the spare room and that he was hurt. And that she couldn't think how.

Denis put an arm around her and told her not to worry—that Kim had probably fallen off the bed or something and that puppies never really hurt themselves. Then I took poor little Kim from Nic and he started to yelp again. So March examined him. He looked jolly grim and said there were no bones broken but the poor little creature was bruised on one side and badly frightened. Nic turned round to Denis and said: 'But how *could* it have happened?'

Denis said he really didn't know and that they must get on or they'd never catch their train.

Nic seemed awfully upset but she asked me to look after Kim which of course I am doing, and he seems quite all right tonight. But what happened to him is a *mystery*. And then the *Awful Thing* was when I heard March talking to Ron. March said: 'I hate to say so, my dear fellow, but it's my considered opinion that somebody *kicked* that little dog, and kicked him hard. And you know who I mean.'

I didn't hear what Ron answered but I felt *awful because who could have kicked him? Nobody was upstairs at the time but Denis. March meant Denis. But I'm quite positive it couldn't have been him, and that March was quite wrong.* But whatever it was, it did upset Nic and spoil her wedding day a bit because when she kissed me good-bye I could see that her lips were quivering and her eyes were still full of tears. She begged me to take care of little Kim and said: 'Oh, Flip, I wish it hadn't happened, today of all days!' I felt like crying, too.

Then they drove away and everybody except Ron and March said it had been a *beautiful* wedding. And now I must end this, and close my diary until tomorrow."

## XI

By the time the bride and bridegroom had reached London and the beautiful room reserved for them at the Savoy Hotel Nicola had almost forgotten the incident about her little dog. Denis was sympathetic and at his most charming and attentive during the train journey to London and practically convinced her that somebody must have put Kim on the bed and that he had fallen off and hurt himself—but not seriously. She also forgot Denis's moment of irritability when the playful puppy had twined the ribbon around his leg just as Verona

Dale took their photograph. He had snapped, *"Damn and blast the little brute! . . ."* under his breath, and once again Nicola had become conscious of his quick temper. Then that had passed and now he was an adoring lover again. She felt content. The wedding had been wonderful. Everything had gone off without a hitch and they were going to have two whole days together in London. More than that Denis could not spare from the theatre. One of the first lessons that the new Mrs. Denis Avon had to learn was that, in the mind of an actor, *'the show must go on'*—no matter what happened in his personal life.

For her own part, Nicola had secretly hankered for forty-eight hours' honeymoon in the depths of the country, or by the sea, but Denis adored London and, while leaving it to her to choose, had also left her with the impression that he *wanted* to take her to London. So they went.

A friend who was playing in a popular musical show in the West End at the moment had sent him two stalls for a wedding present (they were going to that tonight). She was to put on her new evening dress and look her loveliest and they were having supper afterwards at the Caprice, which was one of Denis's favourite places.

"Much too expensive for us as a rule so we might as well go haywire with the pound notes tonight. Our Big Night!" he had laughingly told her when he informed her of his arrangements.

She had thought that it all sounded a tremendous thrill. She was not sure where the pound notes were coming from unless Denis meant to spend some of the cheques various relatives had given them for a wedding present. And those really ought to be put by for their future home. But such a practical thought did not stay long in Nicola's mind. She was much too young and excited and eager to enjoy her wedding.

Denis had done just the right thing and ordered roses to be put in her room to welcome her. When they were first shown by the page-boy into the big luxurious room—which had a view of the river—and she saw the array of flowers, she gave a gasp.

"Oh, what magnificence!"

They were alone then, and Denis swept her into his arms, pulled off the gay little going-away hat, and kissed her until she was breathless.

"Nothing is too magnificent for my wife!" he asserted.

"And you are *Denis the Magnificent*!" she laughed back, full of passionate tenderness and pride in him.

Between kisses and laughter, they unpacked. When all his things were laid out beside hers she felt very thrilled and important and much married and a long way from home—even though her thoughts turned sometimes to her parents and to Ron and Flip *and* the little salon which was closed down until its owner should return to work. Truly, the advent of Denis Avon to the Welbridge Rep. Theatre had wrought a miraculous change in her life.

Denis left her to tidy her ruffled hair and went downstairs 'to reconnoitre' as he put it. He was sure that he would meet pals of his in the bar. He wanted to gather a little crowd together and organize a drink party to welcome Mrs. Denis Avon to London.

Nicola acquiesced. She was in the happy mood to want anything *he* wanted. But she was very tired and had, as her mother said, been doing too much lately. She was horrified to feel quite an overpowering desire to sleep, rather than make up her face and go downstairs.

But Denis did so adore people and publicity. Naturally, she thought, it was his *métier*. And it was sweet, the way he loved to show her off to his friends. He liked to make out that she was the most beautiful girl in the world. What could be nicer? But he had a high standard with all his stage and film 'stars' and she felt a little awed at the thought of what she must live up to.

When she was ready she took a look around the room. It was at once obvious that her husband was not a tidy man! Denis had thrown his things in wild confusion on to one of the twin beds and over the chairs. They were very nice things . . . expensive-looking silk pyjamas, a wine-coloured silk dressing-gown—piles of silk shirts, and ties, and socks. Assuredly, her Denis was not a man with many economical ideas! In her quiet life with the family, Nicola was so used to being careful . . . and 'making things do'. Denis's clothes all looked new and elegant.

Smiling, she picked up a piece of paper that she suddenly saw on the floor. It was a typed letter. She scanned it idly, without thinking. Then its meaning struck her rather suddenly and brought a slightly anxious look into her eyes.

It was a letter from the manager of a certain Man's Shop in Regent Street and was one of those beginning with '*Dear Sir, Unless* . . .' intimating that Mr. Denis Avon owed a considerable amount of money and that unless he sent payment (or part payment) shortly, he would receive further communication . . . from a firm of solicitors.

Nicola went rather pink and thrust the letter back into Denis's suitcase from which it must have fallen.

So Denis had debts! And that was a thing she was not used to. The Boyd family did not run up bills. What they bought they paid for at once. Mr. Boyd had brought Nicola up on the Shakespearian philosophy: '*Neither a lender nor a borrower be.*' But of course, Nicola argued with herself, in defence of Denis, people on the stage were different. They hadn't always the cash for the initial outlay and they must keep up appearances—must always look smart.

She went downstairs and joined Denis and forgot about the letter.

Of course Denis had found friends. Two men, and a girl . . . all three on the stage . . . glamorous-looking, smart and very friendly, ready to shower Nicola with congratulations and with flattery. Denis was a 'darling' and a future star. She was 'too divine' . . . they were not surprised he had forsaken freedom for her . . . and so on.

Nicola found herself in the middle of the gay crowd drinking cocktails. She had not caught any of their surnames. They all called each other by their Christian names or 'darling'. The girl was 'Pippa' . . . the two men 'Jack' and 'Victor'. The conversation was mostly about the theatre . . . how long one had been out of work . . . what expectations another had of getting a good part . . . how lucky Denis was with his chance of coming to a London show, *etcetera*. Nicola sat on a stool, sipped a cocktail which Denis had persuaded her to try and watched and listened. Denis seemed in tremendous spirits and every now and then gave her a long ardent look which made her heart plunge. She thought how much she loved him and that she wouldn't mind anything that he did so long as they could be together and he would go on loving her.

She was a bit confused as to who paid for the drinks . . . one round after another . . . but Denis seemed to do most of it, pulling out the pound notes in a lordly manner. Goodness, Nicola thought, it was going to be quite a new thing living with somebody who was so reckless about finance. But if she disapproved he immediately counteracted the disapproval by giving her a brilliant smile and whispering:

"I feel like a prince distributing largesse tonight . . . because it is our wedding night, *angel*!"

She smiled back and squeezed his hand. But she wished that Pippa and her men friends would go. She did so want to be alone with Denis. She had to remind him that if they did not go upstairs soon they would be late for their theatre. That settled it. Denis, being an actor, disapproved of an audience arriving late. He broke up the party and they rushed upstairs to bath and change.

Nicola was exhausted by the time she had put on her new white evening dress and pinned two of the white carnations from her wedding bouquet into a coil of golden hair. Denis, splendid in faultlessly-cut evening clothes and with a flower in his buttonhole, looked at Nicola and drew a deep sigh.

"What a heavenly-looking wife I've got! That's a superb dress, darling. Absolutely right, and you look as though your slenderness has been poured into it."

She blushed and laughed. He had such a wonderful way of putting things. But she did wish her eyelids were not so heavily weighted. The evening was only just beginning! She was dead tired. But Denis seemed inexhaustible. Of course he was used to late nights and a hectic existence. *She* would have to get used to it, too, she told herself ruefully. But she had been awake so early, and what with the wedding and the past week of rushing around . . . she was unusually out of sorts.

She was glad that the white dress suited her so well and that Denis approved.

The musical show was a first-rate one and she enjoyed it and felt a little less tired in the interval when Denis took her round to the dressing-room to see his friend Sally Lee, who played the part of a young dancer and who seemed to know Denis quite well.

Sally was a typical show-girl . . . a little flamboyant with her red curls and big brown eyes but enormously gay and ready to be friendly with Nicola—like all of them. Only when Nicola listened to the rapid flow of conversation between Denis and Sally did it strike her that perhaps there had been a little more than mere friendship between these two. Just the way Sally looked up at Denis and one or two things that she said . . . intimating that she used to see a great deal of him when they were in Rep. together and that she had been 'staggered' to hear of his marriage.

"But I sent you the seats to show you that I forgive you, Denny darling," she finished.

Denis said something charming and kissed her. Only lightly on the cheek, but somehow Nicola resented it. She would not have wanted any man in the world but her husband to kiss *her* tonight. Were all these people so free and easy with their kisses and 'darlings' and so on? Well, if it was so, it meant nothing and she was stupid to mind even the tiniest bit.

But her heart sank when she walked beside Denis back to their seats in the stalls and he said:

"I think we might make a party of it at the Caprice instead of just the two of us for supper. When I spoke to Sally just now, she said she might be going there herself with Oscar Bellamy. He produced this show and he's a very important man for me to keep in with. I haven't met him yet, but it might do me a spot of good. I think we'll try and fix it, darling."

Shocked and surprised, Nicola said:

"But it's . . . it's *our wedding night* . . . surely we ought to be alone? . . ."

He gave her his ardent sidelong look and secretly felt for her hand and caressed it.

"My adorable wife, I quite agree and . . . it's always lovely being alone with you . . . but it only means for an hour at supper and I don't think I ought to lose the chance of getting in with Oscar B. I've just *got* to get on, for your sake as much as mine . . . it's a sacrifice giving up our *tête-à-tête* . . . but we'll be alone afterwards. And we're together for always now, my darling," he added on a passionate note.

At once she was mollified and resolved to do whatever pleased him. But somehow it spoiled things . . . not to dine alone tonight . . . and to have to include the pretty silly little dancer Sally Lee, who had such an intimate way of looking at Denis.

Nicola laughed at herself. It wouldn't do for her to start married life by being jealous of her handsome actor husband!

So the supper *à deux* developed into a party and they joined up not only with Sally and Oscar Bellamy but with another couple whom the producer wanted to talk to. Nicola hardly caught their names, although Denis quickly whispered that they were 'show people' from America.

During the meal, none of them allowed Nicola to forget that she was the bride and there was champagne (ordered, of course, by Denis, who seemed to be running up a huge bill) and toasts were drunk and the American woman called her a 'honey' and told her that she thought Denis 'a wow' for looks and that he ought to go out to Hollywood and that her husband, Pete, would give him an introduction to Metro-Goldwyn.

Everybody was gay and excited and talkative. Denis at the top of his form, flushed and handsome, talking about Hollywood as though he were already there, drinking in all the flattery that was being directed at him. He was 'too good for Rep.', he must get out of it quickly, and if this show in which he was supposed to be having a part did not find the producer for whom they were waiting, he must make further efforts to get into a London show. And so on.

All the time Nicola smiled and listened but could take very little part in the conversation. Indeed, she began to feel that it was not really a wedding celebration at all but a 'business' meal! And as midnight approached she grew deadly tired.

She cast an appealing glance at Denis, who finally caught it and immediately felt remorseful. He was genuinely in love with his newly-made wife and he had not meant their first night together as a married couple to be like this. It had just happened this way and, having been given the chance to join Oscar Bellamy, Denis's vanity and ambition would not allow him to miss it. But now, when he saw the languid shadows under Nicola's lovely eyes, he turned to Bellamy with an apology.

"Do forgive us if we break up the party. But we must go. I had no idea it was so late. . . ." He signalled to a passing waiter and asked for the bill.

Oscar Bellamy said :

"My show, my dear boy."

"Most certainly not . . . it's *ours* . . ." said Denis in his grandest fashion and with a hand on Nicola's shoulder. He added with a gay smile : "My wife and I have great pleasure in inviting you to the dinner which is now over. Exit!"

Everybody laughed. Denis paid the bill. Nicola blinked as she saw the little pile of pound notes he placed on the plate. Truly Denis was distributing 'largesse' in a big way tonight. But she wished somehow that his generosity need not have included his ex-girl-friend and a theatrical producer. Being with these strangers had spoiled it all for *her*.

She was very quiet in the taxi going home, although Denis had an arm round her and murmured charming things to her all the way back to the Savoy. He added profuse apologies about the intrusion of the others but again impressed upon her that it was all for her future good as well as his. She only nodded. She could not speak. The long day, the excitement, and the disappointment of tonight had taken all the joy out of her heart. When they were in their beautiful room together, alone at last, the tears rushed to her eyes and she suddenly hid her face in her hands.

Denis stared at her, aghast. He was most sincerely upset to see her . . . his bride . . . in tears. His happy laughing Nicola. He caught her close, pulled the slender fingers away from her face, and kissed the tear-wet eyes and quivering lips.

"Oh, my darling, my angel . . . don't cry ! You must be so

terribly tired! What a monster I've been! . . . I wish I'd never let Bellamy and Sally and the Yanks join us. You're upset. You're cross with me. Oh, Nic, my sweet, *sweet* love . . . don't be cross with me tonight of all nights. Smile again, darling. We're alone now. I adore you. I'll always adore you, so you've no need to cry!"

Gently he pulled the white flowers from her hair, unpinned her curls and ran his fingers through the pale gold silk which floated down to her shoulders. He was completely hers now, with no thought for anything, anybody else in the world. And Nicola was quick to respond and let all other thoughts be blotted out . . . remembering only that she loved him. In her turn she reassured him.

"I'm just silly . . . it's tiredness . . . nervousness . . . nothing else. Oh, Denis we must always be happy together."

"We always will be," he said and looked down into her grey eyes with an expression of utmost sincerity, adding: "Sometimes you may find me selfish and difficult, but I do love you, Nic, and I'll try to make you the sort of husband you deserve."

Those were the most genuine and humble words that she was ever to hear from him and she remembered them long afterwards—when she had need for comfort. But tonight his kisses, his warmth of passion, and the exquisite tenderness which Denis was capable of showing (he was first and foremost a good showman) lulled her to a sense of contentment and security again.


## XII

THERE were two anxious hearts in Welbridge following upon the wedding of Mr. and Mrs. Denis Avon. March Foster's was one. He had to leave home on business the following day, for which he was thankful. He was due up in Yorkshire. He was glad to get away from the place which was so much connected with memories of the girl he had grown to love too late and lost so completely; and he shrank from the unspoken pity in his mother's eyes. Her sympathy at this moment could do nothing but irritate him.

The other sore heart belonged to Nicola's mother. For not only had she lost a most admirable and devoted daughter—which left a blank in the Boyd household—but she was none too happy about the marriage itself.

She had been charmed by Denis in the beginning, but by the time her husband and son had finished with her she was not so sure of him. And she was a little afraid for Nic. They none of them really knew anything *about* Denis, and Ron seemed so certain that he was bad-tempered and selfish. It appalled her to think of her generous and tender-hearted Nicola living with a man like *that*. However, Mary did her utmost to pooh-pooh all the adverse criticisms, and to re-assure herself that Nicola had chosen wisely and would be quite happy. But she could not help feeling relieved to know that for the next few weeks—and perhaps longer—her darling would be living in the same town and they all of them could see her quite often.

Directly after the wedding Mary Boyd had little time for brooding because the house had to be cleaned up, and there were all the wedding presents to sort out and pack away. Then Ron went back to Bristol and Aunt Frances to her home in Worthing. The Welbridge house returned to normal. It was on a warm June day that the honeymoon couple came back. . . .

Flip was at school and Mr. Boyd out when Nicola, alone, walked into her old home. Mrs. Boyd heard the familiar step and rushed downstairs to welcome her daughter, feeling that she had been away two years.

"Oh, darling, how *lovely*!" she exclaimed.

Mother and daughter fell into each other's arms laughing and hugging. Then Mary Boyd held her Nicola at arm's length and gave her a long searching look. Ah! she was just the same . . . thank God, the mother thought . . . she looked radiant—glowing as though with a new secret happiness. There was nothing to worry about.

They went out into the garden for a chat. Nicola looked round her with a contented sigh.

"It's good to see it all again. I feel I've been away from you a *century* instead of two nights, Mum darling. Isn't it stupid?"

"It's exactly what I was thinking," agreed her mother, and thought, too, how beautiful her Nicola looked. She had a new and smart hair style and wore a beautiful grey flannel suit; and she had more make-up than usual on her face—which gave her a sophisticated air. Yes, this was Mrs. Denis Avon and not Miss Nicola Boyd any more, thought the mother with a sudden pang.

But Nicola was delighting her with a flow of happy talk, saying what a wonderful forty-eight hours it had been; how marvellous Denis was as a husband; what an exciting time they had had at the Savoy.

"But of course it was much too short," she finished; "we haven't had much time to get used to each other . . ." she gave a little laugh.

The mother, ultra-sensitive, over-anxious, wondered secretly if that laugh held a touch of nervousness or uncertainty. But dismissed the idea as Nicola went on talking . . . giving details of their splendid bridal suite overlooking the river . . . the special roses that Denis had ordered for her . . . the musical show they had seen. Mrs. Boyd heard about everything except the dinner with Bellamy, Sally Lee and the Americans. Nicola avoided mention of that. Her mother would not understand Denis allowing those strangers to intrude—even for the sake of his career. She was much too old-fashioned in her theories about newly-weds being *alone*. But, Nicola told herself, she wanted to feel as Denis felt . . . think as he thought . . . absorb herself in *him*. Only in that way could she achieve the complete unity with him which in her generous and romantic heart she yearned for.

Her enthusiasm on the subject of her brief honeymoon was honest enough. Following that one mistake, Denis had made no more. He had put aside his own ego completely . . . striving to please her—to do what she wanted in London. She had the most tender memories of their companionship and he had made her feel proudly confident at length that she had made no mistake in choosing him for a husband. She had been deliriously happy. Last night particularly so, for they had dined alone in a small Soho restaurant and met none of his theatrical friends, and Denis abandoned all talk of the theatre and concentrated upon Nicola. He even consented to go with her to the salon in Bond Street where she had been trained, and meet her old friends. She was so proud of his good looks, his charm and his ability. The girls were all thrilled by him and said so. They made her feel frightfully pleased with him and herself. It had been tremendous fun.

And then, as though to show her his absolute wish to please her, he had of his own free will taken her into a dog shop and bought a small tartan collar and lead for Kim.

That gesture had pleased her ridiculously. Later, in his arms, she had thanked him again and whispered:

"It was so sweet of you, for I know you don't care for dogs."

His answer had been:

"Anything that makes you happy I intend to try and care for in future, my sweet."

All this passionate demonstration of love—particularly the physical rapture that they shared—was like a narcotic for the time being, rendering Nicola oblivious of everything and everybody else except her attractive husband. The bitterness of awakening had not yet come. For the time being the sheer emotional ecstasy dominated her mind—her more practical and perceptive qualities. She ceased to bother about finance and bills or to query Denis's reckless spending. He had blown the bubble of a new life for her . . . it floated iridescent and fascinating before her dazzled vision, and she followed it blithely . . . perhaps foolishly . . . with a child-like belief that it could go on for ever without exploding.

There had been only one slight setback . . . that was connected with the visit to Denis's Aunt Emma.

"It's a nuisance and a bore but I think we ought to look the old girl up. She hasn't much, but she might leave me what she has!" he had laughed.

Nicola had gone with him willingly. She was always nice to and compassionate for the old and ailing. Not that she found Denis's sole surviving relative very attractive. Miss Emma Robinson was a spinster approaching her seventies, an embittered, suspicious, uncharitable old woman. She had a two-roomed flat in the upper part of a dreary little house in

Putney where she had lived for years. Nobody knew how much money she had. Denis thought perhaps a hundred or two a year.

Her only companion was an ancient tabby whom she called Queen—a sad mangy old cat which meowed continually and bore no resemblance to her imperial name. Denis said that he remembered Queen as a kitten. Nicola did not care for the somewhat odorous old thing, but she was fond of all animals and pleased Aunt Emma by making a fuss of her. She thought it rather pathetic that Denis took so little notice of the old woman, who had always been generous to him and craved for his attention.

It was when he went out to buy cigarettes and Nicola was alone with Aunt Emma that the old woman, peering over her glasses at Queen, who was seated purring on the young girl's knee, suddenly said:

"Denis was lucky to get *you*."

Nicola had laughed and stroked poor Queen's shabby coat.

"I'm lucky to have Denis."

Aunt Emma suddenly let out a cackle of laughter, showing her toothless gums.

"Young Denny always did get the girls. Looks! Fascination! That's what they like. But in my opinion 'handsome is as handsome does'."

Nicola had felt her cheeks reddening and cast her eyes downwards. She was not sure that she liked Aunt Emma's suggested malevolence. Then she said:

"Denis has everything. He is nice as well as good-looking."

Another cackle from Aunt Emma.

"Long may it last. I've always spoilt him. So did his Granny. She thought there was no one in the world like Denny. *You'll* spoil him, too. Oh, yes—he's fascinating. But it's all show. No real kindness underneath. Ask Queen! When Denny was a schoolboy he used to torment Queen. She's one of the few females that *don't* like him. You watch her spit at Denny if he gets too near."

Another discordant laugh from the old woman. Then Denis came back, smiling, amiable, quick to put an arm around Nicola. But she felt suddenly cold and anxious to get away from this sinister little room and the miserable old woman with her aged tabby. She hated Aunt Emma for what she had inferred. *It wasn't true* that Denis was 'all fascination', with no kindness under the surface. Nicola could not bear to think that he had ever been the type of schoolboy to torment cats. But inevitably she had remembered Kim and his 'accident' on her wedding day. She tried not to think about it. It made her vaguely uneasy.

Once they left Putney and got back to the Savoy, in the warmth and beauty and excitement of Denis's love, Nicola forgot Aunt Emma and her ugly innuendoes. She did not want to remember them now. She continued to give her mother an account of all the lovely things that had happened in London. Then the baby Boxer appeared out of the house and sent her into raptures.

"Oh, the darling! I must take him back to the hotel with me!" she exclaimed, and added: "Have you seen March?"

"No, he's been out of town on business."

Denis came to fetch her. He had been down to the theatre to see the Company. He was to appear tonight in a new play which he had been rehearsing before his wedding. He seemed in good spirits, embraced Mary Boyd tenderly, said how lovely it was to have a 'mother' and asked her what she thought of Nic.

"Do you think my wife looks as though I've been beating her?" he asked gaily.

Mrs. Boyd laughed—quick to respond to the charm which Denis always managed to exude.

"Oh, yes, she's shown me all her bruises. And has she been nagging *you?*"

"Without stopping . . . I'm rapidly becoming a hen-pecked husband," he declared.

He drew Nicola close to his side and ruffled her hair. She felt suddenly very happy. They had a very nice front room at the Welbridge Park Hotel, she told her mother. She was sure they would be very comfortable there and she was longing to settle down.

"But of course," she said, "I'd rather have a home of our own."

"Well, you'll get that in London, I presume, once Denis starts work there," said her mother.

Nicola drew her husband's attention to the puppy, who was gnawing a bone on the sun-warmed grass.

"Kim seems to have recovered from his accident," she said; "you don't mind if I take him back with us, do you, darling? I must put his tartan collar on!"

"Of course, darling," he said, in the best of humours. He had just received a very warm welcome from the Rep. Company and was looking forward to 'playing to the gallery' again tonight. But he made no effort to stroke or talk to the puppy.

They walked back to the hotel. Nicola's arm through his. She sighed happily.

"It's so lovely, and so *funny*, walking through Wellbridge with my own husband!"

"Well, don't you dare walk with anybody else's," he teased her.

"When *will* we go to London, do you think, Denis? I suppose I ought to start putting *NICOLETTE* up for sale."

"No hurry. I found a letter waiting for me at the theatre, and there are still one or two hitches about the London production. I doubt if I shall leave the Rep. much before the end of July now."

Her eyes sparkled.

"Oh, Denis, I'm glad! I'd much rather stay here and carry on with my own job."

He narrowed his gaze.

"H'm . . . well, the money will come in useful, I must say. We're none too flush at the moment."

The dreaded spectre of finance confronted Nicola once more.

"Oh, Denis, don't you think we are a bit extravagant, even though it's still our honeymoon? I mean . . . if we're going to stay any length of time in Welbridge, oughtn't we to try and find rooms or a tiny flat? It's awfully expensive at the Welbridge Park."

"I'm not very keen on starting married life in cheap digs," he muttered.

"Neither am I, but——" she broke off, chewing her lower lip.

"It's a pity your old home isn't a bit bigger," he broke in.

"I wouldn't dream of asking Daddy to let us live at home, even if it was," she said quickly.

He saw that that had not gone down very well, and covered it up by a more outrageous suggestion.

"What about your friend March Foster allotting us a wing in Heron's Hall? It wants some livening up—it's like a Hapsburg palace—full of decaying splendour."

"Oh, you are silly!" she giggled.

But sometimes the things Denis said worried her. He was such a queer mixture. Either he behaved in the most arrogant fashion, throwing money about and paying for everybody, or he seemed disposed to accept charity from people he openly disliked. She did not altogether understand him. That fact troubled her. It was as though forty-eight hours ago before their marriage she had invested him with all the virtues in the world and since then, just in small ways, she was being disappointed.

The real jolt came later that evening when Denis, with a bright smile on his handsome face, and just before he left for the theatre, said:

"Can you lend me a quid, darling?"

Wide-eyed, she answered: "As a matter of fact, darling, I think I've only got ten shillings in my bag."

They were standing in their hotel bedroom. It was a beautiful June evening. Nicola had been feeling very happy now that she had unpacked and got everything into order. Through the windows she could see the gracious gardens, the park and a shining strip of river. She had felt a glow of contentment at being back in Welbridge and so near Mummy and Daddy and Flip—as well as with her attractive husband.

Then Denis said:

"Oh, lord, darling, can't you rake up a few quid somehow? We're a bit short. I don't get my pay till Saturday."

"But, darling, can't you cash a cheque? The hotel know me. They'll cash one."

He grinned and hummed an old melody.

" '*No more money in the bank*' . . ."

Nicola grinned back at him.

"Idiot! With all our wedding cheques! . . ."

Denis dropped his lids. He was not for the moment pre-pared to tell Nicola that most of those cheques had gone to pay his overdraft at the bank. He said :

"I don't want to touch those for the moment. Besides, I haven't even sent them in."

Nicola's heart gave an uneasy jerk.

"Darling Denis . . . you're a real artist. Most unpractical about money."

"That's why I married a practical woman, so that she could look after me," he said, and pulled her towards him and dropped a kiss on her lips.

She drew back and looked at him with grey earnest eyes.

"Darling, haven't you a bean of your own?"

"Nothing much," he hedged.

"Then how are we going to live in an expensive place like this hotel?"

"Oh, don't worry, my sweet. We can run a bill here. And there's my pay from the theatre—and yours. You can fish a bit out of the till from *NICOLETTE* now and again can't you?"

For a moment she was too flabbergasted to answer. She had never known much about Denis's financial affairs, but she had imagined he could at least support his wife. It had never entered her head that he would expect her to subscribe substantially to the upkeep of whatever home they had. After a pause she said :

"As a matter of fact, darling, Ron lent me most of the money to start my business and whatever comes out of it belongs as much to him as to me. And if I sell up—most of it should go back to Ron. Naturally, I shall keep anything exceeding the amount he lent me."

Then Denis frowned.

"It's a bit of a nuisance."

"Oh, darling," said Nicola in a tone of distress, "if I'd realized this, I wouldn't have let you spend all that money in London."

His good humour vanished. He turned from her.

"Oh, don't, for heaven's sake, nag me about that!" he said in a surly voice.

Speechlessly Nicola stared at him. To be married only two days and to have him speak to her . . . look at her . . . like that . . . to find that he was a reckless spendthrift . . . without security . . . *without integrity.* . . . That to Nicola, with her fine strong nature and orderly mind, seemed catastrophe. Worse than that. The first faint disillusionment.


## XIII

ALMOST immediately Denis seemed to think again and, turning back to his wife, took her hand and gave his most winning smile.

"Sorry I snapped, Precious, but I always hate the subject of money."

Nicola was a little slow to respond (each time this sort of disappointment cut through the surface of her absolute love for and belief in him, that response was slower to emerge). After a pause she said :

"And I hate muddles about money, darling. It's the way I've been brought up, I suppose. Daddy's always preached against our running up bills."

Now Denis laughed tolerantly and tucked an arm through hers.

"Daddy's quite right, but I can't always live up to such a high standard, my sweet. Life in the theatre is a bit precarious and one has to keep up appearances into the bargain."

She made no answer. She was wondering whether it had been really necessary for Denis to do all that wild spending even on their honeymoon. Also, the insidious memory of that letter from Denis's outfitters beginning '*Unless*' crept back into her mind. Why in the face of such bills did he give a champagne dinner to a lot of theatrical people, even if Oscar Bellamy was among them? But she said nothing now. The last thing in the world she wanted to become was a wife who 'nagged'.

"Walk with me to the theatre, sweet," murmured Denis.

"Of course."

He turned her round to him and brought his lips close to hers, looking at her with those handsome eyes which were so blue, so full of apparent depth of feeling.

"Have I told you how much I love you during the last hour or two?" he whispered.

She surrendered to that look—to those words—her senses swimming. She was still too newly-married, too much in love, to be censorious for long of her attractive husband.

That night she sat in the back of the stalls to watch the opening of the new show. The Rep. were playing *The Importance of Being Earnest*, with Denis in the lead. He looked the part—an exquisite young man of the period. He was not really a very good actor but he 'got away with it' in this small town because of his appearance and charm. Nicola felt a thrill of pride as she watched. It was great fun to be Mrs. Denis Avon and know that she could have a seat for the play any night she cared to drop in at the theatre. On Saturday night her whole family were coming at Denis's invitation. They were to have one of the boxes which were not often taken in the little theatre.

She went round to the dressing-room and saw both Denis and Verona Dale. Verona was, as ever, friendly and sweet.

"And how's our Mrs. Avon getting on?" she asked gaily.

"Splendidly—it's simply marvellous being married to Denis!" said Nicola with enthusiasm.

Was it her fancy or did Miss Dale give her a look which was faintly pitying—or ironic? But she said:

"Bless you . . . Isn't Denny playing well? I adore him as Ernest . . ."

After the show Nicola walked home with her husband, as delighted as he was with the applause he had received after the show. He was always in the highest spirits following upon any personal victory. He was lover-like and at his most amusing while he ate the cold supper which had been left for them in their room on a tray by an accommodating manageress. And afterwards, as the night was so warm and beautiful, with a full moon silvering the lovely grounds of the hotel, he even suggested taking the Boxer puppy for a walk.

That, of course, touched Nicola's heart. When Denis laughed at the little animal's capers, chasing his own shadow, she said :

"I do believe you'll get quite fond of my little dog."

"Oh, he's all right," said Denis carelessly.

"He seems to have recovered from his accident after the wedding."

Denis appeared not to have heard this. He put an arm around her.

"Your hair looks absolutely silver in the moonlight and you are as slender as a nymph. Oh, what a lovely wife I've got!" he said with a deep sigh of satisfaction.

She drew close to him, feeling soothed, flattered and content.

Later that night she told herself that she would never allow anything—either great or small—to come between her and this delirious happiness. There were bound to be ups and downs . . . little disappointments . . . differences of opinion . . . and Denis's way of living was quite certainly not her own. But she would get used to it. And she was sure that they would always love each other, which was what mattered most.

There were so many attractive sides to Denis. In the morning, for instance, he was never bad-tempered or unattractive even after a late night's work at the theatre. With his bright chestnut hair ruffled, his cheeks newly-shaven, and in his gorgeous silk dressing-gown, he looked clean-limbed and handsome enough to please the most critical eye. It was a tremendous thrill for Nicola to breakfast with him and—on a morning like this—read the reviews of last night's play in the local paper and share Denis's pleasure in the rather fulsome praise of the Welbridge critic.

Affecting an arrogant drawl, Denis quoted to her :

*"In the delightful rôle of Ernest so recently played by Mr. John Gielgud, who has set a high standard, Mr. Avon gave us a rare treat. It is a part for which he is admirably suited, and I doubt if we have seen a better performance from him this season. . . ."*

Denis looked over the paper at his young wife.

"How's *that*?"

Her eyes sparkled at him.

"Wonderful! Congratulations, darling!"

He did not bother to read out the next paragraph, which added that it was a pity, however, that Mr. Avon had not been word-perfect, which had somewhat spoiled the otherwise excellent performance, and that at times he had muffled some of the sentences so that he could not be heard at the back of the pit stalls or the dress circle. He tossed the paper down and finished his breakfast.

"What are you going to do this morning, sweet? I've got to go to the theatre for an hour or two."

"I'll take a look at *NICOLETTE*," she said.

"But you're not working?"

"Not till Monday. I'm still on my honeymoon," she murmured, with a smile.

Denis cleared his throat.

"Er—darling—with regard to this horrid subject of £ *s. d.* Any chance of raking up a fiver until I can draw my salary?"

She coloured slightly and gave a nervous laugh.

"I'll have to see."

"I'll pay it back, of course," he exclaimed.

After he had gone she thought seriously about the financial position and wondered if Denis always conducted his affairs in this way . . . spending too much . . . borrowing . . . paying back. . . . Somehow it grated on her.

And somehow, when she opened up her little salon and picked up some of the business mail which had accumulated while she was away, she felt quite a pang because the place looked so deserted. She did not like the idea of neglecting her beloved job even for a week's honeymoon. She sat down at her desk and tried to straighten things out in her mind and wonder, for instance, what was going to happen should this London job materialize and she sold *NICOLETTE*. It would put an end to her own resources. When it was first suggested that she should give up her job in order to follow her actor husband, she had somehow taken it for granted that he could always earn enough for the two of them. But even after these few brief days of marriage she had discovered that there was little security to be found with Denis. He just 'hadn't a clue' over money matters, she told herself ruefully.

Her parents would disapprove, and so would Ron, who was a hard worker and, without being mean, a fairly thrifty young man. Of course, there was money in the *NICOLETTE* account if she cared to draw on it but, as she had told Denis, she did feel that most of it belonged to Ron who had enabled her to start the salon.

However, it seemed that for the moment there was a slight crisis in Denis's life, so she drew ten pounds out of the *NICO-LETTE* account and gave Denis half of it at lunch-time.

"Mind you pay me back," she grinned at him.

He kissed her and grinned back.

"Miss Stingy!"

"Miss Nothing . . . I am *Mrs*. Denis Avon and don't you forget it."

"I like to remember it every moment, every hour, every day," he said in a low ardent voice.

"*Darling!*" she responded with equal ardour.

They had a happy lunch together. And they were happy for the rest of the week. The Rep. Company was doing well and playing to packed houses. Nicola had a lovely, lazy time, basking in her husband's ardour and the gay companionship which he unfailingly gave her when they were together. It was lovely, too, being able to see so much of her family while Denis was out. They had great fun on the Saturday night, when all the Boyds sat in a box at the theatre and applauded Denis. Flip was in a wild state of excitement. She rushed home to write a vivid description of it all in her diary. To see her brother-in-law come before the footlights and re-ceive all that applause was a great thrill for her.

It was on Sunday morning that Nicola suddenly remem-bered her five pounds.

"Hi, you!" she called to Denis, who was brushing his hair. "Yesterday was pay day, wasn't it? And I ought to put my fiver back into the business tomorrow."

Denis raised his brows and, without looking at her, said:

"It can wait, can't it, sweetie-pie? You see, I shall have to pay the hotel bill tomorrow, and there are one or two other little items which want immediate attention."

Her heart sank a little and her brows contracted.

"But Denis, darling, you *must* have a bit in the bank. I mean . . . we had a hundred from Daddy and lots of odd cheques. Haven't you paid them into your account yet?"

"Darling, it's a divine morning . . . let's not spoil it by a sordid discussion on filthy lucre. You know I hate it," he said, and came towards her with outstretched hands and pleading smile.

But Nicola's stubborn streak asserted itself and she was not to be put off. When she persisted that they *must* discuss their financial situation, Denis grew cross.

"Do leave it to me. It's the man's job to deal with the money. And I *don't* like bossy women," he said haughtily.

Nicola went scarlet.

"I'm sorry you think me bossy, Denis, but I dare say I am a little out of the ordinary, because I'm a business woman with a banking account of my own and I'm used to dealing with money matters."

"Do what you like in your Beauty Parlour, my dear girl, but in our personal life *I'm* the boss," he said in an arrogant voice.

"In that case you can return the money that came out of my business," she said heatedly.

He glared at her. She remembered it afterwards . . . how cruelly it hurt her . . . that unfriendly glare. He said :

"It's queer how after marriage one discovers unattractive qualities in one's better half. I never dreamt that you could be so frightfully mean."

Then her colour changed from red to white.

"Denis, that's most unfair . . . no one has *ever* called me mean. Ask Mummy . . . ask any of my old friends. I'm *not* mean. But I do try to be *sensible* about money, and you're not. I just don't understand the way you arrange things. You ought not to borrow from me and not pay it back when it comes out of my business."

"I see," he said frigidly, looking her up and down. " 'With

all my worldly goods I thee endow', but *you* have no intention of sharing yours with *me*."

Her heart beat fast. She could not bear quarrelling with her adored husband. She thought his arguments illogical and unkind. And rather rude, too.

"Denis, I'll share anything in the world with you, but most of the proceeds of my business belong to my brother until I've paid back what he lent me. That's the way I look at it. You ought to understand."

"Your brother! Your father! I'm for ever having your family thrown up at me," said Denis pettishly. "I'm getting rather sick of it."

*That* was so illogical and childish that she could hardly believe her ears. A few more illusions came tumbling about her ears. A man who said that sort of thing, who thought that way, would hardly command a girl's respect. She was horrified. So horrified that she made a rapid and furious effort to build him speedily up again into the idol of her dreams. She *must* be able to respect Denis if she were to continue to adore him. She went up to him, took hold of his arm and pressed it close to her side.

"Oh, Denis darling, we can't talk like this! I know you don't mean it, anyhow. You love my family. You *can't* mean it."

He capitulated immediately. One of Denis's best points was that he did not sulk and his tempers were soon over. He always liked to shine in the eyes of the world. And in Nicola's particularly. He was swift to regret his ill-humour. He immediately hugged his young wife and apologized.

"Of course I didn't mean it, sweet. Sorry! I think I must have a hangover this morning. Forget it. You're quite right and I'm wrong. I'm a damned fool about money. I didn't want to tell you, but I *am* in a bit of a jam at the moment. I was so afraid you might be worried, or even try to postpone our marriage, which I couldn't have borne. I love you so much. I needed your sensible practical side as well as your loveliness. Oh, Nic . . . don't be cross with me, darling. I've run up a few bills, but I'll soon pay them off and we'll start afresh, then we must never argue about money again."

He was holding her close now, covering her hair, her eyes, her lips with kisses. He quickly broke down what little resistance she had and she clung to him almost desperately, anxious to banish that spectre of financial insecurity . . . the unstable side of Denis's nature which bit by bit was ruthlessly being revealed to her.

He went on kissing her until at last she extricated herself from his arms with a little laugh.

"Darling . . . how ridiculous of us! We must behave!"

"Then promise you won't worry about money, Nic. And if you really want that fiver for the business, I'll rake it up somehow."

She found herself weakly surrendering and telling him that it 'didn't matter'. Whereupon he recovered his good spirits and pushed the whole matter aside as though it had never arisen between them. As though to show his penitence for the ill-tempered way he had spoken of her family, he then suggested they should hire a punt and take young Flip with them on the river for a picnic tea that afternoon.

It was only much later when they were in the punt and Nicola lay back watching the golden sunlight filter through the green lace of the leaves on to the dimpled water that the dispute over money returned to her mind. She looked thoughtfully at Denis, who was imitating some comic stage character, and making Flip hysterical with laughter. She thought how young he looked in grey flannels; his white sports shirt open at the neck. How blithe—she told herself ruefully—how *inconsequent* he was. At times he did not seem to her to be the Denis with whom she had first fallen in love and in whom she had invested all the virtues—including great depth of feeling and manliness. This Denis was a stranger. Just as handsome and charming, but quite unbelievably superficial. He seemed to want to blow the froth on the champagne of life; never to delve down into its depths. Nothing had any profound meaning nor lasted long with him. Quarrels . . . kisses . . . arguments . . . they were all mere emotions of the moment. He never seemed to analyse life as she did, and he *never* seemed to think of the future. He lived only for the present. That was what worried her most.

Was she being too serious? she wondered. Ought *she* to learn to take things as lightly as Denis? She could not believe that it would be better. She could see nothing ahead but disaster unless one of them were a little far-seeing and sensible.

She listened to Flip's laughter, then to Denis—joining in like a schoolboy. And suddenly she felt terribly alone. She wanted to talk seriously to somebody about Denis and money matters—about what she ought or ought not to do. But she would have died rather than let her own family know about the feckless Denis whom she was just discovering. And it would be disloyal, she thought, to discuss him with any friend. No—she was isolated in her anxieties.

She trailed her fingers in the cool water, biting her lip, frowning under the weight of her thoughts which spoiled the tranquility, the pleasure of the summer's afternoon. And strangely enough, in that moment she lifted her head and saw across the river bank the distant outline of March Foster's home, Heron's Hall. And there rose in her a sudden yearning to see March; see him come across that green grass with Kimbo at his heels and his pipe in his mouth . . . solid, thoughtful, dependable March who had always been her friend and who had wanted to be something more.

Then she drew a sharp breath and coloured guiltily as though she had no right to remember March, or any need of him. *But the need was there.* And it frightened and astonished her to admit it . . . after little more than one week's marriage to another man.

## XIV

It was not for two months after Nicola's wedding to Denis that she actually came face to face with March Foster again.

Once or twice she had seen his car, but he always seemed to drive past her at a furious pace without looking in her direction. Once Flip had told her that she had spoken to him and that he had asked after Nicola but seemed what Flip called 'jolly casual'. He said that he was often away as he had a lot of business on hand in the Midlands.

Nicola went no more to Heron's Hall. Denis, in his airy fashion, had suggested once or twice that they should call on the Fosters because he liked the big place with the aura of money which clung to the family, but Nicola always made some excuse not to go. Her friendship with March seemed to have been spoiled. His declaration of love for her had spoiled it. She knew that he had been hard hit, and with the passing of time that knowledge seemed to become more distressful. She regretted losing their old comradeship. Yet she had thought that once she met Denis she would never want any man in the world but him again.

Her marriage had brought passionate love and excitement but little real companionship with Denis. The grim bogey of money would keep cropping up continually, rubbing the bloom off her once perfect happiness.

When March Foster saw her again this evening towards the end of August she was walking along the towpath, not far from St. Giles', with the little Boxer capering around her. Kimbo was the first to see them, and with a loud bark made a dash towards his small nephew, who immediately lay down on the ground and put back his ears as though supplicating for a gentle approach. March, like Nicola, was taking advantage of the beautiful summer's evening, which was still light at eight o'clock. Denis was at the theatre. Nicola had had a long and rather tiring day of beauty treatments, and craved for fresh air and exercise.

March had so far deliberately avoided meeting Nicola, but there was no escape from it this time. He put his pipe in his pocket and greeted her in a manner which Flip would have described as 'jolly casual'.

"Hello! How are you?"

"Oh, awfully well," she replied, and added with frank simplicity, "and awfully pleased to see you, March. It's been ages since we met."

He knew exactly how long it had been. Despite all his efforts to throw himself into the business (and he had delighted his father by his recent hard work and attention to detail), the memory of this girl persistently haunted him. Nicola, his boyhood's friend; Nicola as he had last seen her, as a shining exquisite bride. The bitterness of losing her had not lessened and he knew when he looked at her now that he was still hopelessly in love. He was also struck somewhat disagreeably by the unexpected change that so short a time had wrought in her.

She was thinner—much older-looking. Her cheekbones stood out sharply and there were shadows under the wide grey eyes; even a pinched look about her lips which shocked him. He had expected to find her still a glowing bride. She had been married less than three months, he thought, surprisedly.

But he made no comment. They fell into step together and talked about this and that.

Kim had grown enormously, March said, and he reflected that he was glad the puppy had recovered from that unattractive and still unexplained affair on the wedding day. Nicola gave him a vague résumé of the family news. Flip was doing big things at games this term, and much to her delight had been made captain of the lacrosse team. Daddy had had a touch of sciatica but recovered. Mummy was very well. Denis was rehearsing for a new production of three one-act plays by Noel Coward which the Rep. Company had decided to do in place of the Wilde comedy.

Then March said abruptly :

"And how about you? How do you like life at the Welbridge Park?"

"Oh, we're not there any more," she said with a slight flush, "we moved into a flat about a month ago."

"But I thought you were going to live at the hotel?"

"So did I, but . . . it didn't quite work out. They didn't like giving Denis later supper every night and—oh, for lots of reasons we decided to move—especially as Denis's London show doesn't seem to be coming off now until winter and he'll be with the Rep. Company at least another three or four months."

"Where's the flat?" asked March.

She told him. They hadn't been able to find anything self-contained. Only two rooms with the use of kitchen and bath in one of the big Victorian buildings in Market Square. Over a grocer's shop in fact. March knew the shop—Sopers. Not very nice. Not a nice part of Welbridge—Market Square. Noisy, and in summer somewhat odorous, with all the fish and fruit barrows—particularly on Saturday afternoons. He frowned and stared at the smooth shining river. What on earth was Nic doing in a place like that? They must be hard up. No doubt Denis wasn't a big money-maker. March could not help thinking, with bitterness, of Heron's Hall . . . the quiet beauty and luxury of it and all the loveliness that should have belonged to her if she had been *his* wife.

He said :

"Oh, I expect you prefer your own niche. Kimbo and I must come and leave a card sometime."

"Let me know when," she said hurriedly, and added with some confusion : "Of course I'd love to see you both, but I . . . I'd like to have it all nice for you."

He could not guess what was at the back of her mind. He could not know the real reason why the young Avons had moved from the Welbridge Park Hotel to 31 Market Square. But Nic had an uncomfortable recollection of a series of disputes about bills and money generally between herself and Denis, which had finally accumulated into a serious row. Desperately serious from Nicola's point of view, because Denis had been forced to tell the truth on that occasion. And it had completely shattered her morale. He had shouted at her and accused her of nagging. She had seen him in one of his real tempers and it had been an eye-opener. But she did not intend to be shouted at, even by her own husband, and she had started to walk out of the hotel. Then with one of his swift changes of mood he had showered her with apologies and excuses. He was tired . . . he was over-worked at the theatre . . . he was hot . . . he was worried to death about money. After which she stayed to hear all the grim facts. She knew now that every single cheque they had received for their wedding, including her father's hundred pounds, had gone to pay Denis's debts. Had been infiltrated into his overdraft . . . one or two bankers' orders . . . and odd bills like the Regent Street outfitters who had sent a solicitor's letter.

She had to face the hideous fact that there was nothing left with which to buy the carpets and curtains and other things which they needed for their future home. As for the five pounds she had lent him from *NICOLETTE*—that was just a drop in the ocean which she would never see back, nor any other money she might lend Denis in the future.

She had learned once and for all that he was utterly untrustworthy—both with money and women. The latter hurt more than the former—much more. In his usual careless way he left letters lying about. Silly amorous epistles from glamour girls like Sally Lee . . . and actresses like the new girl in the Rep., Carole Fray. Carole was younger than Nicola, ravishingly pretty, and rather ingenuous. Nicola knew now that Denis liked them like that . . . he had no time for experienced women. Verona Dale, for instance, who 'knew her Denny'. He preferred the inexperienced kind who could be easily taken in. *Like herself*, Nicola had thought in her bitterness when it first came to her notice that Denis was being rather attentive to little Carole. On the surface he still seemed to be his wife's most devoted and adoring lover. But Nicola was beginning to find that under the surface Denis was shallow and enormously vain. Perhaps Carole had become infatuated and made the first advance, but he could never resist flattery, and so things began. Nicola had found herself answering various telephone calls . . . mysterious feminine voices asking for Mr. Avon . . . little notes being sent by hand to the hotel— and later to the flat. Denis disappeared for rehearsals which might or might not be taking place. Nicola did not even bother to ask. If ever she did mention that she saw too little of him he took the wind out of her sails first by fervently agreeing, then reminding her that it was her fault, too, that *she* worked all day at *NICOLETTE* when he was free and could have been with her.

It was true. She knew that maintaining her job—with Denis never at home in the evenings—was a serious hindrance to her domestic happiness. It wasn't going to work out as she had hoped. And she would gladly have thrown up her precious work *now*, if only to give her more time with Denis and put an end to the awful loneliness which had become her lot . . . that loneliness of the hungry heart which these days none of Denis's poetic love-making could assuage. But there was a perfectly good reason why she could not abandon *NICOLETTE*. *She needed the money.* She needed to work harder than ever—stick to it—even enlarge her little salon in order to pay back Ron *and* get something for herself. And *for Denis*!

The shock about the wedding cheques had decided her that they must at once leave the expensive hotel. So they had moved into the horrid little flat . . . the only one within their means. The rents of nice furnished cottages in Welbridge or a luxury flat in a modern block like River Court were far too high.

While she walked and talked with March this evening, Nicola thought with deep depression of the conditions under which she was now living. Denis had made every effort to dissuade her from leaving the Welbridge Park, maintaining in his usual airy fashion that they would 'find the money'. But she refused to run up heavy bills and eventually she forced the move. And much as she had loathed it, she had to use a threat . . . she would go to her father, she said, and tell him about the wedding money unless Denis consented to economize and try to lead an existence more in keeping with their income.

Denis had no wish to face an angry father-in-law so he gave in. He had at first been sullen and ungracious about the flat and finally indifferent. He let her do all the work. He had a new part to rehearse, he said. So she put away some of the ugly things and tried to make the place look gay and attractive with their own bits and pieces. Fortunately they had some good plate and silver, and all their wedding presents. And Nicola's linen and books and pictures. But they had to share the bathroom and the kitchen with another couple— which Nicola disliked. The other two were a little shop assistant and his wife whom Nicola knew by sight but had never met before. They were nice, and Nicola was no snob. But they moved in a different world from the one in which Nicola had been brought up in Welbridge. She worried less about it than her mother. But Mary Boyd felt that her daughter had 'come down' and disapproved of the home in Market Square.

Nicola, however, offered no explanation of their finances. She would have died rather than let her family know the truth. Neither could she explain anything to March tonight. But there were many reasons why she did not want him to 'drop in' unannounced. For Denis had made one or two cutting remarks about her friendship with March and under no circumstances did she want him to come home and find her alone in the flat with March or any other man. She did not wish to give Denis an opportunity to criticize her. She had a shrewd idea that because Denis, himself, was so often at fault, he would like to get the chance to turn the tables on her.

That was a horrid thing to think. But there were a lot of horrid little suspicions and thoughts in Nicola's mind these days. She sometimes hardly knew what she was thinking or doing. Her whole life was so revolutionized . . . so unlike the romantic and dazzling existence she had dreamed of . . . and at times both painful and distasteful to her.

It frightened her to realize how suddenly a passionate love can die. Barely two months after her marriage she was having a struggle to maintain her deep feelings for Denis. His fascination was still there . . . his looks, his charm—the physical attraction which she could not resist. And at times he seemed still to be the adorable Denis who had first captured her heart. But he had lost her esteem. And that loss was a funeral-pyre in which the fine flame of her love was slowly but surely being extinguished. Nothing left but ashes.

With March, in particular, she maintained an attitude of bravado. Deliberately she took pains to assure him that 'life was wonderful' and that she did not in the least mind being in a tiny flat, and that she was delighted at being able to go on working at *NICOLETTE*.

March gave her a brief critical glance. She had changed . . . not only physically . . . but in her manner, he decided. She did not meet his gaze with the old frank happiness. Somehow her laughter had a hollow ring. He loved her, and the very power of his love produced in him a psychic reaction which convinced him that all was not well with his Nicola.

Nevertheless they went on chatting merrily. When they parted, he left her outside the flat in Market Square, which at this hour was deserted and not quite so grim as during the busy day. She said :

"I'll fix a little supper one Sunday evening . . . it's the only time I have Denis home for an evening meal. And we'll ask one of the girls from the Rep. to make a four."

March stuck his pipe between his teeth.

"Don't ask any girls for *me*!"

Nicola laughed nervously.

"Have you seen the new show? Don't you think our new addition—Carole Fray, who replaced Irene Hale—is awfully pretty?"

"I haven't seen the show and pretty girls usually bore me," said March, "and if I come, it'll be to see *you*—and your husband," he added politely.

He saw her bite her lip and colour. She turned and with a final "Good night, March," disappeared through the side door adjoining Sopers Ltd. It was dusk now. March stayed a moment filling his pipe. He saw a light go on in the room over the shop. He did not know why, but somehow he had an uneasy feeling about Nicola being up there all by herself in that place. It couldn't be much fun for her. She must be lonely.

He turned his steps in the direction of the old Boyd home and called on the family. They were all pleased to see him, but when he brought up the subject of Nicola he fancied that he saw John and Mary Boyd exchange glances, and that they talked rather guardedly about her. John Boyd made only one open comment and that was briefly to announce that he was 'a bit put out' that his son-in-law could only provide such a cheap shoddy home for Nicola. Mrs. Boyd made haste to explain that they had suggested, as Welbridge Park was too expensive, that the young couple should come here. But Nicola had flatly refused to do it. Flip—ever honest to the point of being tactless—chimed in here :

"I think Nic's flat is a beastly little place, although she's made it look quite nice. But the paint's a *horrible* colour and so are the carpets and curtains. And I think Nic's miserable and I don't like Denis as much as I did. He's too jolly conceited all the time. And . . ."

125

"Darling, it's your bedtime," interrupted Mary Boyd with heightened colour. She could not bear to hear Flip saying things like that . . . things which the mother knew were true, but did not want to *admit*. She had been far too worried about Nic lately. The girl had certainly lost a lot of weight and had become far too silent; withdrawn into herself. She avoided all discussion of her personal life, which made Mary Boyd quite certain that things were not right.

Flip's childish outburst brought a sense of shock to March Foster also. But it only confirmed his own presentiments. However, they talked no more about Nicola. March answered Mrs. Boyd's enquiry about his mother's health, which, he said, was unfortunately none too good, then launched into a discussion on present-day politics with Mr. Boyd.

Later, he walked home with Kimbo, feeling deeply troubled. *Could it be possible that Nicola was not happy with Denis Avon?* Of course he had disliked the fellow at sight—and so had Ronald. But Nic had been so sure of him—and of herself.

"Oh, God," March cried from the depths of his soul, "I couldn't bear her to be miserable. She'll never show it. She'll never let any of us know. She'll just suffer. God! If he doesn't make her happy, *I'll want to kill him!*"

## XV

ONE sultry afternoon towards the end of August, Nicola wiped the cream from her hands with a tissue and then proceeded to wipe little pearls of sweat from her forehead.

Phew! It was hot today, she thought—and unpleasant. No sunshine . . . just that grey heaviness hanging over Welbridge and a threat of thunder in the air; dark menacing clouds banking across the rim of the distant hills. The very river ran sluggishly and looked like molten lead.

Nicola had been suffering from a violent headache ever since she got out of bed this morning. This sort of weather did not suit her. Like the farmers, she longed for rain and hoped that the thunderstorm would end the drought.

Never had she worked so hard as of late. Business was

flourishing and she was rarely without a client. She wished that little Ann Williams could do more than take on the odd manicure or eyebrow plucking. But she really wasn't yet fit to do 'facials', which meant that Nicola was on her feet all day.

Things were not like they used to be in the old days when she could go home and relax and then eat the good supper Mummy served. Now she had to go back to the flat and prepare supper for herself and Denis. And he liked her to wait up until he got back from the theatre at night. Supreme egoist (which she now knew him to be), he could not bear to come home and find her in bed, asleep. He wanted someone to be there to amuse and talk to him. And she did as he asked, fighting against her weariness not only because she felt it to be her duty, but because she liked to see and chat with her husband. She saw so little of him. Just a rushed breakfast in the morning when he was barely awake, and an hour or two between tea and the time when he went down to the theatre.

Young and strong though she was, the strain was beginning to tell on Nicola. And she had been suffering lately from *migraine*—and a perpetual ache in her back. She knew that her family thought that she looked ill. Flip bluntly said that Mummy was 'fed up about her'. But Nicola offered neither explanation nor any suggestion for altering her régime. While their finances were in this present parlous state she must do as much work as possible at *NICOLETTE*. They needed the money.

She looked at her watch and sighed. Only three o'clock. If only she could go home now. Denis had been in an unusually grim mood this morning and had snapped her head off. When he snapped it made her wretched. Yet she was beginning to think that even when he said lovely extravagant things and made love to her she felt just as wretched. All the delight of being in the arms of her handsome actor husband existed still . . . but it was bitter-sweet . . . left her with the taste of ashes in her mouth . . . wondering how much of what he said he *meant* . . . wondering if, when he told her that he was clearing his debts, and that things would soon be normal, he spoke the truth. Wondering, when he maintained that he was happy with her, if he had not already begun to chafe at the matrimonial shackles.

It was quite all right when she came home and told him that there was an increase in *NICOLETTE*'s takings. Then he would be delighted and congratulated her and call her 'his clever little Nic'. And if she gave in to all his whims and moods, he was absolutely charming and could still make her laugh. He could impersonate well-known comedians and speak in half a dozen different dialects, according to his mood, and find in her an appreciative audience. He was never done 'playing to the gallery'. But now that she no longer saw him through rose-coloured spectacles it amazed Nicola that she had not realized in the beginning how tiring all this could become . . . and how the actor in him which she had once hero-worshipped would eventually get on her nerves and drive her to exasperation pitch. She who had never had such a thing as 'nerves' and been the placid one of the Boyd family.

Above all she longed for peace . . . and understanding . . . and Denis afforded her neither of these. There were nights when she would have given anything in the world to be able to lean on his shoulder; feel a strong protective arm about her; the security of living with a man who was integral . . . whom she could *respect*. But she had linked her life with a handsome charming showman without a heart. It wasn't that Denis really meant evil or was deliberately cruel. He was just *heartless*. He felt deeply only where his own ambitions and desires were concerned.

To admit all these things was, Nicola knew, to admit defeat . . . to accept the fact that her choice of Denis as a husband had been a mistake and that their marriage was a ghastly failure. But whatever she thought or felt, she kept it to herself. And because her old passionate love for Denis was not yet wholly dead, she entertained the forlorn hope that things might alter once they got straight financially and Denis's London job materialized. She felt it would be better, really, if she could leave Welbridge where she was well known and start life afresh with him in London. He would get bigger pay there and more chance of becoming a 'star'. It would be better for both his morale and hers if he could keep her entirely. Also, once rid of *NICOLETTE*, she could be more of a companion to him. He was always complaining about her absence from the home when he needed her, which was typical of Denis's illogical nature, for he was the first to enthuse over her earnings.

She looked at the consultation book. Her heart sank at the thought of two more hours of massage. Ann, who had been washing bowls and rearranging the couch, glanced at Nicola and thought how white and drawn she looked. Young Ann had told her mother last night that she thought Mrs. Avon had changed a lot since she got married and never seemed gay or natural these days.

"Can't you let me say that you are ill and cancel the next few appointments?" she asked with childish concern for the employer whom she adored.

Nicola smiled and shook her head. She wasn't ill, she said, only a bit overcome by the heat.

"I think we'd all feel better if there could be a jolly good storm," she said.

A boy came to the door with a note. Nicola, stifling a yawn, sat down and kicked off her shoes to give her aching feet a rest. Her cheeks coloured as she read the note. It was from Denis, and typical.

*"My Fairest, prithee tarry a while from thy work and come with me and we will walk together by the river ere the rain falls. There cometh one helluva storm. Let us be in it together. I am sick of my aloneness. Abandon all and come to thy yearning lover and husband. . . ."*

She smiled a little crookedly. Denis could never do anything naturally. He always liked to raise a laugh, or extract admiration somehow. He was not worrying abut *her* being tired—only sick of being alone. He could never bear to be by himself for five minutes and, presumably, none of his various girl-friends was available, Nicola thought bitterly. Immediately afterwards, she reproached herself. One shouldn't be bitter or suspicious without actual proof, she reflected.

She scribbled a reply and told the boy to deliver it to Market Square. She did her best to play up to the humour of Denis's note.

*"Mine own sweete husbande, prithee pardon me but I cannot come to thee whom my soul yearneth for mine work is heavy and I am grievously overburdened and must tarry a while at 'Nicolette'. I send thee my heart's love. . . ."*

She hoped that there the matter would rest. Once or twice before Denis had tried to wheedle her away from her job. He had no conscience about her breaking appointments. But as a rule he left her to it, for which she was thankful. Today, however, he came down to the salon in person. The moment he entered the shop she saw that he was furious with her because of a certain spark in those blue eyes of his and a tightness of mouth—familiar signs when Denis had been thwarted. But he gave Ann a dazzling smile.

"My *my*!" he chose to ape an American accent, "you sure are losing weight, honey, and it suits you plenty. She's getting a peach of a girl, isn't she, Nic?"

"*I* think so," said Nicola.

Ann, ever aware that she was much too plump, went red with pleasure and gave Mr. Avon a grateful smile.

"Oh, thank you . . . thanks terribly!" she said in her young gauche way.

Denis, hands in his pockets, turned his gaze upon his wife. He didn't like her in that pink overall and secretly he thought that she was beginning to lose her looks. He admired slenderness, but she had become positively angular, and why didn't she put on more of her own make-up? . . . he didn't see why she should give all her time to beautifying other women and neglect herself. He liked Mrs. Denis Avon to shine.

He began to grumble.

"Why can't you come out with me? You never give me a single damned afternoon except at week-ends. . . ."

She broke in an undertone, wearily:

"Darling, I know . . . it must be dull for you and our times of work do clash, but we've had it all out and———"

"It's too hot for a lecture," he broke in rather rudely. "After all, I'd paid my wife a compliment in saying that I wanted her with me, and I just get back a raspberry."

"Oh, darling, you know perfectly well it wasn't meant to be one," she said with the patience she would have exhibited to a spoiled child.

But Denis was in a contrary mood and went on.

"Show some spirit for once . . . cancel your appointments and shut up the damned shop. Come on, Nic."

Her heart sank. She was so afraid that Ann would over-hear. She couldn't bear anybody in Welbridge to know that she and Denis even had a difference of opinion. With the pathetic wish to ensure this, she ignored Denis's remark and quickly asked Ann to go down to the fishmonger's and try to get another block of ice. Her next client wanted a 'pack' and the ice melted so quickly in this weather.

Once they were alone, Denis gave way to all his grievances. Nicola listened in silence, her lids lowered. She knew every word by heart. It always irritated Denis when she wouldn't go out with him or do what he wanted . . . and he had no scruples about her clients or her job.

When he had finished, she felt her heart beating quickly and the pain in her head had increased. The last thing she wanted was a trying scene with Denis when she already felt exhausted, and the next client was due in five minutes' time. At last, goaded, she flung back her head and retorted:

"It's all very well. I don't come and try and drag you out of the theatre in between acts."

"Don't be silly, that's different," he muttered, and lit a cigarette and threw the burnt match angrily on the floor. It was Nicola who bent down, picked it up and mechanically put it on an ash-tray.

"Your job is always different," she said, "but the principle is the same. We both of us have *got* jobs and neither can expect the other to neglect them."

He hunched his shoulders.

"We don't seem to be hitting it off very well just now, do we?"

It was the first time he had ever made such a blunt

statement. It went through her heart like a knife. She felt physically sick.

"*Please* don't say things like that, Denis."

Immediately he relented. He put an arm around her and drew her close to him.

"Sorry, sweet. That was rotten of me. I don't mean it. Of course we get on." He tried to kiss her, but she felt no urge to kiss him back and turned away her cheek.

"Sometimes I don't know what you *do* mean. You never say the same thing twice, Denis. I haven't a clue as to how you really do feel about our marriage. I only know that I don't seem to please *you* very much these days."

He relented still more, flung his cigarette through the open window and hugged her.

"Darling, you do please me. I adore you. It's just that what you said a moment ago is true . . . our jobs clash and I want more of you to myself. Isn't that natural?"

It was Nicola's turn to relent. She was so tired and wretched that she could easily have relaxed in his arms and wept. But Denis hadn't much patience with tears, and anyhow it wouldn't do to give way to her emotions, with Mrs. Oswald Rennie—one of the richest women in Welbridge—coming in at any moment for her 'facial'.

So Nicola fought with her distress and tried to laugh.

"Oh, darling, of course it's natural and I feel the same, but it's the old business of money. I must make as much as I can."

Now he released her and scowled.

"My fault you have to work at all, I suppose. I know you blame me for the whole position."

"Am *I* to blame?" she was driven to retaliate.

"Oh, I didn't come down here to quarrel with you and if you don't want to come out with me—stay here and go to hell!" he said with childish violence.

Nicola went white.

"I don't know how you can speak like that when you know the full facts and it's obvious that I'd much rather go out with you than stew indoors doing massage."

He gave a brief laugh and avoided her gaze.

"Oh, well, don't blame me if I find another girl to go out with me, will you?"

Now, out of sheer misery, Nicola retaliated again with a bitterness unusual for her.

"Haven't you done that already, my dear Denis?"

He flushed and gave her a haughty withering look.

"If you're accusing me . . ."

"Not now, *please*," she interrupted, for, parting the curtains at the sound of an opening door, she saw Mrs. Rennie, an elderly woman with a much-painted face and dyed auburn hair, sail into the shop. Nicola forced her features into a glittering smile.

"*Good* afternoon, Mrs. Rennie . . . *do* sit down . . . I'll be ready for you in just one moment. . . ."

To Denis she whispered:

"Don't let's quarrel, darling, *please*. I'll be home at five. Take me for a walk then. *Please*, Denny."

He whispered back, unsmiling.

"Oh, no! You've accused me of having a girl-friend. I'll go out and find one. . . ." He turned and walked through the salon. She heard him stop and speak to Mrs. Rennie. Now he was piling on the charm.

"Good afternoon. May I introduce myself? I'm Denis Avon. I just ran in for a moment to see my wife."

And Mrs. Rennie's gushing reply:

"How delightful to meet you, Mr. Avon. Of course I've seen you act often in your delightful little Rep. I think it is *excellent* this year. And you were delicious as Ernest. You must bring your sweet little wife along for a cocktail some time. You know my address . . . we've just moved into a new place . . . Bridge House, on the river about a mile out of the town."

"That would be delightful," came Denis's answer.

Nicola shut her eyes. She was trembling with nerves and exhaustion. How charming he could be when he wanted . . . and of course he *would* 'play up' to a woman like Mrs. Oswald Rennie. Bridge House was one of the show places of the district . . . Jacobean and full of treasures. Oswald Rennie had paid a small fortune for it.

Somehow or other Nicola managed to pull herself together and go to her client. While Mrs. Rennie divested herself of her hat and gloves, she launched into glowing compliments about Denis.

"Aren't you a lucky girl . . . married to such a clever husband, so good-looking and talented. . . ." Then she shook a finger coyly at Nicola and added: "And can't keep away from his little bride, eh?"

Nicola joined in the accompanying laugh. But she was thankful that now Mrs. Rennie lay on the couch with closed eyes, while a crêpe bandage was being tied over her hair and under her chin in preparation for the massage. So she could not see the hot tears that forced a way through Nicola's eyelids and trickled slowly down her cheeks.

Later, when she walked home with Kim, Nicola felt barely able to drag one foot in front of the other. She tried not to think too harshly of Denis. She had had so many of these little 'scenes' and she knew that he always got over his bad moods and became nice and easy again. But whereas the upsets did not seem to touch him deeply, each one destroyed Nicola afresh. Such petty displays of ill-humour were to her utterly destructive of love and friendship.

But she tried to make the best of a bad job and was always ready to start again. She did not bear malice. She was quite prepared to meet Denis now and be friendly, and make no reference to the stupid dispute at the salon.

She found a note waiting from him when she entered the flat.

*"Don't bother about tea for me—or supper later on as I've been asked to a party at Bill Venning's. He asked you, too, but I said you had too much work and couldn't come.*

*D."*

With a little twist of her lips, Nicola tore up the note. So that was Denis's petty method of revenge because she wouldn't leave her job and go out with him this afternoon. He had gone to Bill's and made sure that she didn't go too. No doubt Carole Fray would be there. Bill often held a beer and sausage party for the Company in his flat after the show.

It meant that Denny wouldn't be home until midnight or later.

Nicola looked at her watch. A quarter past five. The whole evening in front of her—alone. She could have gone along to her old home. She *wanted to*. She wanted terribly to see Mummy and Dad and Flip. To find peace in the old happy family atmosphere—where they had all loved and understood each other. But she dare not go home tonight. She knew she was on the verge of breaking down. Her mother had such a tender anxious heart, and she would grieve if she thought that this marriage was not a happy one. And people like Daddy and Ron would grieve, too. They wouldn't say '*I told you so*.' They would just be miserable because *she* was, and she didn't see the sense in making everybody wretched. No, she had made this bed and she must lie on it and just go on hoping that things would improve.

She felt too tired to get any food for herself, nor indeed did she feel hungry. But she got ready a dish of horsemeat and biscuits for Kim, who had grown into a big strong young dog like his Uncle Kimbo. He had long since outgrown the little tartan collar which Denis had bought her in London. That honeymoon! Thrilling, exotic, extravagant and short-lived . . . like her happiness . . . her belief in Denis, Nicola thought.

While she watched Kim bolting his food, she thought too about the man who had given him to her. Dear March! He and Ron had planned a holiday together this autumn. Ron was getting a fortnight in September, and March was going to take him in the Riley—having saved enough petrol—up to the Lake District for some sailing on Windermere.

March had met Nicola in the High Street one day last week and told her this.

"A pity you can't get away with Denis and join us," he had said lightly.

She had replied, equally lightly :

"I'd have loved it, but not a hope. Denis and I are both up to our necks in work."

But afterwards, she had thought how much she would have adored to drive up to Windermere with her brother and March . . . as they would have done in their extreme youth

together . . . full of fun and laughter. But not with Denis . . .
Oh, Denis would never have fitted in *that* sort of holiday
where there could have been no showing off for him, and no
ulterior motive. Denis seldom liked to go anywhere or do
anything unless it meant furthering his career. She knew now
that he was first and foremost a 'climber'.

That evening, alone in her flat, she thought of that forthcoming holiday which March and Ron were taking and was
horrified to find how very much she regretted not being able
to go with them. It would have been lovely to laugh and joke
with the old frank *joie-de-vivre*—without the incessant need
to keep Denis in a good humour, and sacrifice her wishes to
his.

Kim had finished his supper. He came across and laid a
big head on her knee and looked at her with beseeching
liquid eyes, his tail wagging.

"You want me to take you for a walk, don't you darling? But
I'm too tired . . . and oh, Kim, Kim, I'm so *miserable* . . . !" she
whispered to the dog.

He licked her hand as though to comfort her. Nicola sat in
a little heap on the floor and with her arms around his neck
began to cry in a lost, hopeless kind of way.


## XVI

ONE Saturday afternoon, about a month later, Denis returned
from a matinée to find Nicola struggling up the staircase to
their flat, dragging with her a large shopping bag, full of
parcels. He had just played to a packed house and taken three
curtains and was pleased with himself. Whistling gaily, he
jumped up the stairs two at a time and took the bag out of
his wife's hands.

"I'll carry it for you, sweetie-pie. What on earth is all this?
You oughtn't to tackle such weights."

She smiled at him over her shoulder.

"Somebody's got to do the shopping."

"Now don't blame me if *I* don't do it . . ." he began resentfully and she at once cut in.

"Don't be so touchy, darling. And I suppose you've forgotten that we've got our family lunch tomorrow. . . ."

They were in their flat now. Denis laid the shopping bag on the kitchen table and grimaced.

"Oh, heck! So I had! What a bore!"

Nicola made no answer. These days she rarely, unless driven beyond endurance, allowed such remarks to affect her. But she looked back on the many Sundays that Denis had crammed the flat with his theatrical friends whom she was expected to entertain. How often she had to use a week's rations in order to make cocktail snacks for such parties, and then listen to Denis grousing because they had little left for themselves.

And when he was playing host to any of the Repertory Company, or his London friends who sometimes came down to Welbridge on a Sunday, he would go and buy the most expensive tinned luxuries and think nothing of spending two or three pounds on gin or other drinks. But as she had told him quietly last night, it was high time she entertained her own family who had been so good to them. Mummy gave them hot lunch most Sundays, and Nicola, herself, frequently lunched in her old home, to say nothing of the times that Mummy trailed up these stairs with little presents for Denis and herself.

The sight of all the preparations for tomorrow swept away Denis's former good humour. He had long since decided that his in-laws were all prigs and just out to criticize him. He had no use for them. He had also long since decided in his own mind that he had been a fool ever to get married to a 'nice girl'. It didn't suit his temperament. Nicola was sweet and generous and he knew quite well that he often behaved disgracefully to her, but he wasn't at all sure that he was better off in this home with a good wife like Nic than he had been as a bachelor in digs. And he was at the moment quite a good bit amused by little Carole Fray who worshipped him. It soothed his vanity to be worshipped. A wife was all very fine but she got to know a chap too well and was too apt to criticize.

"Am I to be expected to stay in the whole of tomorrow

afternoon and entertain your parents?" he asked as he flung himself down on a chair and lit a cigarette.

"I don't think you'll find Mummy and Daddy will stay longer than they're wanted," Nicola said with heightened colour. "In any case I think Daddy is going to play bowls."

Denis cast his eyes heavenwards.

"Bowls! Ye gods! What a game! I hope I never come down to that."

Now Nicola, cheeks burning, retorted.

"You won't do too badly, Denis, if you are like my father when you're his age. He's a good soul."

Denis picked up a magazine and flipped through the pages, yawning.

"I don't think I was born to be a 'good soul'," he said with a laugh, then added in an idle tone: "Well, whatever time ye noble game of bowls begins, maybe you'll make an excuse for me if I slip away soon after half past two tomorrow."

Nicola walked to the window which overlooked the Square and closed it. The September day was stormy and the weather had turned much colder. It had begun to rain a few moments ago and a strong wind was blowing the drops into the room. She did not mind the weather. She found it easier to work when it was cold. She had felt so ill all last month until that night of the thunderstorms after which the weather broke. All the same it was rather dark and gloomy in this flat, and she dreaded the coming winter. There seemed no chance of Denis's glowing hopes of the London job being realized until after Christmas. One of the things that was making him ill-humoured was his disappointment over that London production. She said:

"What are you doing at half past two tomorrow, darling?"

She was smiling at him in a friendly way, but he avoided her eyes and focused on his magazine.

"Oh, I've been asked to a party in town which I think might be good for me to go to . . . a theatrical show, and I've been offered a lift up to town in a car, if I like to take it. Providing I leave here at half past two."

"Whose car?"

She asked the question without rancour although she felt

depressed and hurt that he should arrange to leave her for a whole night without even asking her about it beforehand. How times had changed! How tattered was the brave banner of love that had been unfurled between them only four short months ago.

Denis yawned.

"Carole's brother's. Don't think you've met him. Rather pleasant fellow, Tony Fray. In the car business and runs a superb 3-litre Bentley. Carole comes of a family with quite a bit of cash and it seems her people were not at all keen on her going on the stage, but she would do it—that's why she's in the Rep. down here. But she has hopes of a London show— like yours truly. Tony has come down to stay tonight and see her play."

"I see," said Nicola.

Denis rambled on—about the Bentley—the Frays' big flat in a West End luxury block—what a good fellow Tony was —and so on. Nicola listened in silence. Her face was expressionless. She had no intention of launching a grievance—or criticizing. She was beyond it. She knew, in her heart, that Denis was wishing he had tied himself up to a girl in Carole's position, with a wealthy family behind her and a brother with a Bentley . . . instead of *her* . . . with her impecunious family . . . dear Ron, hard working, car-less, and so absolutely decent in every way. And the awful part of it was that *Nicola was beginning to wish it too* . . . wish that Denis had never swept her off her feet in a moment of madness (both his and hers!), never brought her to this state of hopelessness . . . of utter disillusion. Yet she saw no way out. It never entered her head to entertain the idea of breaking up this brief, mistaken marriage. She had married Denis. So far as she could see, she must stick to him . . . to her vows . . . until the bitter end.

"You don't mind if I take the opportunity of running up to town to this party—do you, sweetie-pie?" came Denis's voice, cutting in upon her morbid reflections.

"Not at all," she answered politely.

He glanced at her . . . frowned . . . shrugged his shoulders. He didn't always understand Nic. But he was too full of excitement about tomorrow to mind much what Nicola was thinking or suspecting. Probably she *knew* that Carole would be in the car with him and Tony . . . and that tomorrow night she would be in the party as well. But Nic must 'get on with it', he mentally decided. He wasn't cut out to be a 'good soul', as she had labelled her father . . . the sort of husband to hang around his wife's skirts night and day. Besides . . . an actor had his way to make. Nic was sweet . . . but she had in his mind become more or less a mere background—a house-keeper and someone who fortunately 'paid her whack'. All this money business had, of course, spoiled things between them, and Nic was too anti-spending to suit him . . . too fussy about paying bills on the dot and that nonsense about not taking cash out of her business. He was a fool not to have realized that he would find marriage such a 'bind'.

Quietly, without further reference to Denis's jaunt to-morrow, Nicola went into the kitchen and began to make the cake she had planned for the family—Flip's favourite, with cherries in it. She had saved sugar and margarine this week specially for the cake. She had hoped Denis would like it. How silly of her, she thought, as she plunged her hands into the flour and began to smooth out the lumps of grease. Denis wouldn't be interested in a homemade cherry cake when he was anticipating a ride in a Bentley up to a party with the rich Frays!

She suddenly laughed aloud—but had to bite hard on her lip to keep it from quivering.

Denis strolled into the kitchen.

"Old Nic doing the efficient-little-cook act," he grinned at her, quite good-humouredly.

She looked up at him with grey, deep eyes which gave away none of her heart's sick grief and disappointment.

"Do I suit the part?"

"I rather think you do," he laughed. "What's the mixture?"

"Just a . . . cake. But you won't be here to eat it. I expect Flip will finish it quick enough."

"Too bad," he murmured. Then after a moment's thought and without meeting her gaze—which somehow made Denis feel awkward, though he did not know why—he added : "By the way, I ran into your old flame, March Foster, yesterday

I forgot to tell you. We had a beer together after the show. That's why I was a bit late. He was driving along and saw me in the rain and gave me a lift. I said I couldn't ask him back here as we hadn't any drink, so he took me up to Heron's Hall for a quick one."

Nicola coloured. Her heart jerked a bit. This was news to her. Her slender fingers went on kneading the flour and margarine mechanically.

"How was March?"

"Oh, in good form. He really isn't a bad chap."

"No—he's awfully nice," said Nicola in a low voice.

Denis, with a faintly malicious smile, said:

"Do you think he's the solid type you ought to have married?"

Now her cheeks went scarlet. She looked him straight in the face with a brave show of pride.

"Why should I? What reasons have I to regret marrying you? Good heavens, Denis . . . what a question . . . and less than four months after our wedding!"

It was his turn to colour. He turned away, laughing.

"Can't you take a joke?"

She wondered if it had been a joke. He added:

"I'm so forgetful, honey . . . I didn't tell you either that I asked March along here at six-thirty this evening. I must return his hospitality. I'll nip along when the shop opens and get some beer."

Nicola wiped the flour from her hands. She looked surprised and almost scared.

"You asked March here this evening?"

"Why not? Very nice of me, wasn't it? He's one of *your* friends."

She bit her lip. She was confused. She longed to see March yet did not really want him to come. She had never asked him to their flat because she dreaded lest in his observant way he noticed the fact that she and Denis were not quite so happy as they used to be.

Also, she was afraid of Denis *the opportunist* . . . Denis 'making up' to a man like March because he was well off. She would hate *that*. But she said:

"Oh, I shall be quite pleased to see March. It's nearly a quarter to six now. I'd better do my cake later. I'll . . . get washed and changed."

"That's right, darling—glam-up for the former boy-friend."

He went out laughing. Nicola did not echo the laugh. It had an edge to it . . . like his careless words. It seemed to her this evening that Denis had nothing left for her but the very remnants of his former adoration.

And March was coming here . . . dear March—for the first time. *Whatever* happened she must not let him see how matters were. In an agony of pride, she vowed to do her best to prevent that. She washed and took special pains to put on a new glamorous make-up; lilac eye-shadow, eyelash-black, soft pink rouge . . . till her face looked less pale and drawn; her lips rosy; her eyes almost unnaturally big and bright. She chose one of her trousseau dresses . . . grey wool with frilly organdie collar and cuffs. She brushed her hair until it looked like smooth gold.

When she walked into the sitting-room where Denis sat smoking, he glanced up and exclaimed:

"My *my*! You certainly have put on the war-paint, my sweet. Mr. Foster is honoured. I haven't seen you look like that for weeks."

She flushed dully.

"I'm generally so tired—I dare say I haven't looked my best at times. But I assure you this isn't just for March— but also because I want him to see us *both* at our best."

"Oh, I'm all for it!" said Denis airily. "I think he's a good fellow to have around."

Nicola did not altogether understand, but she accepted gratefully the fact that Denis liked at least *one* of her friends as well as his own.

Denis, opening one of the bottles of beer in advance, whistled a tune. He was thinking that it was as well 'old Nic' didn't know that at Heron's Hall last night he had spun a hard luck story to March—told him that all his shares had lately gone down and that he was very worried about money for Nic's sake, then later had touched the rich Mr. Foster for fifty pounds. March had given him a cheque a bit grimly but without hesitation. He would hate to think Nicola was hard up, he had said, and agreed that the loan should not be mentioned to her. Just as well, Denis reflected, grimacing. He couldn't quite think *what* Nic would do if she *knew*.

## XVII

WHEN March Foster walked into the Avon's flat—his first visit to Nicola as a married woman—his feelings were very mixed.

He wanted to see her. Time had increased rather than diminished his love and longing for her and his unending regret that he had waited too long before recognizing the existence of that love.

He wanted to see her—but dreaded it. He knew now, indubitably, that he disliked Denis Avon and that the fellow was not good enough for her. He had been shocked by Denis's brazen request for the loan of fifty pounds. It was not that he begrudged lending money to a needy friend. March was the most generous of men; sometimes too generous. He remembered a slight 'scene' he had had with the old man, who had opened a drawer in his desk at the office and accidentally found a little pile of I.O.U'S. He never forgot Mr. Foster's cryptic remarks.

"It isn't that I mind you helping a friend, but it's almost an invariable rule that a fellow who borrows is worthless. I say —why waste money on worthless and spendthrift people? Far better give it to someone who is poor through no fault of his own and who has *not* asked."

His father was right, March thought. Why should Denis Avon be so hard up? And if he was—then he had had no right to marry Nicola. A chap should be able to support his wife.

March, however, was agreeably surprised to find the atmosphere in the little flat a happy one. Dingy though the sitting-room was, there were one or two charming touches, expressive of Nicola's personality. Some beautiful roses from the Boyd garden; some fresh frilled net over the window. (Nicola had made the curtains.) A laughing framed snapshot of Flip taken a few years ago with Tessa, the old spaniel. And young Kim, the Boxer, stretched on the rug in front of the fireplace. Somehow it pleased March to see the Boxer there. Nicola looked lovely, too, he thought, although far too thin. But she and Denis seemed on the best of terms . . . calling each other 'darling' . . . behaving most affectionately towards each other.

"Oh, well," March reflected, as he bent down to caress the dog, "if Nic's happy, what's it matter whether I think Avon a wash-out or not?"

But for a moment his heartbeats had shaken his strong body as he had taken one of Nic's slender hands in his, pressed it and caught the soft welcome in the sweet grey eyes. Dammit! How long did it take a chap to get over a unrequited love?

Denis poured out beer. He was very effusive—too effusive to please March—who could have too much of being called 'old boy' and generally flattered. There was something a bit too charming about Denis, and the fifty pounds loan loomed up like a guilty secret between them.

"You've got quite a nice little place," murmured March as Nicola sat down beside him and he lit the inevitable pipe.

"Yes, it's fine," she said with determined cheerfulness.

"A bit of a come-down after Heron's Hall, of course," added Denis with a laugh.

March looked embarrassed and Nicola hastily added :

"One day when we're terribly rich, darling, *we'll* have a lovely home, too."

Denis made a theatrical gesture and cast his eyes heavenwards.

"One day when I, with my fire, my thunder, shake the world of drama, and reduce a hard-hearted audience to pulp."

Everybody laughed, Nicola a trifle too long and heartily. Then she asked March all the things she wanted to know. How he had been getting on in the business all these months; how his mother was; and of course, about the forthcoming holiday with Ronald in the Lake District.

He answered all questions in turn. Business was good despite the restrictions and difficulties of present-day commerce, he said. His mother was a good bit better and on her feet again, but still rather nervy. He thoroughly looked forward to the holiday at Windermere with Ronald.

"Pity you two can't join us," he added, although with one glance at Denis's handsome face, he thought how sadly the trip would be spoiled by *his* presence.

Denis drank down a tumber of beer and wiped the foam from his lips with a graceful gesture, afterwards replacing his silk handkerchief in his pocket. Everything the fellow did seemed to be studied for effect, March thought moodily. He was surprised that Nicola didn't get sick of it. Just *how* sick of it he couldn't begin to guess, nor could he know the gloomy troubled reflections that flitted like sad dark shadows through the girl's mind. She looked from her husband to the other man. She listened to March's quiet voice. She knew that she could have married him if she had chosen and been secure with him in every way. Then she turned back and gazed through her lowered lashes at Denis again. So handsome! So charming like this, when he was doing everything he could to be amiable to a guest. So shallow and unreliable behind that smooth façade. Oh, why, *why* had she been so blind? Why had she ever thought that she loved him desperately? It was terrible to a girl of her temperament to face the fact that what she had felt for Denis was only infatuation . . . to be forced to admit out of the depths of her bitter disappointment that it was this other man she should have married; that it was March whom she should have loved.

March took the pipe from his pocket and, in that instant, looked at her. She returned the look for an unbearably poignant moment. Then hastily glanced away and, rising, put a hand on Denis's shoulder. A slim hand that trembled. In a hard bright voice she said :

"I don't suppose Denis and I will have a holiday this year, and when we do, we'll have it in London, won't we, Denis?"

"You're dead right, my sweet," he said, playing up to her, and covered her hand with his and gave her an upward ardent look which at one time would have roused all her response and love. But now it left her deathly cold. She knew that there was *nothing* behind that theatrical ardour.

March looked away from them. He wanted Nicola to be

happy but he could not pretend to care much for the sight of the intimacy between these two.

Then Denis said :

"Of course, if you'd like to drive up to Windermere with your brother and March, my sweet, I'd let you go. I should be wildly jealous . . ." a little laugh . . . "but I'd be happy if I thought it was doing you good."

March's head shot up.

"*Could* you come, Nic?"

The eagerness in his voice warmed her heart, but she shook her head, smiling.

"Not possible. Denis is only ragging. He knows I couldn't leave *NICOLETTE* . . . or him . . ." she added hastily.

"But really, darling, if you'd like to go . . ." began Denis.

Nicola flushed up. She felt a spurt of anger against him. She knew perfectly well why he wanted her to go. So as to leave him more free to find amusement with his new girl-friend.

Somehow she managed to go on smiling. She murmured :

"Silly! I wouldn't dream of leaving you, much as I'd love to go with Ron—and March," she added the last name in an embarrassed way.

So the conversation went on. It all seemed quite cheerful and normal to March. He began to wonder if the rumours he had heard about Nic's marriage not being a success were unfounded. The end of that visit to the Avons left him unsatisfied and, he admitted wryly, more than ever in love with Nicola. He really ought not to go on seeing her. What an enchanting wife she made! Did this fellow Avon realize how lucky he was?

Just before he left, he held Nicola's hand for a fraction of a moment and was a little astonished to find it so hot and feverish. Was she well? When he was near to her, he could see the tired lines around her eyes and the way her skin was stretched across her face, showing the fine bones. She was wearing a lot of rouge this evening. Was it to disguise her pallor? He was filled with tenderness and unspoken anxiety. He said :

"Thanks for a very good drink, and nice to see you again, Nic."

"Nice to see you," she answered gaily. "Why didn't you bring Kimbo?"

"Oh, I thought he'd be far too large and obstreperous for your small room, but young Kim will soon be the same size," laughed March.

"What about asking March in for a bite tomorrow evening?" Denis suggested with sudden cunning. "I've got to be away the night, and I don't want you to sit alone."

March saw Nicola's face suddenly grow scarlet.

"Oh, no . . . I mean . . . I shall probably go home," she stammered.

"If you've nothing to do tomorrow evening, I'd be only too pleased if you'd come out with me," said March. "Come up to Heron's Hall for a bite. Mother'd love to see you."

Even as he said the words, he wondered if they were true. If his mother would approve of his renewing his friendship with Nicola now that she was married. Only last night he had felt unusually irritated with Mrs. Foster because she had bemoaned the fact that he never brought any girls back to the house.

"When are you going to settle down and find a wife?" she had asked. "I want to see you happily settled and with children of your own before I die."

He had laughed it off . . . telling her that there was plenty of time, and that she wasn't going to die yet. But he had felt her dark brooding gaze upon him; felt suffocated by her concentrated mother-love and all her ambitions for him. He always tried to be gentle, to be affectionate, but he knew that the shadow of Nicola lay between them. Mrs. Foster wanted him to forget Nicola and put her right out of his life.

Nicola started to refuse the invitation, but Denis cut in. He seemed to want to encourage her to go out, which March found a bit odd. He even spoke pettishly.

"You spend far too much time with your own family, my darling. Do you good to snap out of it. And I'm sure Mrs. Foster would like to see you. Why not go, Nic?"

March looked at Nicola. She *knew* that he was looking at her. She refused to meet that searching gaze. She was afraid of it. Afraid of giving herself away. She felt furious with

Denis for putting her in this invidious position. For a long time now he had been trying to establish an intimacy with the Foster household, just because he liked the things that their money could buy, and the lavish hospitality that was always to be found at Heron's Hall. But that stubborn little streak that was in Nicola asserted itself now. She swallowed hard and said:

"I'm sorry. I would have loved to go and see Mrs. Foster, Denis darling . . . but I think the family will expect me to go to them, especially as Mummy has my godmother staying with her. I don't think you've met her. She used to be a singer—Nicola Perry. I was called after her."

Denis was not interested in Nicola's godmother and he was angry now because he had been thwarted. Knowing that he was going up to town to have a good time with the Frays, it would have salved his conscience to think of Nicola in the company of her former admirer. But he could not argue the point without it appearing curious to March. So there the argument ended and March took his departure.

"So long, Nic . . . see you sometime . . . and I'll send you a p.c. from Windermere." March said the words in the most casual voice, although he was filled suddenly with a bitter envy of the fellow who had a right to live here in this little flat with her . . . to have all that grace and beauty and sweetness for his own.

She looked at him with a surge of wild regret in her heart. But her good-bye was as casual as his.

"Drop in sometime, March. Denis and I will aways be pleased to see you."

On the doorstep, March fumbled in his pocket for pipe and tobacco-pouch and was annoyed to find he had left the pipe up in the Avon's sitting-room. He trailed up the stairs again. Their flat was not self-contained and he could walk straight into their room. But outside the door, he suddenly paused. In the dim light of the hall his face changed colour. His brows came togther. For he heard voices . . . raised voices. Denis's and Nicola's. They were having a dispute. And March was aghast at what he, the unwilling eavesdropper, heard.

Denis was saying in a violent voice:

"Oh, you're too good to live! The family! The *family*! Every spare moment spent with your family. It's an absolute bore. I'll be finding *you* a bore if you go on like this."

Nicola's voice, raw with bitterness, answered:

"Why not put it in the past tense? Aren't you bored with me already?"

"If I am, it's your fault. If you're not working in your damned Beauty Parlour, you're talking about your family or preaching at me because I run up a bill or two. It gets a fellow down."

"Perhaps you might consider that I'm being 'got down' too," came from Nicola.

March Foster stood like a figure of stone. There was sick surprise in his eyes. He was flabbergasted. So *this* was the truth! All the brightness and friendliness had been a show before *him*. *This* was what Nicola's marriage of four months' duration had come to! How horrible! Poor, poor little Nic! All his and Ronald's fears had been justified. Denis Avon was a hypocrite and a cad. How dared he speak to her like that?

Denis went on:

"Why couldn't you have gone to Heron's Hall tomorrow night? You stick to the friends who don't matter and can't be of use to you, and you avoid those who *are* of use. The Fosters are made of money. You're such a little *idiot*."

March's hands doubled at his sides. He had an overpowering desire to go through that door and smash both fists into Denis's face. Then came Nicola's reply:

"I can't *use* people as you do. If I went to Heron's Hall it wouldn't be because I wanted to cadge, but because I *like* the Fosters."

An unpleasant laugh from Denis.

"Isn't that putting it mildly? Haven't you always had a bit of a penchant for March? And isn't it true that everyone in Welbridge knows that he wanted to marry you—before I came on the scene?"

March's heart missed a beat. He wanted to turn and run down the stairs, yet stood there fascinated. He knew that he *must* hear Nicola's reply. It came in a low voice.

"It may be true. But if it is, all the more reason why I shouldn't see much of him now."

Then from Denis:

"My dear, you should have lived in the days of Queen Victoria. I had no idea you were so old-fashioned. Dear prim little thing!"

Then Nicola cried out as though driven beyond endurance.

"Oh, stop bullying me, Denis! I can't stand it. I'm too tired. And the whole thing is so wretched. I thought we would always love each other and that our marriage would never develop into this. Oh, *Denis*!"

She began to cry. Denis's voice said:

"Oh, I'm sorry, I'm *sorry*. Dammit, you get upset so easily . . ."

March waited to hear no more. He had heard too much. He was hot with disgust for Denis Avon. A quite frightening hatred of the young hypocrite filled his being. He felt anguished with pity for *her*. His sweet gentle Nic . . . Nic reduced to such a state of mind. Nic with all her hopes and dreams in tatters. Nic who used to be so happy and serene. The stark revelation of how things stood between those two shook March Foster to the core. Nothing would have induced him to go in and fetch his pipe now. He rushed out of the building into the Square. He needed fresh air. He wondered what in heaven's name Ron would say if he knew the truth about his sister's marriage. That *damnable* fellow! Jibing at Nic . . . trying to force her into a position from which she shrank because she was decent and good. Taunting her with her very goodness. Just because he wanted to cover his *own* tracks.

March walked blindly through the dark quiet streets. He was haunted by the memory of Nicola's voice.

"*Oh, stop bullying me . . . I can't stand it . . . I'm too tired . . .*"

His poor love! And he could do nothing about it. She herself had said that she ought not to see him, because he loved her. And she was dead right. For knowing the truth now, he would find it hard not to ask her to leave Denis and go to him. And that would be impossible. He knew his Nicola. He knew himself. To break up a marriage was unthinkable. But equally was it unthinkable that Nicola should spend the rest of her life with a man who was a bully; eaten up with his own conceit . . . a man who, into the bargain, was financially unstable.

She certainly had made a poor choice and it had been brought home to her too late.

There was no more miserable man on earth than March Foster as he walked home that night, knowing that he could do nothing . . . nothing to help the girl he loved but leave her alone and hope that the quarrel he had overheard was only a temporary misunderstanding between husband and wife, that matters would, in time, adjust themselves.


## XVIII

*Extract from the diary of Miss Frances (Flip) Boyd. Entry made on December first.*

"EVERYTHING seems to have gone wrong. The weather has been jolly awful and the ground is so hard with frost all week that stupid Miss Pym won't let us play hockey. It's jolly awful. And I got into a row this morning in the geography class because I didn't know what the capital of China was. I don't care about the silly old Chinese anyhow. And Nic has been ill for the last fortnight and has had to close down NICOLETTE and she says she's hard up and can't afford it because she has to go on paying Ann Williams. She has had 'flu. Mummy went to sleep in the horrid little flat and nurse her. And then Mummy got it too, and we had to send for old Winnie. Winnie was Mummy's cook when she was first married in the days when there were servants and she's about a hundred, but she's jolly decent. She came all the way from Plymouth to look after Mummy and do the cooking. She said she would never see us 'in a jam' because Mummy was once so kind to her.

Mummy's better now but she's awfully worried about Nic and so is Daddy. They won't tell me what's wrong. But I've guessed. And now I'm going to write a DEADLY SECRET.

Pam and I discussed it and we think we know. *My sister has married the wrong man*. We neither of us like Denis any more. He's changed since his marriage and become very bossy and conceited and I know he isn't very nice to Nic behind our backs, although he's smarmy to our faces. But sometimes Mummy and Daddy let things out and when Nic was so ill and had a huge temperature, Mummy came home one day looking grim, and I heard her tell Daddy that Nic was just skin and bones and that she blamed Denis and that he was a rotten husband. She said something about 'betraying a trust' and Daddy said: 'I knew it, Mary. I knew it. Poor child! But she would marry him.'

Pam and I went to see Nic when she was getting better and I must say she looked awful, but she's still jolly pretty. Denis wasn't there. Nic said he didn't want to get the 'flu and not be able to act so he had been staying with Bill Venning, and she hadn't seen him for days. Pam and I didn't say anything but we agreed after that we thought it jolly cowardly of him. If he'd really *loved* Nic, he would have gone to see her and cheer her up because she was so depressed, and risked the 'flu.

Her room was full of flowers. I asked her who'd sent the lovely hothouse roses and she said they were from Mrs. Foster and March. Then I giggled and said that I bet they were from *March* and not Mrs. Foster and Nic told me to shut up and looked quite cross—all red. But she soon said she was sorry for snapping and that it was because she was feeling ill.

I told her that March came to our house every day to ask after her and she went redder than ever and had an awfully queer look in her eyes as though she wanted to cry. But she just smiled and said, 'Please thank him, but tell him I can't ask him round because of the infection.'

Well, Pam and I thought *that* funny, because we knew she was past the infectious stage or Mummy wouldn't have let us go to see her.

As we walked home, Pam said that she bet Nic was sorry she hadn't married March instead of Denis. Well, I think so, too, and I wish it, because Denis is *hateful*. I won't go and see him act any more. He offered Pam and me two stalls when he met us in the High Street the other day coming home from school. He was with that pretty girl who acts with him, Carole Fray. He introduced her to us and she was jolly snooty, and didn't talk to us but took a mirror out of her bag and began to push waves into her hair. Silly thing! Denis said to us: 'Wouldn't you like Miss Fray's autograph, Flip? She's going to be famous one day.'

We didn't want her autograph so we didn't answer and she looked livid and so did he. Then when I got home and told Mummy that I'd met Denis with Miss Fray, Mummy tightened in her lips as she does when she hears a crash in the kitchen and knows that Mrs. Tunny has broken something. But she didn't say anything.

Pam and I think that *Denis is keen on Carole Fray* and we think it's a jolly shame for Nic.

But the worst thing happened this morning. At lunchtime, I went round to the flat to take Kim back to Nic, as I'd been looking after him while she was laid up. It was a beastly cold morning with a sort of sleet falling and I was all wet and frozen and so was Kim by the time we got to Market Square. His paws got all muddy and wet, but I couldn't help that. When I walked into the flat, he was so pleased to see Nic that he sprang at her, barking and licking her all over. She was up and sitting in a chair, huddled over a little electric fire. The room was freezing and not like ours with a lovely coal fire at home. Nic looked worse now that she was up— all eyes and dreadfully thin and white. And she was a bit weak still, she said. Kim nearly knocked her over. He put his paw marks all over the place. But she hugged him like anything and said how much she'd missed him.

Well, we were sitting, talking, when Denis came home. Nic said he'd been down to the Rep. for a rehearsal and when I asked her when he was going into a London show she said there was nothing definite and I think she seemed glad that she didn't have to leave Welbridge and *us*. But she said that Denis was in touch with the film world now and wanted to go to Hollywood. I said how super if she had a chance to go to Hollywood and see my favourites like Frank Sinatra and Gregory Peck, but Nic didn't seem to be at all thrilled. She said she didn't suppose she'd go, anyhow.

Then Denis walked in. He looked awfully bad-tempered when he saw me and hardly said 'Hello'. Then he saw Kim's paw marks, and went red. He muttered something about *'Hell take that dog.* He messes up everything and I don't want him back at the flat. Flip, take him home again. I've never liked him here anyhow.'

Nic looked very pale and said: 'I'm sorry you don't like my dog, Denis, but he's a great companion for me when you're not here, and I don't see why I should give him away. I'll wash the marks off the carpet later.'

Then Denis said in a beastly voice that he was master of the house and that it was what *he* wanted that counted, and that I was to take Kim home—and quickly.

'I need peace and quiet when I get back from the theatre,' he said, in a lordly sort of way. I made Pam giggle when I imitated him later for her, although I was jolly sorry for Nic.

But Nic stuck it out, and said she wouldn't part with Kim, neither would she have me turned out of the flat when I'd only just come.

Denis lost his temper. IT WAS AWFUL. He said either the dog went or *he would go.* Nic looked ghastly, but tried to laugh and told him not to be silly. Then he said:

'Oh, you and your precious animal! March Foster's wedding present, eh? That's why you're so incredibly attached to him, my dear Nic. It makes me sick.'

Nic looked at me and I looked at her. I could see she was trembling and I thought it a shame as she's not well yet and I wouldn't have *believed* Denis could be so awful. But she didn't say a word. And there was a frightful sort of silence and then Denis seemed to be sorry that he'd said all those things in front of me, and he sort of laughed and shrugged his shoulders.

'Oh, well, keep your hound. Anything for peace's sake. How's school, Flip?'

I didn't feel like answering. Poor Nic looked so unhappy and he'd *made her.* After a moment, he said he was going out to get a beer before lunch, and that he'd bring her back a bottle of Guinness which would be good for her. She didn't even thank him. I've never seen her look so ghastly.

After he'd gone she burst into tears. She cried and cried like I did when our spaniel died—as though her heart was broken. And she kept saying :

'Oh, Flip, I'm so unhappy. But, Flip, don't tell Mummy and Daddy. Please . . . please don't tell anybody. Denis doesn't often behave like that in front of people.'

I knelt beside my chair and put my arms around her. I cried too. And dear old Kim kept trying to shove his nose between us and snuggle a way in, out of pure sympathy. I promised Nic that I wouldn't tell, and I told her that we all loved her and so did March, and that everybody said he would never get over losing her. But that didn't seem to comfort her, for she only gave a long long sigh, and just whispered that I mustn't say things like that. Then she added that Denis was very nice sometimes, and it was just that he got into bad moods like today, and she seemed sorry that she had let me know that she was unhappy.

I said I thought it was awfully sad because she had such a beautiful Wedding and had seemed so terribly happy with Denis. And she sighed again and stroked my hair and said : 'It was a beautiful wedding and I was happy. But perhaps I married Denis before I really knew or understood him.'

Then I said, 'Is that what people call infatuation, and not real love?'

Then she laughed awfully sadly and said : 'Yes, Flip darling, perhaps that's what it is. But I've got to make the best of it and I could still be happy with Denis if he would let me. He can be so unutterably charming when he chooses. I'll try not to despair.'

I told her that if she did despair she could always come home—she always had us. Then we both started to cry again, and she got up and begged me to go and that she must hurry and wash her face, as she didn't want Denis to see she'd been crying. But I'm jolly glad she wouldn't let him have his way about Kim. She was going to keep him whatever Denis said. She fetched a wet cloth and started to clean the paw marks. I wanted to do it for her because she is so pale and trembly after her 'flu. But she wouldn't let me, and kissed me and sent me home.

I felt dreadfully miserable and I told Pam and swore her to secrecy. But I didn't let Mummy or Daddy know a thing. I think if Daddy knew that Denis shouted at Nic he'd have gone there and carried her home against her will.

March came to ask after Nic this evening. Mummy and Daddy were out. They'd gone up the road to see old Mr. Straker, our Vicar, who's got lumbago. Daddy promised to play chess with him while Mummy and Mrs. Straker do their knitting. They left me because I've got my homework. March brought Kimbo in and sat and talked to me for a bit and smoked his pipe. I think I must have looked funny when I answered his enquiries about Nic. March has an awfully funny way of knowing things. It's his searching eyes. I think he's jolly deep, old March. He asked me if anything was wrong.

'Is it only '*flu* that's the matter with her, Flip?' he asked me.

Then I know I looked guilty because he immediately said:

'Tell me, Flip. I'm very fond of Nic. When I last saw her I thought she looked frightful.'

I know when that was because Mrs. Foster told Mummy in front of me that she had had Nic and Denis for lunch at Heron's Hall about a month ago, and that Nic had seemed very changed and quiet but Denis was full of himself, and although jolly handsome, she did not much care for actors.

Then I told March what had happened. It was a bit awful of me when Nic asked me not to, but he dragged it out of me—honestly he did—and he swore he wouldn't tell. When I told him about how beastly Denis was over Kim's paw marks and how Nic cried, he got up and stood by the fire, put his arms on the mantelpiece and leaned his head on them. He was awfully upset. After a moment he turned back and looked at me and his face was grim.

'Flip,' he said, 'never repeat that story to anybody else, will you? Nic wouldn't like it.'

I swore that I wouldn't. He shook his head from side to side and he was terribly worried. He said he would like to 'wring Denis's neck' and it was as well old Ron didn't know or he would do it. I said that I wished we could help Nic. March's face all twisted up and he put an arm around my shoulders and said: 'So do I, Flip, so do I, my poppet. But we can't. That's the hell of it. None of us can do a thing.'

'Oh, March,' I said, 'it's what they call a "Mistaken Marriage", isn't it?'

His eyes looked kind of tragic.

'Yes, Flip,' he said, 'I think it's what you'd call a mistaken marriage, but marriage is for keeps. That's why it's so hard for Nic. Unless that fellow goes off one day—and I wouldn't put it past him—she'll never be free. But he *may* get fed up living with somebody whose shoes he isn't fit to clean.'

Then I said:

'I wish she'd married you, March. You're fit to clean her shoes.'

He went all red and laughed and put a finger against my lips.

'Infant,' he said, 'that's the sort of remark one doesn't make. But I entirely agree with you. About her marrying me, I mean. Only nobody must know. I think we can best help Nic by pretending that everything's okay. She's so proud.'

After he had gone, I thought a lot about March and all he said. He's going to be My Hero in future. I think he's wonderful and full of ideals. I found a snapshot of him and I've framed it and put it up in my room. But I couldn't help thinking about my poor darling sister! At this very moment Denis is on the stage making people think how splendid he is. And Nic will be alone with Kim, and perhaps she's crying again.

I think I'd better stop writing in my diary, or I shall start crying too. Oh, I wonder how it's all going to end . . .?''

## XIX

ONE week later, Denis's Aunt Emma suddenly died after a stroke. Denis hurried up to London, taking Nicola with him. By that time she had recovered from her long depressing bout of 'flu.

They were the sole mourners at the funeral of the lonely old woman. Nicola was quite glad she had accompanied Denis because—strange man that he was—he showed some genuine grief for the old woman who had been his sole surviving relative for so long, and who had always been so fond of him. Of course he dramatized his grief.

"I am quite alone in the world now, except for you, Nic," he said emotionally as they drove back from the funeral.

Although disillusioned and no longer in love, Nicola still could not help but feel some of her old tenderness for Denis when he was in this sort of mood, holding on to her, craving sympathy like a small boy.

"Well, I'm always here when you want me, Denny," she said.

He looked at her with some remorse, not unaware of the fact that she had altered a lot this winter and was looking much older and thinner and that he was partially responsible. He put an arm around her shoulder.

"I don't think I've made you much of a husband, have I, Nic?" he sighed. "I'm infernally selfish."

She did not meet his gaze but sighed with him and rubbed her cheek against his shoulder.

"Oh, you're not too bad," she murmured in a joking way; "perhaps I've been a disappointment to you as a wife."

"You've been marvellous," he said with sincerity. And with equal sincerity he wished that it was in his nature to love his young wife as she was meant to be loved. But nobody knew better than he did how transient his emotions were, and that he was fundamentally incapable of carrying out many of his best intentions. He could behave really well only for short periods. This was one of them. After Nicola's illness he had fallen out with Carole Fray, who had not been as patient or understanding of him as his wife, and there was no other girl on the horizon at the moment, so he was prepared to be exceptionally nice to Nicola.

Then the reading of Aunt Emma's will revealed the fact that after paying death duties and one or two minor bequests to a church mission in which she was interested, Denis inherited a capital sum which would bring him in about four pounds a week for life. It wasn't much, but it was something, and there was the lease of the little flat to dispose of and the sale of furniture and effects which would bring in a hundred or two more.

Denis, who had never had anything in his life that he

hadn't worked for, felt quite rich. His sorrow at the death of his old aunt rapidly altered to elation.

Nicola had grown used to the fact that he was an unknown quantity and that she never knew what to expect from Denis. Now he decided that he could afford to be generous and that it was Nicola who must benefit, rather than his friends or hangers-on in the theatrical profession.

He bought beautiful extravagant presents and showered them on his wife. A fur coat. A new radio-gramophone which she had coveted for some time because she loved music. Handsome presents, too, for the whole of her family, including a brand new bicycle for Flip. He had these things sent down to Welbridge from Harrods.

Nicola was overwhelmed and a little embarrassed. She could not truly say that she wanted Denis to spend money in this way. The capital sum left to him by his aunt was so small that it would soon go if he went at it recklessly. She felt that he ought to keep the investments Miss Robinson had so wisely made and go carefully. But Nicola said nothing. The last thing she wanted was to be a 'spoilsport' and damp down Denis's desire to be generous. She felt that perhaps he was trying to make up for some of his past misdemeanours. But she did hope he would clear all his debts. She ventured to remark this to him.

"But of course, darling," was his airy reply. "I won't have a bill left in the world by the end of this week."

And he kept to his word, with the exception of the fifty pounds which, unknown to Nicola, he owed March Foster. Somehow he had no wish to repay March—for the moment.

He had a twisted way of thinking and he condoned his own conduct by reminding himself that 'March had money and would not miss the fifty.'

He was altogether in the best of moods when he and Nicola returned together from London to Welbridge. He had even been nice about poor old Queen, Aunt Emma's tabby. He had agreed with Nicola that the kindest thing would be to have the old cat put to sleep before they left London, and when Nicola had wept a little when they took Queen to the vet, he had been understanding and sympathetic about it.

"Poor old Queen, and poor Nic. You're so fond of animals; such a dear, kind little thing," he had said on the way home.

Almost she could have found it in her heart to love him again during this period of well-being. He was the old lovable splendid Denis who had swept her off her feet six months ago.

She sensed that the affair with Carole was over and that she, Nicola, was once more the centre of existence for him. Yet she found it difficult, and even impossible, to respond wholly, as she used to do. She was afraid now of loving and believing in Denis. Afraid of being hurt and disappointed all over again. Besides, deep down within her she had become aware of the fact that it was March Foster whom she really loved and needed. That knowledge was now a painful certainty. It rose like a wall between Denis and herself. But nothing on earth could have dragged such an admission from her to a single soul.

Christmas, however, was a little happier than she had imagined it would be. Denis's good humour and goodwill towards her was maintained. The whole Boyd family was slightly overwhelmed by the magnificence of his Christmas gifts.

Flip accepted her bicycle with a reluctance which was in keeping with her honest, independent character. Denis was no longer her hero and she found it difficult to take something that she really wanted, like the bicycle, from a man who had made her sister so unhappy. On the other hand, it was impossible to refuse. And the family, talking among themselves, confessed that things were better between Nic and Denis and that having a little money to spend seemed to have greatly improved him.

Only Nic—and perhaps her father—worried a little as to how long Miss Robinson's legacy would last if Denis continued to draw out capital at such an alarming rate.

Another person in Welbridge looked on all this with some cynicism and misgiving. March Foster. He was thankful to see Nicola looking better and less strained. He heard about all the presents. But he could not believe that his lovely Nicola was any happier in herself because of Denis's 'windfall'. Nor that all this *bonhomie* on Denis's part would last. March could not forget the things that he had heard Nicola's husband say to her on that evening March had spent with them in Market Square. The fact that Denis had not repaid the loan of fifty pounds stuck in March's mind. It was not that he needed the money. It was the principle that worried him. The fellow *ought* to pay it back now. He was incensed against Denis for Nicola's sake. He knew how the existence of that debt would distress her.

But money was not mentioned between the two men when they met. They ran into each other once or twice just before Christmas, and then at Heron's Hall on Boxing Night when Mrs. Foster gave a party. A small supper-dance for the Fosters' intimate friends.

Mrs. Foster was still something of an invalid but she was on her feet again and she considered it her duty to her son to waken up the old house and give at least one good party for him. It was, of course, at the back of her mind that he might meet some nice girl in the locality and be wooed away from his old passion for Nicola. She asked several pretty girls to the party and March knew it and let her have her way. But pretty girls meant nothing to him. And the party meant nothing until the butler announced Mrs. Denis Avon. Then, when he looked at Nicola—slender, fair, very beautiful, wearing a tight black velvet evening dress and an old-fashioned locket on a ribbon around her slim throat—he knew that he loved her more than ever. His whole being ached with love for her. And stronger than his desire was the selfless wish to see her happy—*really* happy, again.

Denis was playing in the Boxing Night performance and coming on later. So, for a little while, March felt that he would have Nicola to himself.

"I'm so glad that you were able to come," he said and then bent and kissed her cheek and added in a low voice: "Happy Christmas to you, Nic, my dear."

Her heart leapt at the look in his deep hazel eyes and that fleeting touch of his lips. But she said calmly:

"And to you, March, dear."

Looking around the big reception-room, festooned with holly and mistletoe and banked with flowers, listening to the dance music and watching the gay crowd—most of whom she knew—she added :

"It's like old times being here. Your mother always used to throw a party on Boxing Night, didn't she?"

March nodded.

"Yes, and you and Ron always came together. I wish he could be here tonight."

"So do I," said Nicola regretfully.

But her brother was one of the unfortunates who had to go on working. He had spent Christmas Day and night with the family but had gone back to Bristol that morning.

March looked at her in silence a moment. Her eyes were deep and shadowed. He wondered bitterly how much she had suffered to make her look so grave—so mature. But there was still something strong and fearless about her. He thought: "She is very courageous. Things have improved, but I wonder how much life with Denis is really worth to her now. And how long it will be before he goes off the deep end again."

He said aloud.

"Are you sticking to Market Square, or moving in the New Year?"

"Moving, probably," she said, "Denis hates it and so do I. But everything's in the air. Denis is in touch with some film producer, you know, whom he met up in London. He thinks Denis extremely photogenic. There is some chance that he'll go to Hollywood for a test."

March felt a pang and gave her an anxious look.

"And you'll go with him?"

"I don't know," she said quietly, "I don't know anything just yet."

"Would you like to go?"

She hesitated. He saw the colour mount to her cheeks as though she found it a difficult question to answer. Then she said :

"Not much. I don't think Hollywood is up my street, but Denis, of course, would love it."

March looked gloomily around the room, which was rapidly filling with his mother's guests. He thought that it would be the end of everything for him if Nicola left Wel-

162

bridge . . . left England . . . to go to Hollywood with Denis. Yet what was the good of nourishing this hopeless love for her?

He saw his mother leading a young thing in a pink dress, with pink flowers in her hair, towards him. That must be Dorinda Morris, whose father was Lord-Lieutenant of the county. It was her first appearance at Heron's Hall. She was only nineteen and had just left finishing-school in Paris. He knew perfectly well that his mother wanted him to marry somebody like Dorinda. With a heavy heart he dragged himself away from Nicola. She was swept into the dance by an old friend.

But later, when March had done various duty dances, he went in search of Nicola again. He had seen her a few moments ago walking by herself through the doors that led into his father's study. It was quiet there and dim except for one shaded lamp on the desk and the red embers of a coal fire which had been burning. The house was centrally heated but Mr. Foster favoured an old-fashioned fire.

Nicola had seated herself on the brown velvet cushions of a leather sofa opposite the fire. March thought that she looked tired. He sat down beside her and offered her his cigarette-case.

"You've chosen the right place, Nic. I think I must be getting old. I can't cope with all these young things my mother has invited. I'm worn out, talking about nothing."

Nicola smiled at him. She thought that strong blunt face of his had a troubled air. She wished he looked more content. It was nice to sit with him here in the quiet study.

"I'm getting old, too," she laughed. "I must conserve my strength—because Denis will want to dance every dance once he gets here, and show off his new samba."

"Oh, of course, he's an expert," said March.

"That was a very pretty girl—the one in pink you were with just now," she remarked after a pause.

"Was she pretty? I didn't notice," he said. "She giggled. I don't like women who giggle—except Flip, who has a specially endearing kind."

"Flip will soon be old enough to come to dances like this."

"Time surely rushes by, Nic."

She stared at the fire. Life for her was dragging by—not rushing. These six months of her marriage had seemed like six years. Into them she seemed to have crowded a lifetime of experience, sweet and bitter. But unfortunately the bitterness had triumphed. Once upon a time a dance like this would have been a terrific excitement for her. She knew that she should have been bubbling over with *joie-de-vivre* and that she and March should have been on the top of their form, joking with each other tonight instead of behaving like two bored old cynics.

When he looked at her it seemed to mean something so much more than it should. She thought:

"I believe he is still in love with me. . . ."

If that were so, then she ought to run away from him and from her own half-formed unconfessed desire to respond. She looked at her wrist-watch. Denis would be here at any moment. The sooner the better. In a sudden panic she said gaily:

"Now, I think it would be nice if you got engaged to a lovely girl like Dorinda Morris."

March pursed in his lips. His eyes narrowed.

"Do you?"

She gave a confused laugh.

"Don't you think it's time you did get married and settled down, March?"

He got up and flung his half-smoked cigarette into the grate.

"No, I don't," he said roughly. "And neither do you."

She too gained her feet and smoothed a crease in the black velvet of her dress. She did not look at him. Nervously she said:

"Let's go back to the ballroom, shall we? I think I heard the front-door bell. It might be Denis."

March came nearer her. For a moment his gaze held hers with frightening intensity. Then with all the will in the world he could not entirely restrain the inclination for closer contact with her . . . something more than their childhood friendship. He said hoarsely:

"Nic, are you happy? Is all well between you and Denis?

It's got to be. If I'm to have any peace of mind I've got to know that you are all right. Oh, Nic, my darling . . ."

He caught her hand. For a moment he pulled it up to his lips. She went white. Her whole body grew taut as she felt the burning passion of the kiss which he laid against her palm. The violence of it and of her own feverish wish to respond terrified her. She snatched the hand away.

"March . . . *please* . . ."

He, too, was white. It was a tense moment. They looked into each other's eyes as though they could not look away. Then he controlled himself.

"Sorry, Nic. You go to my head a bit. I don't change easily, you know."

She felt a sense of overwhelming tragedy . . . for it *was* tragic that she should have chosen the wrong man. *This* was the one who could have brought her the peace and happiness and the love that she could never know with Denis. But her loyalty to her husband still struggled to prevail. She whispered :

"It's all right, March. I understand. And please don't worry about me. I . . . I'm perfectly all right, really I am. I expect I shall go to Hollywood with Denis and enjoy it thoroughly."

She lied and March knew it. But he followed her lead.

"Good show," he said with an effort. "You might find it just the job, you know."

She made a blind movement towards the study door. She wanted to cry. She wanted to stay here and seek for peace and understanding—in March's arms. But she told herself in despair that this was only the beginning of her married life with Denis and that whatever she had to put up with, she must do her best to make a success of that marriage. Besides, she had to hand it to him that lately—certainly since Aunt Emma's death—he had been so much nicer.

He was there . . . she saw him walking into the ballroom with the grand air which Denis could put on so easily for his entry into a roomful of people like this. He looked very handsome and splendid in white tie and tails and with a white carnation in his lapel. He was darting smiles right and left, and lazy glances into the eyes of the pretty girls who looked at him through their lashes. But he went straight up to Nicola. A whim led him to take the hand which March had just kissed, and draw it up to his own lips.

"May I introduce myself?" he said. "I am Denis Avon. And you are undoubtedly the most beautiful girl in the room. May I have this dance? Tell me your name."

Nicola gave a stifled laugh. So Denis was in this sort of mood! Well, she must play up to it and shut her mind to the memory of March. *"Tell me your name,"* Denis repeated. And she thought with tragic irony that she would like to have answered with Rossetti's immortal words:

> *"Look in my face. My name is Might-Have-Been. I am also called No-more. Too-Late. Farewell."*

She said nothing. Denis seized her in his arms and glided smoothly with her into the crowd of dancers.

March Foster from the doorway had witnessed that meeting between husband and wife, and Denis's kiss on the hand which he himself had only just pressed against his own hungry lips. He turned and walked out of the ballroom. He could not bear to see them dancing together. Not just for the moment, anyhow, he thought. Later, he would go and dance with Dorinda Morris and flirt a little with her. But with the arrival of Denis Avon the dance was spoiled for March. The fun was *finished. He did not know that he could hate a man so much.*

## XX

DENIS'S orgy of spending Aunt Emma's money lasted well into January, during which time the two sides of his nature which Nicola found so hard to reconcile were alternately displayed to her with bewildering rapidity.

He still continued to be on good terms with her and as agreeable to her family as he used to be in the early days of their engagement. He gave Nicola more presents than she wanted. None of them brought her any particular pleasure, for she had an uneasy feeling that he was running up debts in the old careless way.

166

Parcels arrived from London . . . new suits and expensive underwear and shoes for Mr. Avon . . . expensive-looking luggage, too (he firmly believed that he would shortly be on his way to Hollywood), always with the glib excuse of '*my public*'. Denis must be smart so as to impress his public and theatrical producers. His wife must be smart with him. He told everybody that they were only staying in their 'horrid little flat' until his plans for the future became more definite. But he no longer gave parties there. He entertained the whole Repertory cast at the Welbridge Park Hotel. He charmed everybody and was a little intoxicated with his own powers of charming.

Nicola would watch him amazed and with a sinking feeling in her heart that this was not a man for whom any girl could feel a profound love and respect. He was just an irresponsible schoolboy . . . acting, always acting. At times making her laugh despite her soul's despair. At times becoming again her passionate lover, demanding passion from her and expecting her to give it without backward glimpses into the uncomfortable past . . . astonished if she should remember a time when he had made her unhappy, or hurt and disappointed her.

He excused himself for those unattractive moments—even spoke about them boldly and frankly.

"I used to be very bad-tempered at times. Poor little Nic! I'm afraid the first flush of matrimonial responsibility without a sou rather got me down. But thanks to old Aunt Em I've felt a lot better and happier lately. You've been happier, too, haven't you, sweet?"

She always found it hard to answer that sort of question. She had none of Denis's incredible ability to change his moods in a lightning flash—gloss over defects, wipe out grievances as though they had never existed. It was not that she bore a grudge or sulked. She had far too sweet and even a disposition for that. But the discovery of Denis's true nature had been a kind of shock and those moments of careless cruelty and occasional bullying had left a mark which could not easily be erased. To one of her simple straightforward mind it was all far too complicated. But she never dreamed of trying to spoil Denis's good moments or repulsing his overtures of love and good will. Deep down in herself she felt miserable and horribly alone . . . right outside the circle of Denis's magnificence. Always afraid that there might be a crash and an end to it all just as there had been an end to her dream of perfect love.

Then there was March . . . that memory which nothing could obliterate of that emotional moment between them in the study of Heron's Hall on Boxing Night. She had seen little of him since then. She was torn between an ever-growing need of him and a terror of giving way to her desire. So she avoided meeting him and flung herself more arduously than ever into her work at *NICOLETTE*. She spent most of the evenings when Denis was playing with her own family.

The bills, of course, began to pour in, mostly from London . . . to which Denis paid frequent visits. He had even bought himself a second-hand smart little car. Sometimes Nicola accompanied him—never very willingly because he drove too fast for her liking. More often than not he went alone, and Nicola would hear from him only casually and at a later date that he had taken some girl up to town. But she could not even be jealous any more. She seemed to feel *nothing* . . . just went on from day to day telling herself that she must be thankful that there was no longer active friction between Denis and herself, yet conscious that no matter how hard she tried, she could not wholeheartedly love him again.

For one thing she was supremely thankful . . . that Denis continued in the Welbridge Rep. and that she could live in her old home town and go on seeing her parents and her young sister. And, of course, Kim, now grown into a big strong dog like March's Kimbo, was a faithful and endearing friend, always there to welcome her when Denis was away.

There were, of course, flashes back to that other unattractive Denis. Occasionally she asked him about money matters, then he either snapped at her or assured her in an airy way that 'everything was all right'. When she handed him bills he stuffed them in a drawer and said that he would deal with them later. Then there were mysterious 'phone calls . . . one woman's voice in particular Nicola was beginning to recognize. At times she asked to speak to Mr. Avon; at other times when she heard Nicola's voice she rang off. These calls came from London.

Denis's explanation was that the caller was a Miss Ursula King, on the staff of an important film agency, and that it was through her that he hoped to get a test and contract in Hollywood.

Nicola accepted this explanation only half believing in it. Miss King rang quite often at night, which seemed strange hours for business, but nothing would induce her to question Denis. She was far too proud. And she preferred that things should be as they were, comparatively peaceful, rather than that they should slip back to the open hostility of last autumn.

But it was the lull before the storm.

There came one bitter afternoon in February when Welbridge lay white and silent under a heavy fall of snow, that Denis returned from one of his trips to London in a bad mood. He did not even kiss Nicola when he entered the flat; muttered that he was frozen, poured himself out a stiff drink and sat staring gloomily at the fire.

Nicola, too, was cold and very tired. She had been out for rather too long a walk with her sister and young Kim this afternoon, and the week's work had been heavy, with Ann laid up with a bad chill, and Nicola herself single-handed in the salon.

She started to lay the table for supper. Denis flung her a frowning look.

"What have we got?"

"I wish I could say roast chicken and champagne," Nicola laughed, trying to bring in a cheerful note, "but it's only one of my made-up dishes I'm afraid, darling. There isn't much one can do with a meat ration like ours, is there?"

He grumbled. He grumbled all through supper. He cursed the weather, the Government, the theatre. Nicola listened in silence, her grave eyes fixed on him. Then she said:

"What's gone wrong, Denis?"

"Well, if I tell you, for heaven's sake don't do the 'I told you so' stunt," he muttered, reaching for a cigarette and scowling as he lit it.

"Do I often do so?" she asked with heightened colour.

"Well, I know you are *thinking* things, even when you don't say them."

Nicola twisted her slim fingers nervously together. It certainly didn't look like being a good evening and she dreaded what she already knew she was going to be told. Denis in his glorious feckless fashion had been running through Aunt Emma's legacy; no doubt of that, and now he admitted it. There was still some left, shares which he had been strongly advised not to sell out, but he had spent more than he intended and run up far too many heavy bills. The trouble was, he told Nicola sullenly, that he had been expecting long before this to get his summons to America, or even go into a London production. And it hadn't come off. In his conceit, he had never imagined that Denis Avon would have to remain in a third-rate Repertory Company.

"So you see," he finished, "things aren't too good."

She bit hard on her lip—determined not to reproach him.

"I'm sorry, Denny," she said. "What can I do?"

With one of his quick sunny smiles which transformed him he reached up a hand to her and touched her cheek.

"You're a darling, Nic. I wonder you don't bite my head off. I'm so hopeless. But I don't mean it. And we've had a heck of a good time lately, haven't we?"

*Have we?* she thought, her misery welling slowly up inside her. *Have we? Oh, Denis, Denis, it wasn't fur coats and cars and parties that I wanted so much as to share a home with somebody whom I could love and trust and who would want no one but me.*

"The trouble is," added Denis, "that I have one or two outstanding accounts I must settle. And I can't sell out any more shares for the moment. And I've got a pretty heavy overdraft."

"Oh, Denis!"

Inevitably, the evening ended in bitterness. They were scarcely on speaking terms when they went to bed that night. But long after Denis calmly slept Nicola lay awake staring into the darkness, wondering what she ought to do . . . if she ought to help her husband out of this crisis by drawing on *NICOLETTE*'s funds, despite the fact that she wanted badly to repay her brother . . . or leave him to get out of his own difficulties.

Whichever way out, the future seemed unattractive. How hard it was to preserve a romantic love when this sordid question of finance kept cropping up, she thought drearily. If *only* Denis could be a little more responsible. *If only*.

During the week that followed, Denis was more often than not in a poor humour and Nicola suffered in consequence. Mary Boyd, who had begun to think that things were better between her daughter and young actor-husband, read the unspoken anxiety in Nicola's eyes and lost heart again.

February drifted into a wild blustering March. Denis sold his car to pay some of the outstanding debts. Some of the new expensive things which had been bought for the flat disappeared. Nicola endeavoured loyally not to let her family know what was going on, but young Flip's sharp eyes took in quite a good deal and she wrote feverishly and secretly in her diary.

April came to Welbridge—full of the nostalgic beauty of early spring. And then, at last, the day of Denis's triumph dawned. A telephone call from Ursula King. A cable from America. That long-looked-for, much-dreamed-of, summons to Hollywood.

Denis went wild with excitement. Debts and troubles and bills were forgotten. When the news reached him he seized Nicola's arms and danced her around the little flat, his eyes brilliant with excitement.

"They've fallen for me. I knew they would, sweetie-pie! Ursula said those photographs we sent over would knock them sideways. It was only a question of time. I'm to fly over at once and they're going to pay all my expenses."

Nicola's heart beat quickly. She was thankful for him. Even thrilled. But she saw suddenly a complete upheaval of her whole life . . . another aspect of this marriage which had brought her so little fulfilment or tranquillity.

"And I?" she asked breathlessly.

He stopped dancing and released her, his face flushed with victory.

"Ursula suggests that I should fly over first and then send for you. And if I get a good contract you can come out by air or on a super-ship like the *Queen Elizabeth* and have a good rest."

She drew a deep breath.

Last summer it might all have been so wonderful—so exciting. But now she knew, deep down in her heart, that she did not want to cut loose all her ties in England and go to America with Denis. It would never do. He would never stand up to the spoiling and flattery. His extreme good looks and charm would be his ruin there. He would be surrounded by glamour-girls. She, Nicola, would just be the dull little wife in the background, waiting for him to come home. It would not mean the domestic life—the children—the close companionship that she had always wanted.

She had been warned by her parents . . . her friends . . . even by one of *Denis's* friends, like Verona Dale, that she could never get these things with Denis. But she had not listened. Why, *why*, she asked herself hopelessly, had she ever thought it would be possible?

He could not really need her in Hollywood. There would be so many lovely girls to amuse him. She herself would be desperately lonely there in a strange country. She would have to say a long good-bye to Mummy and Daddy and Flip. *And to March*. But perhaps that was as well, she thought. The aching need for March was far too deeply rooted now and a long period of separation might be the best thing.

Yet her heart sank at the thought of going to America with Denis. Almost with a sense of guilt she was *glad* that he had to go first—without her.

"We'll begin a new life together, Nic," she heard Denis say enthusiastically. "We'll have a lot of fun. Ursula's the person who's put this deal through, you know. I must run up to town and say thank you with orchids."

Nicola said nothing. Yes, that was typical of Denis . . . to be madly excited before he even knew that Hollywood would be as pleased with him as he was with the idea of going there

. . anxious to send orchids to somebody, when he hadn't a shilling to spend, and that drawer in the desk was still full of unpaid bills.

And she, his wife, would be left to clear up the muddle after he had gone.

## XXI

DENIS did not wait for his wife's approval—or otherwise—of his plan to rush up to town and send orchids to Ursula King. Once more he was elated and filled with the desire to be generous and to include not only Nicola but everybody who knew him. He immediately 'flung a celebration party', and after the show ended that night gathered the cast at the Welbridge Park Hotel for supper.

There was champagne for everybody. Only Nicola sipped that champagne wondering who was going to pay for it and when. Everybody else warmed to the occasion and showered Denis with congratulations—the party was hilarious. Denis was alternately flattered and teased.

"So this is where our Denny leaves the Rep. and starts life among the stars," Verona Dale said gaily, lifting her glass to him. "We shall have him in neon lights as the second Robert Taylor in due course."

"And I," put in one of the younger feminine members of the cast, "shall be able to say once I acted with Mr. Avon before he was so famous . . ." and she fluttered her lashes coquettishly at Denis, who rose gallantly to his feet and kissed each of his flatterers in turn.

Bill Venning, a little more sceptical, put his tongue in his cheek. He had no wish to appear a wet blanket but he was not at all sure that young Denis would be all that success in Hollywood. He had the looks but not enough fire and imagination ever to make a really fine actor. However, these Hollywood chaps did wonders with good direction and photography. Bill added his good wishes and then turned his attention upon Denis's young wife.

Sweet girl and with a lot of character, he always thought, but she didn't look awfully happy. Bill was a bit of a psychologist and he fancied that behind Nicola's smiles lay a trace of sadness. Had their marriage worked out? He wasn't at all sure. Most of the women were crazy about Denis, but there had been moments in the theatre when, personally, Bill found his leading man insufferably conceited.

"When are you going to follow our future star?" Verona asked Nicola.

"Later, when he's had a look round," Nicola smiled back.

"Will you keep on your little flat?"

Denis promptly answered for his wife.

"I'll say she won't. It never has been good enough for her." Nicola coloured.

"Oh, I expect I shall go home and live with my people until Denis sends for me," she murmured.

Miss Dale looked at the girl and her thoughts ran on much the same lines as Bill's. She was not at all sure the Denis-Nicola marriage had been a success. But then she had always thought Denny, so charming as a friend, would be impossible as a husband. Poor little Nic! A pity Denny hadn't left her alone to carry on in peace with her life. She had been so happy when Verona first met her in *NICOLETTE*. Lately she had had a decided look of strain. She was far too gentle for Denny, of course. The sort of person who could easily be broken on the wheel of his colossal egotism and conceit. And of course Verona knew all about that little affair with Carole Fray, whom she frankly despised.

Carole was rather silent and sulky during that party. She was more than a little sorry that she had quarrelled with Denis. She had never thought he would really get to Holly-wood.

Walking home through the cool spring night with an arm tucked through Nicola's, Denis talked enthusiastically about the future.

"Enjoyed your party, sweet?"

"Very much," she lied.

"Well, I'm glad I'm getting this chance. It will mean you can quit that damned Beauty Parlour, and I'll be able to buy you everything you deserve," he said on a sentimental note.

She forced her reply.

174

"It'll be wonderful . . ."

He was far too wrapped up in himself and his glowing prospects to notice the lack of sincerity and enthusiasm in Nicola's voice. She looked at the tall spire of St. Giles' silhouetted against the starlit sky, and at the little sleeping town in which she had been so happy—and so unhappy—and thought:

*It's too late. He should always have been like this. If only I could love him again . . . if only I could want to go to Hollywood.*

"When do you think you'll be off, Denis?" she asked.

"Ursula's going to book me on the first flight possible at the end of the month. Bill says he can't let me go till then. They've got to find someone to take my place in the Rep., and that won't be too easy," he added with a boastful laugh.

"I'm sure it won't."

"I shall nip up to town in the morning. So much to see to. Do you want to come?"

"No, I've far too many appointments," Nicola said.

"Well, you'll be able to stop working soon."

She bit hard on her lip. She didn't want to stop working. She loved her job. But before this news about Hollywood had come she had made up her mind to brave Denis's wrath and have another straight talk about the financial situation.

They just couldn't go on in the way they were going. He hadn't given her any housekeeping money for the last three weeks, and now she was quite sure she wouldn't get any. He would want every available penny, even though the Hollywood film company was paying his expenses. He had run up a big bill at the Welbridge Park. That champagne party tonight must have cost him a packet. . . .

It was so hateful always having to think in terms of cash. It wouldn't have been like that with a husband who paid his bills and had some sense of responsibility, she thought sadly.

But nothing was said, and Denis maintained his high mood of jubilation. When they were alone in the little flat he took her in his arms with a passion which she could have sworn was sincere. He couldn't bear to leave her behind even for a few weeks, he declared.

175

"I may be a bit of a cad now and again, but I do really love you, Nic," he said.

She buried her face against his shoulders, her cheeks wet with tears, her body shaken with wild sobbing. He kissed and comforted her. He took it for granted that she was in a state of emotional ecstasy, like himself. It did not enter his head that she wept for her lost love and the tragic realization that his kisses, caresses, and whispered words of love meant nothing to her any more. Nothing at all.

He came back from London next evening still in the best of spirits and bringing a huge bottle of special lotion which she had mentioned, in course of conversation, that she needed at the salon. The very fact that he had remembered that need touched her, and almost drew her near to him again. But after he had gone to the theatre she started to brush the suit he had worn up to town, and found a handkerchief in it stained with lipstick . . . of a dark orange shade which she certainly never used, and which reeked of perfume. *Ursula's,* no doubt. He had told Nicola he had had a 'business lunch' with Ursula. But it must have been followed by a little more than that. Nicola's tender feelings evaporated as she stared at the handkerchief; and then she made another discovery. A flimsy sheet of notepaper. Unwilling though she was to pry into Denis's affairs, Nicola was only human. She read what was written on that piece of paper. It had neither address nor date. It said :

*"This is for you to read in the train, my splendid Denis. Just that I love you and to tell you that it means everything to me to have been instrumental in getting you your heart's desire. You alone are my heart's desire.*

*Ursula."*

The words danced before Nicola's sight. The hot blood suffused her cheeks. She felt suddenly sick and her whole body trembled. Ursula ! Yes, of course, all the way along she had guessed that Denis was having an affair with his 'theatrical agent', who was a very clever business woman as well as a pretty one, and older than himself. So even after last night when he had told her, his wife, that he loved no one in the world but her, he had been able to go straight to the arms of the latest 'girl-friend'. Nicola felt anger and disgust rather than jealousy. And if Denis could behave like this so soon after their marriage, what would happen in Hollywood?

She sat down suddenly and put her face in her hands.

She could not go with him. She *could not*.

It took her a long while to regain sufficient composure to do the ordinary little things that she had to do—prepare supper for Denis . . . take Kim out for his last walk.

The last person on earth whom she wanted to meet in her present mood was March Foster. But she ran straight into him striding down the High Street with Kimbo at his heels and a pipe in his mouth.

He greeted her cheerfully:

"Two minds with but one single thought. The welfare of our canine favourites. How are you, Nic?"

"Oh, fine!" she answered brightly and was thankful that it was dark and that he could not plainly see her face or note that she had been crying.

"Aiming for the river? If so, we might stroll together."

The two Boxers were already leaping playfully around each other and breaking the silence of the little town with loud joyous barks.

"Shut up, you two!" growled March, and repeated his invitation to Nicola.

She wanted to walk with him and yet shrank from the thought of a *tête-à-tête* with March on this particular evening. She felt far too sore at heart, too disgusted with Denis—and life. It would be heaven to be alone with March—to feel his strength, his kindliness and honesty of purpose, emanating towards her. God knew she needed it . . . needed to be assured that there *was* something decent and concrete left in the world. The world in which she had once had so simple a belief—an almost childlike faith which Denis had ruthlessly spoiled for her. Ruthless? Perhaps *thoughtless* was the right word. He was weak and irresponsible. He could never resist flattery. Ursula King, successful, useful, smart, had made an easy conquest. But Nicola could not look upon infidelity in a light fashion. To her, the marriage tie was sacred. Even now she could not have brought herself to have a cheap revenge upon her husband by entering into some sort of emotional episode with March. She had too much self-respect and too much real feeling for March.

She said :

"No, we've had our walk. . . . I'm going in now, thanks, March."

He took his pipe from his mouth and tried to see her face more closely, but she kept it averted. He sensed that something untoward had happened and that Nicola did not particularly want to be with him. He was mystified and a little hurt. He said :

"I'm not going to like it much when you desert Welbridge for Hollywood, Nic."

She kept her lashes lowered.

"You've heard about Denis, then?"

"Yes. Congratulations."

"Well, I don't know that I shall go," she added. "Certainly not for the moment. I shall probably pack up and stay at home for a bit."

His heart leaped. It would be good to see her back there in the old house, he thought. The old Nicola . . . *without a husband*. He said :

"Your people will enjoy that."

"So shall I," she said, and then with another excuse turned and walked away from him.

He stood puffing at his pipe, frowning, watching her slender figure retreat with Kim at her heels. He wondered what was wrong. And in one of his sudden moments of dislike for Denis Avon, he thought :

"I wish the fellow would get lost in Hollywood and stay there . . . and never come back."

Just in what sinister fashion that wish was to be fulfilled he was not to know just then. He walked Kimbo back to Heron's Hall in a sombre mood. It never did him any good seeing and talking to Nicola, he reflected. Each meeting only reopened the old wound. Last night there had been an unfortunate scene with his mother, with whom he so rarely

178

held even the smallest dispute. He knew how much she adored him, and even though that adoration frequently irked and exasperated him, he tried to preserve a sense of humour and amiability towards her. But last night she had nagged him about that silly little girl Dorinda Morris until he could stand no more. Why couldn't he fall in love with Dorinda and bring her as a bride to Heron's Hall? His father was retiring from business this summer. He had promised that they should go down to Cornwall to live once he had retired and handed the business over to March. Heron's Hall would be his, March's. Then Dorinda with her youth and beauty, and a father in such a big position, would be the ideal wife for March.

After an hour of this talk March had grown irritated and eventually told his mother that he had no intention of marrying Dorinda Morris.

"She would get on my nerves in a week with her giggles. She's absolutely empty and interested in only one thing . . . having a good time. I have no interest in good-time girls, Mother," he said.

Then Mrs. Foster had tactlessly laid the blame at Nic's door.

"You don't seem able to forget that Nic. I hate her for spoiling your life."

March had grown ice-cold and rather white. He had said in a low voice :

"If you are really so fond of me, Mother, you will try not to hate somebody whom I devoutly care for."

"But that's why I *do* hate her!" Mrs. Foster had wailed.

"Then don't, because I will never change and, since she has married Denis Avon, I shall probably never marry. There it is," he snapped.

It had ended of course in tears from Mrs. Foster and March walking out.

But it was true, he told himself tonight with bitterness. The fact that Nicola had become Mrs. Denis Avon could not destroy his, March's, love for her. It was indestructible. A pity perhaps, and a disappointment to his parents if he did not marry, but without real love marriage could never mean anything to March. As for Dorinda Morris—she just faded into insignificance beside his conception of Nicola as a woman.

Nicola went back to her flat after that short interrupted walk, and with a heavy heart tried to work out in her mind what she was going to say to Denis when he came back from the theatre. Should she show him the note and the handkerchief and accuse him . . . or leave it? She decided to leave it. What use was an ugly scene? He was going in less than two weeks from now. Whether she would eventually join him or not was a thing which she must decide in the future. She decided for the moment to say and do nothing and to let things work themselves out.

There came one moment, however, when it was beyond her control to dissemble or lie too thoroughly. That was the night before Denis went to America.

Everything had been arranged. He had said good-bye to the Rep. and the little Company with whom he had worked so long. They had given him a beautiful silver cigarette-case, inside which the whole cast had inscribed their names. A young actor had been installed in his place and Denis had even had the satisfaction of seeing the first newspaper notice and finding it a poor one. He felt tremendously excited and confident of his success in Hollywood, and he had been far too occupied rushing around and doing this and that to notice how silent and preoccupied Nicola had become, and how indifferent to his love-making.

He had wanted her to go up to London and stay the night before his departure. He had suggested a farewell party with Ursula King and one or two other theatrical friends. But Nicola had refused and maintained that she would sooner say farewell to him here in Welbridge.

He had not been slow to agree with this, airily observing that she was right . . . that the journey back without him would be so miserable. And Nicola looked at him with shadowed eyes and heavy heart, thinking:

*He'll be only too pleased to have the evening with Ursula.*

Then, before he left, she asked if he had settled the Welbridge Park account and one or two other outstanding bills, and he said, yes, of course, and wished, he said, that she would have more faith in him.

With a sudden wrench of his mind away from himself and the tremendous events awaiting him, he then turned his thoughts to her. It struck him suddenly that she had been a little cool these last few days and extraordinarily silent. He had put it all down to the fact that she was unhappy at the prospect of their temporary separation. In his way he was fond of his young wife. Other affairs like the one with Ursula were of no great importance to him. Nothing really was important except *Denis* and the furthering of Denis's career. He put his hands on Nicola's slender shoulders.

"Nic, darling," he said, "do you love me just as much as you used to?"

The colour stained her face and throat. Quickly she lowered her lashes. He had not asked a question like this for a very long time. She had hoped he wouldn't. Her silence filled Denis with sudden anxiety.

"Don't you?" he asked uneasily.

With an effort she answered.

"Does it matter so much to you, Denis?"

He laughed and shook her gently.

"Of course, silly!"

"Are you sure?"

"Hey, what's gone wrong with you? Naturally it matters whether my wife still loves me or not. You know that I love *you*."

Glib words. The old glib Denis. And no doubt he meant it. But she thought of the lipstick stains on his handkerchief. The love-letter from Ursula. The affair with Carole Fray. All the telephone calls and notes from all the other girls. His petty cruelties and selfishness . . . even before they were married, when he had shown such dislike of the puppy March had given her. So many bitter things which had ruined and changed the very face of love between them.

"Nicola," Denis spoke anxiously, "you're not going to tell me on the very eve of my departure that you don't love me any more!"

Then with a great effort she replied:

"I don't think we ought to start probing into how much we love each other. Really I don't!"

"Then you've got some grudge against me. I knew it!"

"Denis, please . . ."

"It's typical of you," he broke in sullenly, "when everybody else is so nice to me and wishing me luck and so on, you criticize me. I *know* you do. Just trying to make me unhappy before I go. It's rather a petty revenge for anything I've done that you don't like."

She could have told him then all that she knew, but she could not face what would follow in the way of explanations or self-reproach or glib excuse . . . whatever method he would have of wriggling out of it. So soon he would be gone. How did she know whether or not she would ever see him again? Accidents happened. It would be awful if anything happened to Denis after parting from him in anger.

She felt utterly miserable and sick at heart—worn out after the exhausting fortnight which had followed Denis's summons to Hollywood. She burst into tears.

"Oh, Denis, Denis, don't let's be unkind to each other tonight. It may be our last night together for so long."

He melted. That was better. That was the sort of thing he understood and could cope with. Nicola was a funny difficult little thing at times. He gathered her into his arms and started to kiss and caress her. He probed no more into what she did or did not feel. And when he left her he was confident that he still held her in the hollow of his hand.

Within forty-eight hours of their last good-bye Nicola was to feel utter thankfulness that she had controlled herself sufficiently to avert a sordid row. That her last memory of the man with whom she had been so wildly infatuated, and whom she had married so hastily, held some kind of tenderness.

For Denis never reached his goal and never was to realize his ambitions on this earth. The big air-liner which was taking him across the Atlantic reached no further than Ireland. In a thick mist, it bumped against a hillside in Shannon, burst into flames and crashed. Of all the passengers and crew there was not a single survivor.

It was young Flip in the Boyd family who first learned of the disaster.

Cycling back from school, she met March Foster walking grimly down the High Street with a local paper in his hand. He stopped her and asked her if she had heard the news. When she shook her head he said:

"Perhaps Nic hasn't either. But Denis was on that Sky-master which crashed at Shannon this morning, you know."

Flip nearly fell off her bicycle. That bicycle which Denis had given her. Her eyes goggled at March.

"Oh, goodness!" she gasped. "Do you mean that Denis is *dead*?"

March handed her the paper.

"Looks like it. Rather an appalling show. Poor wretched fellow!"

"Oh, *poor* Denis!" exclaimed Flip with a natural pity for the dead which erased any unkind memories, "and *poor* Nic. Goodness! It means she's a *widow*, doesn't it, March?"

"Yes," said March quietly, "it does. Better nip home and tell your parents, Flip."

Flip needed no second bidding, but seized the paper and cycled furiously down the High Street.

March walked home. His feelings were indescribable. That such a thing as this should have happened had never so much as entered his imagination. In an automatic sort of way he went straight to his desk when he got to Heron's Hall, pulled out Denis's I.O.U. for fifty pounds and tore it into little strips.

That was one thing Nicola need never know about.

Later he telephoned the Boyd house to make sure that Nicola was all right. Mary Boyd answered him.

"Yes, Nic is all right, my dear, but horribly shocked. She is in bed at the moment quite collapsed. Doctor gave her a sleeping draught."

"Poor Nic."

"You know how sensitive she is," Mary Boyd added in a low voice, "and ever since she heard the news she's been haunted by awful pictures of that crash. She keeps saying she hopes Denis didn't suffer."

"I hope he didn't," said March.

"So do we all," said Mrs. Boyd. "It's a frightful thing—just when he was about to make the grade. Poor boy."

"Give her my love and tell her that if there's anything I can do to let me know."

Nicola's mother said :

"Thank you, dear March. And I know she'll want to see you very soon. She must just have time to get over the shock. Her father and I have been talking . . . and as soon as she has settled up about the flat and everything we're going to try and get her away. There's an old married school friend of hers who has a farm in Worcestershire. That would be the very place for her to go. What she needs now is complete rest. She was very nearly at the end of her tether before Denis went away, you know."

"I know," said March curtly.

"And this, of course, has finished it," sighed Mrs. Boyd. "But she'll be all right in time. And she'll just have to let *NICOLETTE* go. Her father's going to insist. What my darling needs is a long rest and she must have it."


## XXII

" 'THE spirit is willing'," said Nicola, " 'but the flesh is weak.' "

She uttered this well-worn quotation with a rueful laugh, sitting in a deck-chair outside the thatched cottage in which she had been staying with her friend Patty Coran. Patty, engaged upon the darning of a very holey small sock which belonged to her eldest child, aged four, glanced up at Nicola and gave a little sigh and nod in response :

"How right you are, dear. I feel that way at the end of most days after I've cooked three meals, pushed a pram round the village, done my shopping, washed and ironed Johnny's shirts and my own smalls, rinsed through baby's nappies and . . ."

"Oh, stop, for heaven's sake!" broke in Nicola, laughing. "You make me feel positively ashamed, the way I've been lazing around here for the past month."

"It's been grand having you," said Mrs. Johnny Coran, who looked in her short skirt and gingham blouse more like a girl of seventeen than a young married woman of twenty-seven with a family. "I've never had such peace in the home and you're a huge help. Micky adores you and you give Caroline her bath and bottle in a soothing fashion that any nanny would envy. You couldn't do more."

Nicola said nothing but shook her head. She felt that Patty had done more than enough for her. This little home had been a haven of rest since Denis died.

Lucky Patty was in England just now. She had only just come back after three years in the Middle East, where her husband had been serving with the Air Force. Caroline had been born out there three months ago and now Johnny's tour was finished and he had been posted to a unit in the Midlands. But for the moment Patty and the children were occupying the cottage which they had bought and furnished when they first married, six years ago.

Patty was the best person that Nicola could have come to after Denis died. The Corans had not been home for Nicola's wedding so they had never met Denis. Nicola had felt that she need not talk about him if she did not want to. She shrank from all the well-meaning friends who had been friends of his—who wrote to her, talked about her 'terrible loss' or met her in Welbridge, sounded Denis's praises and drenched her with sympathy. She did not want their pity. She had been shocked and grieved by the suddenness—the awfulness—of the death which had overtaken Denis in the flower of his youth. But her tears had been all for him—not for herself. She knew that she preferred to be alone. Ever honest, she could not pretend that the world for her had ended with his going. Love had died between them . . . love and trust and all the things that had mattered. Only the husk of glamour remained. But for *him* she had wept long and bitterly, and the shock of the whole affair had a curious physical effect upon her. It had temporarily robbed her of power in her legs. She walked only slowly—with difficulty. It was impossible for her to carry on with her Beauty Parlour, but the specialist whom her parents had called in had assured them, and Nicola, that it was only a temporary phase. It would pass with rest —complete rest of body and mind. And that was what she had found in this little cottage with Patty and the children. Today—a month after Denis's crash—she was back to normal. But she still felt that she could not have stood upon her feet and done even six hours of massage in the salon.

So she had taken a working partner into *NICOLETTE*.

A friend of Miss Dale's from the Repertory Company had come in with her. Ann Williams was remaining as assistant. This woman was an experienced beauty specialist with a little money behind her. She was anxious to enlarge the premises and the business as a whole, and as soon as Nicola recovered her full strength she was going back to work with her. Nicola needed hard work. She wanted to wipe out the memory of her brief marriage. Even those happy days when she had first loved Denis. The whole thing had been such a bitter disappointment that she felt it better somehow to try and begin life all over again. To look upon her marriage as a dream which had now finished.

Her mother had been magnificent. It was she who had cleared up the little flat in Market Square and seen to all the business side of things. There had been little enough to see to, for Denis had left no will and what remained of Aunt Emma's legacy was swallowed up in the sea of debts which continued to pour in after his death. Mrs. Boyd had found a little deed-box belonging to him and brought it to Nicola so that she might sort out what papers were in it. Most of these papers had been letters . . . foolish letters from foolish girls or hysterical women fans . . . pandering to poor Denis's vanity; leaving no room for doubt that he had responded. It had finally proved to Nicola how incapable he had been of stable affection. She tore everything up without feeling.

"Poor Denis," was all she said, as she asked her mother to make a bonfire of the pieces. She felt curiously bereft of emotion when one by one the Repertory cast called at the house to see her and offer their condolences.

"Denis was so marvellous," they all said.

And to each one Nicola smiled and nodded.

"Yes, he was marvellous," she replied.

But Carole Fray did not come to see her and Ursula King did not write.

March visited her several times before she left Welbridge. Each time armed with lovely flowers. But he never mentioned Denis's name. He talked about everything except her marriage, for which she was thankful. He showed no emotion and was cheerful and friendly. But whenever he looked at her she saw what lay in his eyes and it brought balm to her bruised spirit and the vague stirring of hope to a young heart which had been almost broken.

On this warm day of early summer, Nicola sat lazily back in her deck-chair, looking at the border of Dutch tulips in front of her . . . at the small rustic garden full of heavenly flowers . . . to the orchard beyond, exquisite with blossom. She felt the sun warm on her face and heard the ecstatic song of a thrush in the hedge close by. And she felt better, spiritually and bodily, than she had been since Denis died . . . and indeed long before that.

On her lap there was a letter which had just come for her. From March. Telling her that he missed her and that every time he took Kimbo down the towpath by the river Kimbo looked dismally for his nephew. He said that he would very much like to come down and see her and that he was saving some petrol for the journey, but that he did not wish to come until she said that she wanted to see him.

She *did* want to see him; badly. And yet after the disastrous emotional experience of marriage with Denis which had so devastated her . . . she shrank a little from any kind of new feeling. Yet she loved March. She knew that she would always love him now. It was just a question of time.

How she envied Patty Coron who adored Johnny her husband, and her handsome little son, and Caroline—her fat contented baby who slept in her pram under the trees. Patty worked like a slave, but it was the sort of satisfying work which a woman needed. Patty was the happiest person whom Nicola knew.

"She had all that I missed by marrying poor old Denis," Nicola thought.

A boy on a bicycle stopped outside the gate, and walked whistling up the path with a telegram in his hand.

"For Mrs. Avon. . . ."

Patty took the telegram and handed it to her friend.

"It's probably from Mummy," said Nicola; "she said she was going to come down on Sunday with Flip and spend the day, you remember, and that she'd wire us."

But the telegram was not from Mrs. Boyd. It was from March.

Nicola read it aloud to her friend.

*"Father wants me to go abroad on business. May I come see you before I go. March."*

Nicola's face flushed a little. She eyed Patty.

Patty, who knew without being told what lay in the other girl's heart, smiled and nodded.

"You'll wire back 'yes', won't you? Tell him we'll put him up for the night, if he likes. He can have the divan in the sitting-room."

Nicola's heart began to beat quickly. It would be rather wonderful to have March down here in the thatched cottage for a whole day and night . She drew a deep breath and whistled suddenly to Kim the Boxer.

"You'd like it if he brings your Uncle Kimbo, too, wouldn't you?"

"The more the merrier," said Patty. "You know how I love crowds."

So March and Kimbo came down to the little thatched cottage with the flower-filled garden and the blossom-white orchard and air of tranquillity and happiness. And March had the satisfaction of finding his beloved Nicola with a tan and a soft glow on her cheeks which did not come out of any pot of cosmetic . . . with a little more flesh on her bones . . . and with a look of peace in the deep soft eyes and around the gentle mouth such as he had not seen since her marriage to Denis Avon.

He was also infinitely relieved to see her walking again with the old grace of movement. To hear her laugh. It was plain that his Nicola was recovering. And he thought that the most beautiful sight he had ever seen was when Nicola cradled Patty's fat baby in the crook of her arm and gave the little creature its bottle. It was the finishing touch, he thought. Nicola in the rôle of mother. It suited her so well.

That night they strolled together, alone in the soft May night, arm in arm, followed by the two dogs. Nicola felt utterly content.

"It's like old times, March," she said.

He stopped and looked down at her. And then with a touch of shyness stuck his pipe in the corner of his mouth and averted his gaze.

"Nic," he said, "there's a time and place for everything and it's a bit soon for me to say what I really want to. But it's like this—I'm off the day after tomorrow . . . to Durban. I shall be in South Africa about a month studying Colonial business methods. After which the old man wants me to go to Kenya—and then to America. I don't suppose I shall be back in England much before July or August. When I come . . I want to come straight back to you and talk about our future."

Nicola's heart jumped and her face crimsoned. She put a slim nervous hand up to her fair hair.

"Our future?" she repeated.

"Yes, my dear. You know what I'm going to ask—don't you? You know that I know that your marriage to Denis was not what you wished it to be. But I wouldn't like that to put you right off matrimony. In other words, Nic darling . . . I want to feel that in a year's time you might be able to face another marriage . . . with me."

She stood silent, her head bowed. He added gently :

"Don't bother to answer now. Think it all over while I'm away. But you know I'd take care of you. I'd like to live the rest of my time making up to you for anything that you've so far suffered."

The tears rushed to her eyes. She raised her face to his and on an impulse reached up and touched his cheek with her lips.

"March, dear, *dear* March, you've been so good to me, and the thought of life with you is very wonderful. I'll remember all you've said. And when you come back . . . I'll be home in Welbridge . . . waiting for you."

He was answered. Quickly he put his pipe in his pocket,

caught her close and for a moment held her very tightly, hi
cheek against her hair.

"Oh, Nic, I love you more than anything on earth," h
said. "I always have done, and I always will."

*Extract from the diary kept by Miss Frances (Flip) Boyd.*

"In lots of books you read about time 'seeming like
hundred years instead of one'. Well, I feel like that today.
feel it's a hundred years since poor old Denis died in tha
awful air crash and my sister Nic was left a widow. Yet it'
only about twelve months ago. And spring will soon be her
again and our Nic's going to be married to March Foster.

I'm jolly glad, and Mummy and Daddy are thrilled. I thin
they always wanted it. March and Nic have been sort o
secretly engaged ever since March came back from his tou
abroad, but they didn't announce it because of it being s
soon after Denis's death. Some horrid people in Welbridg
might think Nic was mean to forget Denis so quickly. But n
one knows what *we* know about Denis and how unhapp
she was, and that it was a Mistaken Marriage. So it had to b
kept quiet. I was allowed to tell my friend Pam and we use
to be thrilled when old March came to see Nic or take her ou
in the Riley. She always got such a terrific colour and had
shiny sort of look in her eyes when he was with her. Pan
and I think she's REALLY in love this time and we are sur
now that what she felt for Denis was INFATUATION. W
have vowed we will never get infatuated with anyone—it'
much better to wait and marry someone you really love.

Mummy and Daddy never mention Denis's name now
Neither does Nic. She's put away his photo and she is goin
to begin a new life. She told me so. I'm jolly glad she's s
happy because she deserves it. She worked jolly hard at *NICO
LETTE* after Denis died. That partner Miss Dale found for he
has helped make it bigger and better. Now she has bought Ni
out. That's what Daddy said, and Nic is terribly thrilled be
cause she got quite a lot of money and gave Ron a cheque t
pay back all he lent her.

Last night we had an engagement celebration at Heron'
Hall. March gave Nic a super ring. A yellow diamond whicl

he bought for her in South Africa and had specially set. He's always giving Nic terrifically nice things. He's awfully generous. And Pam and I both think he's changed to look at. He never looks gloomy now. He and Nic are always laughing —he makes us laugh, too.

'Due to circumstances,' Mummy says, they've decided to get married very quietly in London. Then March is taking Nic to Rome and Florence and Venice. Nic is longing to see Italy because March has told her it's so beautiful there. March said at dinner last night that it would be a perfect setting for Nic because *she* is so beautiful. I think that's a super thing to have said. Nic blushed and her eyes went terrifically big when she looked at him. Another time, she said she was getting too fat because she'd put on so much weight since Christmas, and March said he'd be livid if she banted, as he liked her just as she was and always would. I bet he will, too. He'll never let her down like Denis did. But Daddy taught me something in Latin, *De mortuis nil nisi bonum*, which means 'Of the dead speak no evil', so I won't.

The dinner at Heron's Hall was gorgeous—a terrific goose and ice-cream. It was marvellous me being allowed to go to a grown-up party. Ron was home for it too. He's thrilled because Nic is going to marry his best friend. All the grown-ups seem crackers about romance. Ron's got one going in Bristol now. He says her name is Eileen and that she's got Irish blue eyes and dimples, and dances divinely. He met her at a dance in Bristol, and her father is a doctor. He's going to invite her to stay with us in Welbridge, so Mummy and Daddy can meet her. I only hope it won't be *Infatuation*. He says it's not.

Well, the party at Heron's Hall was terrific. Mrs. Foster was nicer and weller than I've ever known her and looked awfully good-looking in a black velvet evening dress and mink cape and pearls. Mummy told Daddy she is awfully bucked because March is getting married at last, and that she's very fond of our Nic and glad it is her. Mr. Foster was nice too and said some awfully funny things that made us laugh. Mrs. Foster kept telling him not to be 'naughty'. It made me giggle to think of fat old Mr. Foster being called naughty. He said I was growing jolly pretty and would be the next to fall in love. They all say that but I won't yet. I'm going to stay with Mummy and Daddy for ages.

I do think it's fun to think that the two Boxers, Uncle Kimbo and Kim, will soon be living in the same house. They'll have games all the time. The big moment was when last night Mr. Foster announced the great news that he has 'made Heron's Hall over' to March as a wedding present because he always promised he would take Mrs. Foster to live down in Cornwall when he retired, and that they might as well go now as later. Especially as March was taking over so much of the business. Daddy said March would be very rich one day. I don't think Nic cares two hoots about that, but she does love him tremendously. She told me so when I kissed her good night. She said : 'Oh, Flip, I'm the happiest girl in the world and if March were penniless I'd still love him. He's so thoughtful and sweet to me, Flip. I can't think what I've done to deserve such happiness. Nor how I could have been so stupid as to say "no" to him when he asked me before.'

I could see she was remembering Denis, and looking a little sad. But it didn't last long. Mummy came in and we started to talk about the gorgeous dinner and the flowers and everything up at the Hall and Mummy said to Nic : 'Just fancy you having that place for your home, and we having dear dear March for a son-in-law and both of you to live so near us. It seems too good to be true, darling.'

Nic lifted her hand and the yellow diamond sparkled in the light—she sighed—in such a happy way—and nodded.

'When I grow old enough,' I said, 'I'm going to find a husband like March.'

Then Nic laughed and shook her head at me.

'No luck, Flippet. There couldn't be another March,' she said.

Oh, well—she may be right. But my turn will come. And if it doesn't I'll be an old maid and have hundreds and hundreds of dogs and cats all over the place—nobody to mind about muddy paw marks.

Good night, everybody."